GREATEST
SPEECHES
OF THE
MODERN
WORLD

GREATEST
SPEECHES
OF THE
MODERN
WORLD

RUPA

Published by
Rupa Publications India Pvt. Ltd 2018
7/16, Ansari Road, Daryaganj
New Delhi 110002

Sales centres:
Allahabad Bengaluru Chennai
Hyderabad Jaipur Kathmandu
Kolkata Mumbai

ISBN: 978-93-5304-027-7

First impression 2018

10 9 8 7 6 5 4 3 2 1

The moral right of the authors has been asserted.

This edition is for sale in the Indian subcontinent only.

Contents

We have seen that our nation is more deeply divided than we thought. But I still believe in America and I always will.

Publisher's Note

Speeches are the first conversations of history. When one listens to a speech or when one gives it from a pulpit of wisdom or power or authority, history unfolds. Had it not been for speeches there would not have been ideas and ideologies, religion and rationality. As human beings, we all speak—well mostly—but it is the wise and powerful, influential and initiator whom we follow when they speak. This is a kind of following for a leader which generates in one's mind landscaped by words of power, wisdom, joy, epiphany, catharsis. The list of human emotions could go on.

When the famous Greek orator Demosthenes spoke, men moved and toppled the authority. Centuries later, when Mahatma Gandhi spoke, men moved inwards, looked at their greatest strength, resolved non-violence and toppled the British rule. Speech has the quality of water. It takes the shape of its speaker, can easily make its way, is turbulent when uncontrolled and sustains and motivates life when contained within a receptive ecosystem.

Ralph Waldo Emerson famously said in an industrial American society that, 'If a man can write a better book, preach a better sermon, or make a better mousetrap than his neighbour, though he builds his house in the woods, the world will make a beaten path to his door.' So true! And if we add the element of 'speech' to our man in the woods, the world will surely lighten up that beaten path with a neon light for the world to see and follow this man. Speeches inspire and break the inertia. They move the listener, soliciting her/him to do something and in turn make the speaker a hallowed individual. One great takeaway of a powerful speech is that it immortalizes the speaker. He or she may die mortally but their ideas survive and inspire for centuries.

One common theme runs throughout a great speaker, cutting across centuries, issues and age—*Absence of fear.* And as the granddaddy of all motivators, Dale Carnegie, aptly said, 'Fear doesn't exist anywhere except in the mind.' In this anthology of the greatest speeches of the modern world, our starting point is 1990 onwards. Why 1990? We have chosen this year since in some ways and safely speaking, from this year, twentieth century became more modern and more anxious. Well sort of. Cold War came to an end with the fall of Berlin Wall, overtly communist Soviet Union imploded and gave birth to commonwealth of independent states, technology entered our homes and came to occupy our daily lives, markets became omnipresent and greed good, divisions between the haves and the have-nots increased, religion became more violent and people became scared. And it is in times like these that people who held their nerves and fought their fears inspired us with their famous and testing oratory. So when a sitting President of the United States of America, William Jefferson Clinton, apologizes to everyone about his affair with a White House intern, he has already done half his homework in his mind—has removed all his fears of condemnation. When a 16-year-old Malala Yousafzai speaks at the United Nations about her near-death encounter with extremist elements and challenges her attackers, fear is the last thing on her mind. Or when a Silicon Valley-nurtured Sheryl Sandberg talks about resilience to counter our greatest individual tragedies she has successfully logged out fear of 'loss' from her system. This anthology is truly a catalogue of fearlessness, hope and victory.

In order to compile this compendium, utmost care has been taken to accrue permission from the source wherever it was required and the same has been mentioned against the concerned speech as well.

We hope our readers will enjoy this collection as much as we have enjoyed curating it.

1

Bill Clinton

42nd President of the United States of America
(1993–2001)

We will honour the life and the work of
Martin Luther King.*

*This speech was delivered as remarks to the Convocation of the
Church of God in Christ in Memphis on 13 November 1993.*

Thank you. Please sit down. Bishop Ford, Mrs Mason, Bishop
Owens and Bishop Anderson; my bishops, Bishop Walker and
Bishop Lindsey. Now, if you haven't had Bishop Lindsey's
barbecue, you haven't had barbecue. And if you haven't heard
Bishop Walker attack one of my opponents, you have never
heard a political speech.

I am glad to be here. You have touched my heart. You've
brought tears to my eyes and joy to my spirit. Last year I was

---

*Source: White House website

with you over at the convention centre. Two years ago your bishops came to Arkansas, and we laid a plaque at the point in Little Rock, Arkansas, at 8th and Gaines, where Bishop Mason received the inspiration for the name of this great church. Bishop Brooks said from his pulpit that I would be elected President when most people thought I wouldn't survive. I thank him, and I thank your faith, and I thank your works, for without you I would not be here today as your President.

Many have spoken eloquently and well, and many have been introduced. I want to thank my good friend Governor [Ted] McWherter and my friend Mayor [Willie] Herenton for being with me today; my friend, Congressman Harold Ford, we are glad to be in his congressional district. I would like to, if I might, introduce just three other people who are Members of the Congress. They have come here with me, and without them it's hard for me to do much for you. The President proposes and the Congress disposes. Sometimes they dispose of what I propose, but I'm happy to say that according to a recent report in Washington, notwithstanding what you may have heard, this Congress has given me a higher percentage of my proposals than any first-year President since President Eisenhower[1]. And I thank them for that. Let me introduce my good friend, a visitor to Tennessee, Congressman Bill Jefferson from New Orleans, Louisiana—please stand up; and an early supporter of my campaign, Congressman Bob Clement from Tennessee, known to many of you; and a young man who's going to be coming back to the people of Tennessee and asking them to give him a promotion next year, Congressman Jim Cooper

---

[1] Dwight D. Eisenhower served as the 34th President of the United States from 1953–61.

from Tennessee, and a good friend. Please welcome him.

You know, in the last ten months, I've been called a lot of things, but nobody's called me a bishop yet. When I was about 9 years old, my beloved and now departed grandmother, who was a very wise woman, looked at me and she said, 'You know, I believe you could be a preacher if you were just a little better boy.'

Proverb says, 'A happy heart doeth good like medicine, but a broken spirit drieth the bone.' This is a happy place, and I'm happy to be here. I thank you for your spirit.

By the grace of God and your help, last year I was elected President of this great country. I never dreamed that I would ever have a chance to come to this hallowed place where Martin Luther King gave his last sermon. I ask you to think today about the purpose for which I ran and the purpose for which so many of you worked to put me in this great office. I have worked hard to keep faith with our common efforts—to restore the economy, to reverse the politics of helping only those at the top of our totem pole and not the hard-working middle-class or the poor—to bring our people together across racial and regional and political lines, to make a strength out of our diversity instead of letting it tear us apart, to reward work and family and community and try to move us forward into the twenty-first century. I have tried to keep faith.

Thirteen per cent of all my presidential appointments are African Americans, and there are five African Americans in the Cabinet of the United States, two and a half times as many as have ever served in the history of this great land. I have sought to advance the right to vote with the motor voter bill, supported so strongly by all the churches in our country. And next week it will be my great honour to sign the restoration of religious freedoms act, a bill supported widely by people across all religions and political philosophies to put back the real meaning of the Constitution, to give you and every other American the freedom to do what is most important in your life, to worship God as your spirit leads you.

I say to you, my fellow Americans, we have made a good beginning. Inflation is down. Interest rates are down. The deficit is down. Investment is up. Millions of Americans, including, I bet, some people in this room, have refinanced their homes or their business loans just in the last year. And in the last ten months, this economy has produced more jobs in the private sector than in the previous four years.

We have passed a law called the family leave law, which says you can't be fired if you take a little time off when a baby is born or a parent is sick. We know that most Americans have to work, but you ought not to have to give up being a good parent just to take a job. If you can't succeed as a worker and a parent, this country can't make it.

We have radically reformed the college loan programme, as I promised, to lower the cost of college loans and broaden the availability of it and make the repayment terms easier. And we have passed the national service law that will give in three years—three years from now—1,00,000 young Americans the chance to serve their communities at home, to repair the frayed bonds of community, to build up the needs of people at the grass roots, and at the same time, earn some money to pay for a college education. It is a wonderful idea.

On April 15th when people pay their taxes, somewhere between fifteen million and eighteen million working families on modest incomes, families with children and incomes of under $23,000, will get a tax cut, not a tax increase, in the most important effort to ensure that we reward work and family in the last twenty years. Fifty million American parents and their children will be advantaged by putting the Tax Code back on the side of working American parents for a change.

Under the leadership of the First Lady, we have produced a comprehensive plan to guarantee healthcare security to all Americans. How can we expect the American people to work and to live with all the changes in a global economy, where the average 18-year-old will change work seven times in a lifetime, unless we can simply say we have joined the ranks of all the other advanced countries in the world; you can have decent healthcare that's always there, that can never be taken away? It is time we did that, long past time. I ask you to help us achieve that.

But we have so much more to do. You and I know that most people are still working harder for the same or lower wages, that many people are afraid that their job will go away. We have to provide the education and training our people need, not just for our children but for our adults, too. If we cannot close this country up to the forces of change sweeping throughout the world, we have to at least guarantee people the security of being employable. They have to be able to get a new job if they're going to have to get a new job. We don't do that today, and we must, and we intend to proceed until that is done.

We have a guarantee that there will be some investment in those areas of our country, in the inner cities and in the destitute rural areas in the Mississippi Delta, of my home state and this state and Louisiana and Mississippi and other places like it throughout America. It's all very well to train people, but if they don't have a job, they can be trained for nothing.

We must get investment into those places where the people are dying for work.

And finally, let me say, we must find people who will buy what we have to produce. We are the most productive people on earth. That makes us proud. But what that means is that every year one person can produce more in the same amount of time. Now, if fewer and fewer people can produce more and more things, and yet you want to create more jobs and raise people's incomes, you have to have more customers for what it is you're making. And that is why I have worked so hard to sell more American products around the world; why I have asked that we be able to sell billions of dollars of computers we used not to sell to foreign countries and foreign interests, to put our people to work; why next week I am going all the way to Washington State to meet with the President of China and the Prime Minister of Japan and the heads of thirteen other Asian countries, the fastest growing part of the world, to say, 'We want to be your partners. We will buy your goods, but we want you to buy ours, too, if you please.' That is why.

That is why I have worked so hard for this North American trade agreement that Congressman Ford endorsed today and Congressman Jefferson endorsed and Congressman Cooper and Congressman Clement, because we know that Americans can compete and win only if people will buy what it is we have to sell. There are ninety million people in Mexico. Seventy cents of every dollar they spend on foreign goods, they spend on American goods.

People worry fairly about people shutting down plants in America and going not just to Mexico but to any place where the labour is cheap. It has happened. What I want to say to you, my fellow Americans, is nothing in this agreement makes that more likely. That has happened already. It may happen again. What we need to do is keep the jobs here by finding customers there. That's what this agreement does. It gives us a chance to create opportunity for people. I have friends in this audience, people who are ministers from my state, fathers and sons, people—I've looked out all over this vast crowd and I see people I've known for years. They know I spent my whole life working to create jobs. I would never knowingly do anything that would take a job away from the American people. This agreement will make more jobs. Now, we can also leave it if it doesn't work in six months. But if we don't take it, we'll lose it forever. We need to take it, because we have to do better.

But I guess what I really want to say to you today, my fellow Americans, is that we can do all of this and still fail unless we meet the great crisis of the spirit that is gripping America today.

When I leave you, Congressman Ford and I are going to a Baptist church near here to a town meeting he's having on healthcare and violence. I tell you, unless we do something about crime and violence and drugs that is ravaging the community, we will not be able to repair this country.

If Martin Luther King, who said, 'Like Moses, I am on the mountaintop, and I can see the promised land, but I'm not going to be able to get there with you, but we will get there', if he were to reappear by my side today and give us a report card on the last twenty-five years, what would he say? You did a good job, he would say, voting and electing people who formerly were not electable because of the colour of their skin. You have more political power, and that is good. You did a good job, he would say, letting people who have the ability to do so live wherever they want to live, go wherever they want to go in this great country. You did a good job, he would say, elevating people of colour into the ranks of the United States Armed Forces to the very top or into the very top of our government. You did a very good job, he would say. He would say, you did a good job creating a black middle-class of people who really are doing well, and the middle-class is growing more among African Americans than among non-African Americans. You did a good job; you did a good job in opening opportunity.

But he would say, I did not live and die to see the American family destroyed. I did not live and die to see 13-year-old boys get automatic weapons and gun down 9-year-olds just for the kick of it. I did not live and die to see young people destroy their own lives with drugs and then build fortunes destroying the lives of others. That is not what I came here to do. I fought for freedom, he would say, but not for the freedom of people to kill each other with reckless abandon, not for the freedom of children to have children and the fathers of the children walk away from them and abandon them as if they don't amount to anything. I fought for people to have the right to work but not to have whole communities and people abandoned. This is not what I lived and died for.

My fellow Americans, he would say, I fought to stop white people from being so filled with hate that they would wreak violence on black people. I did not fight for the right of black people to murder other black people with reckless abandon.

The other day, the Mayor of Baltimore, a dear friend of mine, told me a story of visiting the family of a young man who had been killed—18 years old—on Halloween. He always went out with little bitty kids so they could trick or treat safely. And across the street from where they were walking on Halloween, a 14-year-old boy gave a 13-year-old boy a gun and dared him to shoot the 18-year-old boy, and he shot him dead. And the Mayor had to visit the family.

In Washington, D.C., where I live, your nation's capital, the symbol of freedom throughout the world, look how that freedom is being exercised. The other night, a man came along the street and grabbed a 1-year-old child and put the child in his car. The child may have been the child of the man. And two people were after him, and they chased him in the car, and they just kept shooting with reckless abandon, knowing that [the] baby was in the car. And they shot the man dead, and a bullet went through his body into the baby's body, and blew the little bootie off the child's foot.

The other day on the front page of our paper, the nation's capital, are we talking about world peace or world conflict? No, big article on the front page of *The Washington Post* about an 11-year-old child planning her funeral: 'These are the hymns I want sung. This is the dress I want to wear. I know I'm not going to live very long.' That is not the freedom, the freedom to die before you're a teenager is not what Martin Luther King lived and died for.

More than 37,000 people die from gunshot wounds in this country every year. Gunfire is the leading cause of death in young men. And now that we've all gotten so cool that everybody can get a semi-automatic weapon, a person shot now is three times more likely to die than fifteen years ago, because they're likely to have three bullets in them. A hundred and sixty thousand children stay home from school every day because they are scared they will be hurt in their schools.

The other day I was in California at a town meeting, and a handsome young man stood up and said, 'Mr President, my brother and I, we don't belong to gangs. We don't have guns. We don't do drugs. We want to go to school. We want to be professionals. We want to work hard. We want to do well. We want to have families. And we changed our school because the school we were in was so dangerous. So when we stowed up to the new school to register, my brother and I were standing in line and somebody ran into the school and started shooting a gun. My brother was shot down standing right in front of me at the safer school.' The freedom to do that kind of thing is not what Martin Luther King lived and died for, not what people gathered in this hallowed church for the night before he was assassinated in April of 1968. If you had told anybody who was here in that church on that night that we would abuse our freedom in that way, they would have found it hard to believe. And I tell you, it is our moral duty to turn it around.

And now I think finally we have a chance. Finally, I think, we have a chance. We have a pastor here from New Haven, Connecticut. I was in his church with Reverend Jackson when I was running for President on a snowy day in Connecticut to mourn the death of children who had been killed in that city. And afterwards we walked down the street for more than a mile in the snow. Then, the American people were not ready. People would say, 'Oh, this is a terrible thing, but what can we do about it?'

Now when we read that foreign visitors come to our shores and are killed at random in our fine State of Florida, when we see our children planning their funerals, when the American people are finally coming to grips with the accumulated weight of crime and violence and the breakdown of family and community and the increase in drugs and the decrease in jobs, I think finally we may be ready to do something about it.

And there is something for each of us to do. There are changes we can make from the outside in; that's the job of the President and the Congress and the governors and the mayors and the social service agencies. And then [there are] some changes we're going to have to make from the inside out, or the others won't matter. That's what that magnificent song was about, isn't it? Sometimes there are no answers from the outside in; sometimes all the answers have to come from the values and the stirrings and the voices that speak to us from within.

So we are beginning. We are trying to pass a bill to make our people safer, to put another 1,00,000 police officers on the street, to provide boot camps instead of prisons for young people who can still be rescued, to provide more safety in our schools, to restrict the availability of these awful assault weapons, to pass the Brady bill and at least require people to have their criminal background checked before they get a gun, and to say, if you're not old enough to vote and you're not old enough to go to war, you ought not to own a handgun and you ought not to use one unless you're on a target range.

We want to pass a healthcare bill that will make drug treatment available for everyone. And we also have to do it, we have to have drug treatment and education available to everyone and especially those who are in prison who are coming out. We have a drug czar now in Lee Brown, who was the police chief of Atlanta, of Houston, of New York, who understands these things. And when the Congress comes back next year, we will be moving forward on that.

We need this crime bill now. We ought to give it to the American people for Christmas. And we need to move forward on all these other fronts. But I say to you, my fellow Americans, we need some other things as well. I do not believe we can repair the basic fabric of society until people who are willing to work have work. Work organizes life. It gives structure and discipline to life. It gives meaning and self-esteem to people who are parents. It gives a role model to children.

The famous African American sociologist William Julius Wilson has written a stunning book called *The Truly Disadvantaged* in which he chronicles in breathtaking terms how the inner cities of our country have crumbled as work has disappeared. And we must find a way, through public and private sources, to enhance the attractiveness of the American people who live there to get investment there. We cannot, I submit to you, repair the American community and restore the American family until we provide the structure, the values, the discipline and the reward that work gives.

I read a wonderful speech the other day given at Howard University in a lecture series funded by Bill and Camille Cosby, in which the speaker said, 'I grew up in Anacostia years ago. Even then it was all black, and it was a very poor neighbourhood. But you know, when I was a child in Anacostia, a 100 per cent African American neighbourhood, a very poor neighbourhood, we had a crime rate that was lower than the average of the crime rate of our city. Why? Because we had coherent families. We had coherent communities. The people who filled the church on Sunday lived in the same place they went to church. The guy that owned the drugstore lived down the street. The person that owned the grocery store lived in our community. We were whole.' And I say to you, we have to make our people whole again.

This church has stood for that. Why do you think you have five million members in this country? Because people know you are filled with the spirit of God to do the right thing in this life by them. So I say to you, we have to make a partnership, all the government agencies, all the business folks; but where there are no families, where there is no order, where there is no hope, where we are reducing the size of our armed services because we have won the Cold War, who will be there to give structure, discipline and love to these children? You must do that. And we must help you. Scripture says, 'You are the salt of the earth and the light of the world, that if your light shines before men they will give glory to the Father in heaven.' That is what we must do.

That is what we must do. How would we explain it to Martin Luther King if he showed up today and said, yes, we won the Cold War. Yes, the biggest threat that all of us grew up under, communism and nuclear war, communism gone, nuclear war receding. Yes, we developed all these miraculous technologies. Yes, we all have got a VCR in our home; it's interesting. Yes, we get fifty channels on the cable. Yes, without regard to race, if you work hard and play by the rules, you can get into a service academy or a good college, you'll do just great. How would we explain to him all these kids getting killed and killing each other? How would we justify the things that we permit that no other country in the world would permit? How could we explain that we gave people the freedom to succeed, and we created conditions in which millions abuse that freedom to destroy the things that make life worth living and life itself? We cannot.

And so I say to you today, my fellow Americans, you gave me this job, and we're making progress on the things you hired me to do. But unless we deal with the ravages of crime and drugs and violence; and unless we recognize that it's due to the breakdown of the family, the community and the disappearance of jobs; and unless we say some of this cannot be done by government, because we have to reach deep inside to the values, the spirit, the soul and the truth of human nature, none of the other things we seek to do will ever take us where we need to go.

So in this pulpit, on this day, let me ask all of you in your heart to say: We will honour the life and the work of Martin Luther King. We will honour the meaning of our church. We will, somehow, by God's grace, we will turn this around. We will give these children a future. We will take away their guns and give them books. We will take away their despair and give them hope. We will rebuild the families and the neighbourhoods and the communities. We won't make all the work that has gone on here benefit just a few. We will do it together by the grace of God.

Thank you.

◆

This has hurt too many people.[*]

This speech was delivered by President Bill Clinton on 17 August 1998, after his testimony before the jury in the Monica Lewinsky affair. It was a historical day for American presidency.

Good evening.

This afternoon, in this room, from this chair, I testified before the Office of Independent Counsel and the grand jury. I answered their questions truthfully, including questions about my private

---

*Source: White House website

life, questions no American citizen would ever want to answer.

Still, I must take complete responsibility for all my actions, both public and private. And that is why I am speaking to you tonight. As you know, in a deposition in January, I was asked questions about my relationship with Monica Lewinsky. While my answers were legally accurate, I did not volunteer information.

Indeed, I did have a relationship with Miss Lewinsky that was not appropriate. In fact, it was wrong. It constituted a critical lapse in judgement and a personal failure on my part for which I am solely and completely responsible.

But I told the grand jury today and I say to you now that at no time did I ask anyone to lie, to hide or destroy evidence or to take any other unlawful action.

I know that my public comments and my silence about this matter gave a false impression. I misled people, including even my wife. I deeply regret that.

I can only tell you I was motivated by many factors. First, by a desire to protect myself from the embarrassment of my own conduct. I was also very concerned about protecting my family. The fact that these questions were being asked in a politically inspired lawsuit, which has since been dismissed, was a consideration, too.

In addition, I had real and serious concerns about an independent counsel investigation that began with private business dealings twenty years ago, dealings I might add about which an independent federal agency found no evidence of any wrongdoing by me or my wife over two years ago.

The independent counsel investigation moved on to my staff and friends, then into my private life. And now the investigation itself is under investigation. This has gone on too long, cost too much and hurt too many innocent people.

Now, this matter is between me, the two people I love most—my wife and our daughter—and our God. I must put it right, and I am prepared to do whatever it takes to do so.

Nothing is more important to me personally. But it is private, and I intend to reclaim my family life for my family. It's nobody's business but ours. Even presidents have private lives. It is time to stop the pursuit of personal destruction and the prying into private lives and get on with our national life.

Our country has been distracted by this matter for too long, and I take my responsibility for my part in all of this. That is all I can do.

Now it is time—in fact, it is past time to move on. We have important work to do—real opportunities to seize, real problems to solve, real security matters to face.

And so tonight, I ask you to turn away from the spectacle of the past seven months, to repair the fabric of our national discourse and to return our attention to all the challenges and all the promise of the next American century.

Thank you for watching. And good night.

◆

I don't think there is a fancy way to say that I have sinned.[*]

This speech was delivered by President Bill Clinton at the annual White House prayer breakfast on 11 September 1998 to an audience of more than hundred ministers, priests and other

---

*Source: White House website

religious leaders assembled in the East Room. First Lady Hillary
Rodham Clinton was also in attendance.
The speech came amidst the publication of the first report
to Congress by Independent Counsel Ken Starr in the infamous
Monica Lewinsky–Bill Clinton affair. The report laid the grounds
for possible impeachment of the President, accusing him of
perjury, obstruction of justice and other offences as a result of
his attempt to conceal his relationship with former White House
intern Monica Lewinsky. This speech was handwritten by Clinton.
In this speech, the President includes Lewinsky in his apology.

Thank you very much, ladies and gentlemen. Welcome to the
White House and to this day to which Hillary and the Vice
President and I look forward so much every year.

This is always an important day for our country, for the
reasons that the Vice President said. It is an unusual and, I
think, unusually important day today. I may not be quite as
easy with my words today as I have been in years past, and
I was up rather late last night thinking about and praying
about what I ought to say today. And rather unusual for me,
I actually tried to write it down. So if you will forgive me, I
will do my best to say what it is I want to say to you—and
I may have to take my glasses out to read my own writing.

First, I want to say to all of you that, as you might imagine,
I have been on quite a journey these last few weeks to get to
the end of this, to the rock-bottom truth of where I am and
where we all are.

I agree with those who have said that in my first statement
after I testified I was not contrite enough. I don't think there
is a fancy way to say that I have sinned.

It is important to me that everybody who has been hurt

know that the sorrow I feel is genuine: first and most important, my family, also my friends, my staff, my Cabinet, Monica Lewinsky and her family, and the American people. I have asked all for their forgiveness.

But I believe that to be forgiven, more than sorrow is required—at least two more things. First, genuine repentance—a determination to change and to repair breaches of my own making. I have repented. Second, what my bible calls a 'broken spirit'; an understanding that I must have God's help to be the person that I want to be; a willingness to give the very forgiveness I seek; a renunciation of the pride and the anger which cloud judgement, lead people to excuse and compare and to blame and complain.

Now, what does all this mean for me and for us? First, I will instruct my lawyers to mount a vigorous defence, using all available appropriate arguments. But legal language must not obscure the fact that I have done wrong. Second, I will continue on the path of repentance, seeking pastoral support and that of other caring people so that they can hold me accountable for my own commitment.

Third, I will intensify my efforts to lead our country and the world towards peace and freedom, prosperity and harmony, in the hope that with a broken spirit and a still strong heart I can be used for greater good, for we have many blessings and many challenges and so much work to do.

In this, I ask for your prayers and for your help in healing our nation. And though I cannot move beyond or forget this— indeed, I must always keep it as a caution light in my life—it is very important that our nation move forward.

I am very grateful for the many, many people—clergy and ordinary citizens alike—who have written me with wise counsel. I am profoundly grateful for the support of so many Americans who somehow through it all seem to still know that I care about them a great deal, that I care about their problems and their dreams. I am grateful for those who have stood by me and who say that in this case and many others, the bounds of privacy have been excessively and unwisely invaded. That may be. Nevertheless, in this case, it may be a blessing, because I still sinned. And if my repentance is genuine and sustained, and if I can maintain both a broken spirit and a strong heart, then good can come of this for our country as well as for me and my family.

The children of this country can learn in a profound way that integrity is important and selfishness is wrong, but God can change us and make us strong at the broken places. I want to embody those lessons for the children of this country—for that little boy in Florida who came up to me and said that he wanted to grow up and be President and to be just like me. I want the parents of all the children in America to be able to say that to their children.

A couple of days ago when I was in Florida, a Jewish friend of mine gave me this liturgy book called *Gates of Repentance*. And there was this incredible passage from the Yom Kippur liturgy. I would like to read it to you:

> Now is the time for turning. The leaves are beginning to turn from green to red to orange. The birds are beginning to turn and are heading once more toward the south. The animals are beginning to turn to storing their food for the winter. For leaves, birds and animals, turning comes instinctively. But for us, turning does not come so easily. It takes an act of will for us to make a turn. It means

breaking old habits. It means admitting that we have been wrong, and this is never easy. It means losing face. It means starting all over again. And this is always painful. It means saying I am sorry. It means recognizing that we have the ability to change. These things are terribly hard to do. But unless we turn, we will be trapped forever in yesterday's ways. Lord help us to turn, from callousness to sensitivity, from hostility to love, from pettiness to purpose, from envy to contentment, from carelessness to discipline, from fear to faith. Turn us around, O Lord, and bring us back toward you. Revive our lives as at the beginning, and turn us toward each other, Lord, for in isolation there is no life.

I thank my friend for that. I thank you for being here. I ask you to share my prayer that God will search me and know my heart, try me and know my anxious thoughts, see if there is any hurtfulness in me and lead me towards the life everlasting. I ask that God give me a clean heart, let me walk by faith and not sight.

I ask once again to be able to love my neighbour—all my neighbours—as myself, to be an instrument of God's peace; to let the words of my mouth and the meditations of my heart and, in the end, the work of my hands, be pleasing. This is what I wanted to say to you today.

Thank you. God bless you.

◆

2

George W. Bush
43rd President of the United States of America
(2001–2009)

Today our nation saw evil.[*]

This speech was delivered on 11 September 2001 after the deadly terrorist attacks on the American soil. The speech, delivered at the Oval Office, Washington, D.C., is now popularly called the 9/11 Address to the Nation.

Good evening.

Today, our fellow citizens, our way of life, our very freedom came under attack in a series of deliberate and deadly terrorist acts. The victims were in airplanes or in their offices: secretaries, business men and women, military and federal workers, moms and dads, friends and neighbours. Thousands

*Source: White House website

of lives were suddenly ended by evil, despicable acts of terror. The pictures of airplanes flying into buildings, fires burning, huge, huge structures collapsing have filled us with disbelief, terrible sadness and a quiet, unyielding anger. These acts of mass murder were intended to frighten our nation into chaos and retreat. But they have failed. Our country is strong.

A great people has been moved to defend a great nation. Terrorist attacks can shake the foundations of our biggest buildings, but they cannot touch the foundation of America. These acts shatter steel, but they cannot dent the steel of American resolve. America was targeted for attack because we are the brightest beacon for freedom and opportunity in the world. And no one will keep that light from shining. Today, our nation saw evil—the very worst of human nature—and we responded with the best of America. With the daring of our rescue workers, with the caring for strangers and neighbours who came to give blood and help in any way they could.

Immediately following the first attack, I implemented our government's emergency response plans. Our military is powerful, and it's prepared. Our emergency teams are working in New York City and Washington, D.C., to help with local rescue efforts. Our first priority is to get help to those who have been injured, and to take every precaution to protect our citizens at home and around the world from further attacks. The functions of our government continue without interruption. Federal agencies in Washington which had to be evacuated today are reopening for essential personnel tonight and will be open for business tomorrow. Our financial institutions remain strong, and the American economy will be open for business as well.

The search is under way for those who were behind these

evil acts. I have directed the full resources of our intelligence and law enforcement communities to find those responsible and to bring them to justice. We will make no distinction between the terrorists who committed these acts and those who harbour them.

I appreciate so very much the members of Congress who have joined me in strongly condemning these attacks. And on behalf of the American people, I thank the many world leaders who have called to offer their condolences and assistance. America and our friends and allies join with all those who want peace and security in the world, and we stand together to win the war against terrorism.

Tonight, I ask for your prayers for all those who grieve, for the children whose worlds have been shattered, for all whose sense of safety and security has been threatened. And I pray they will be comforted by a Power greater than any of us, spoken through the ages in Psalm 23:

Even though I walk through the valley of the shadow of death, I fear no evil for you are with me.

This is a day when all Americans from every walk of life unite in our resolve for justice and peace. America has stood down enemies before, and we will do so this time. None of us will ever forget this day, yet we go forward to defend freedom and all that is good and just in our world.

Thank you. Good night. And God bless America.

◆

3

Barack Obama
44th President of the United States of America
(2009–2017)

I am married to a black American who carries within her the blood of slaves and slave owners.[*]

The following speech was delivered by Barack Obama in his capacity as a Democratic Senator from Illinois on 18 March 2008 in Philadelphia at the Constitution Center. In it, Obama addresses the role race has played in the presidential campaign.

We the people, in order to form a more perfect union.

Two hundred and twenty-one years ago, in a hall that still stands across the street, a group of men gathered and, with these simple words, launched America's improbable experiment in democracy. Farmers and scholars, statesmen

---

*Source: White House website

and patriots who had travelled across an ocean to escape tyranny and persecution finally made real their declaration of independence at a Philadelphia convention that lasted through the spring of 1787.

The document they produced was eventually signed but ultimately unfinished. It was stained by this nation's original sin of slavery, a question that divided the colonies and brought the convention to a stalemate until the Founders chose to allow the slave trade to continue for at least twenty more years, and to leave any final resolution to future generations.

Of course, the answer to the slavery question was already embedded within our Constitution—a Constitution that had at its very core the ideal of equal citizenship under the law; a Constitution that promised its people liberty and justice and a union that could be and should be perfected over time.

And yet words on a parchment would not be enough to deliver slaves from bondage, or provide men and women of every colour and creed their full rights and obligations as citizens of the United States. What would be needed were Americans in successive generations who were willing to do their part—through protests and struggles, on the streets and in the courts, through a civil war and civil disobedience, and always at great risk—to narrow that gap between the promise of our ideals and the reality of their time.

This was one of the tasks we set forth at the beginning of this presidential campaign—to continue the long march of those who came before us, a march for a more just, more equal, more free, more caring and more prosperous America. I chose to run for president at this moment in history because I believe deeply that we cannot solve the challenges of our time unless we solve them together, unless we perfect our union by understanding that we may have different stories, but we hold common hopes; that we may not look the same and we may not have come from the same place, but we all want to move in the same direction—towards a better future for our children and our grandchildren.

This belief comes from my unyielding faith in the decency and generosity of the American people. But it also comes from my own story.

I am the son of a black man from Kenya and a white woman from Kansas. I was raised with the help of a white grandfather who survived a Depression to serve in Patton's Army during World War II and a white grandmother who worked on a bomber assembly line at Fort Leavenworth while he was overseas. I've gone to some of the best schools in America and lived in one of the world's poorest nations. I am married to a black American who carries within her the blood of slaves and slave owners—an inheritance we pass on to our two precious daughters. I have brothers, sisters, nieces, nephews, uncles and cousins of every race and every hue, scattered across three continents, and for as long as I live, I will never forget that in no other country on earth is my story even possible.

It's a story that hasn't made me the most conventional of candidates. But it is a story that has seared into my genetic make-up the idea that this nation is more than the sum of its parts—that out of many, we are truly one.

Throughout the first year of this campaign, against all predictions to the contrary, we saw how hungry the American people were for this message of unity. Despite the temptation to view my candidacy through a purely racial lens, we won commanding victories in states with some of the whitest populations in the country. In South Carolina, where the Confederate flag still flies, we built a powerful coalition of African Americans and white Americans.

This is not to say that race has not been an issue in this campaign. At various stages in the campaign, some commentators have deemed me either 'too black' or 'not black enough'. We saw racial tensions bubble to the surface during the week before the South Carolina primary. The press has scoured every single exit poll for the latest evidence of racial polarization, not just in terms of white and black, but black and brown as well.

And yet, it has only been in the last couple of weeks that the discussion of race in this campaign has taken a particularly divisive turn.

On one end of the spectrum, we've heard the implication that my candidacy is somehow an exercise in affirmative action; that it's based solely on the desire of wide-eyed liberals to purchase racial reconciliation on the cheap. On the other end, we've heard my former pastor, Jeremiah Wright, use incendiary language to express views that have the potential not only to widen the racial divide, but views that denigrate both the greatness and the goodness of our nation, and that rightly offend white and black alike.

I have already condemned, in unequivocal terms, the statements of Reverend Wright that have caused such controversy and, in some cases, pain. For some, nagging questions remain. Did I know him to be an occasionally fierce critic of American domestic and foreign policy? Of course. Did I ever hear him make remarks that could be considered controversial while I sat in the church? Yes. Did I strongly disagree with many of his political views? Absolutely—just as

I'm sure many of you have heard remarks from your pastors, priests, or rabbis with which you strongly disagreed.

But the remarks that have caused this recent firestorm weren't simply controversial. They weren't simply a religious leader's efforts to speak out against perceived injustice. Instead, they expressed a profoundly distorted view of this country—a view that sees white racism as endemic, and that elevates what is wrong with America above all that we know is right with America; a view that sees the conflicts in the Middle East as rooted primarily in the actions of stalwart allies like Israel, instead of emanating from the perverse and hateful ideologies of radical Islam.

As such, Reverend Wright's comments were not only wrong but divisive, divisive at a time when we need unity; racially charged at a time when we need to come together to solve a set of monumental problems—two wars, a terrorist threat, a falling economy, a chronic healthcare crisis and potentially devastating climate change—problems that are neither black or white or Latino or Asian, but rather problems that confront us all.

Given my background, my politics and my professed values and ideals, there will no doubt be those for whom my statements of condemnation are not enough. Why associate myself with Reverend Wright in the first place, they may ask? Why not join another church? And I confess that if all that I knew of Reverend Wright were the snippets of those sermons that have run in an endless loop on the television sets and YouTube, or if Trinity United Church of Christ conformed to the caricatures being peddled by some commentators, there is no doubt that I would react in much the same way.

But the truth is, that isn't all that I know of the man. The man I met more than twenty years ago is a man who helped introduce me to my Christian faith, a man who spoke to me about our obligations to love one another, to care for the sick and lift up the poor. He is a man who served his country as a United States Marine, who has studied and lectured at some of the finest universities and seminaries in the country and who, for over thirty years, has led a church that serves the community by doing God's work here on earth—by housing the homeless, ministering to the needy, providing day care services and scholarships and prison ministries and reaching out to those suffering from HIV/AIDS.

In my first book, *Dreams From My Father*, I describe the experience of my first service at Trinity:

> People began to shout, to rise from their seats and clap and cry out, a forceful wind carrying the reverend's voice up into the rafters. And in that single note—hope!—I heard something else: At the foot of that cross, inside the thousands of churches across the city, I imagined the stories of ordinary black people merging with the stories of David and Goliath, Moses and Pharaoh, the Christians in the lion's den, Ezekiel's field of dry bones. Those stories—of survival and freedom and hope— became our stories, my story. The blood that spilled was our blood, the tears our tears, until this black church, on this bright day, seemed once more a vessel carrying the story of a people into future generations and into a larger world. Our trials and triumphs became at once unique and universal, black and more than black. In chronicling our journey, the stories and songs gave us a meaning to reclaim memories that we didn't need to feel shame

about—memories that all people might study and cherish, and with which we could start to rebuild.

That has been my experience at Trinity. Like other predominantly black churches across the country, Trinity embodies the black community in its entirety—the doctor and the welfare mom, the model student and the former gang-banger. Like other black churches, Trinity's services are full of raucous laughter and sometimes bawdy humour. They are full of dancing and clapping and screaming and shouting that may seem jarring to the untrained ear. The church contains in full the kindness and cruelty, the fierce intelligence and the shocking ignorance, the struggles and successes, the love and, yes, the bitterness and biases that make up the black experience in America.

And this helps explain, perhaps, my relationship with Reverend Wright. As imperfect as he may be, he has been like family to me. He strengthened my faith, officiated my wedding and baptized my children. Not once in my conversations with him have I heard him talk about any ethnic group in derogatory terms, or treat whites with whom he interacted with anything but courtesy and respect. He contains within him the contradictions—the good and the bad—of the community that he has served diligently for so many years.

I can no more disown him than I can disown the black community. I can no more disown him than I can disown my white grandmother—a woman who helped raise me, a woman who sacrificed again and again for me, a woman who loves me as much as she loves anything in this world, but a woman who once confessed her fear of black men who passed her by on the street, and who on more than one occasion has uttered racial or ethnic stereotypes that made me cringe.

These people are a part of me. And they are part of America, this country that I love.

Some will see this as an attempt to justify or excuse comments that are simply inexcusable. I can assure you it is not. I suppose the politically safe thing to do would be to move on from this episode and just hope that it fades into the woodwork. We can dismiss Reverend Wright as a crank or a demagogue, just as some have dismissed Geraldine Ferraro, in the aftermath of her recent statements, as harbouring some deep-seated bias.

But race is an issue that I believe this nation cannot afford to ignore right now. We would be making the same mistake that Reverend Wright made in his offending sermons about America—to simplify and stereotype and amplify the negative to the point that it distorts reality.

The fact is that the comments that have been made and the issues that have surfaced over the last few weeks reflect the complexities of race in this country that we've never really worked through—a part of our union that we have not yet made perfect. And if we walk away now, if we simply retreat into our respective corners, we will never be able to come together and solve challenges like healthcare or education or the need to find good jobs for every American.

Understanding this reality requires a reminder of how we arrived at this point. As William Faulkner once wrote, 'The past isn't dead and buried. In fact, it isn't even past.' We do not need to recite here the history of racial injustice in this country. But we do need to remind ourselves that so many of the disparities that exist between the African American community and the larger American community today can be traced directly to inequalities passed on from an earlier generation that suffered under the brutal legacy of slavery and Jim Crow.

Segregated schools were and are inferior schools; we still haven't fixed them, fifty years after Brown v Board of Education. And the inferior education they provided, then and now, helps explain the pervasive achievement gap between today's black and white students.

Legalized discrimination—where blacks were prevented, often through violence, from owning property, or loans were not granted to African American business owners, or black homeowners could not access FHA[1] mortgages, or blacks were excluded from unions or the police force or the fire department—meant that black families could not amass any meaningful wealth to bequeath to future generations. That history helps explain the wealth and income gap between blacks and whites, and the concentrated pockets of poverty that persist in so many of today's urban and rural communities.

A lack of economic opportunity among black men, and the shame and frustration that came from not being able to provide for one's family contributed to the erosion of black families—a problem that welfare policies for many years may have worsened. And the lack of basic services in so many urban black neighbourhoods—parks for kids to play in, police walking the beat, regular garbage pickup, building code enforcement—all helped create a cycle of violence, blight and neglect that continues to haunt us.

This is the reality in which Reverend Wright and other African Americans of his generation grew up. They came of

---

[1]Federal Housing Administration (FHA) is a US Government agency.

age in the late '50s and early '60s, a time when segregation was still the law of the land and opportunity was systematically constricted. What's remarkable is not how many failed in the face of discrimination, but how many men and women overcame the odds; how many were able to make a way out of no way, for those like me who would come after them.

For all those who scratched and clawed their way to get a piece of the American Dream, there were many who didn't make it—those who were ultimately defeated, in one way or another, by discrimination. That legacy of defeat was passed on to future generations—those young men and, increasingly, young women who we see standing on street corners or languishing in our prisons, without hope or prospects for the future. Even for those blacks who did make it, questions of race and racism continue to define their world view in fundamental ways. For the men and women of Reverend Wright's generation, the memories of humiliation and doubt and fear have not gone away; nor has the anger and the bitterness of those years. That anger may not get expressed in public, in front of white co-workers or white friends. But it does find voice in the barbershop or the beauty shop or around the kitchen table. At times, that anger is exploited by politicians, to gin up votes along racial lines, or to make up for a politician's own failings.

And occasionally, it finds voice in the church on Sunday morning, in the pulpit and in the pews. The fact that so many people are surprised to hear that anger in some of Reverend Wright's sermons simply reminds us of the old truism that the most segregated hour of American life occurs on Sunday morning. That anger is not always productive; indeed, all too often it distracts attention from solving real problems, it keeps us from squarely facing our own complicity within the African American community in our condition, and prevents the African American community from forging the alliances it needs to bring about real change. But the anger is real; it is powerful. And to simply wish it away, to condemn it without understanding its roots, only serves to widen the chasm of misunderstanding that exists between the races.

In fact, a similar anger exists within segments of the white community. Most working and middle-class white Americans don't feel that they have been particularly privileged by their race. Their experience is the immigrant experience—as far as they're concerned, no one handed them anything. They built it from scratch. They've worked hard all their lives, many times only to see their jobs shipped overseas or their pensions dumped after a lifetime of labour. They are anxious about their futures, and they feel their dreams slipping away. And in an era of stagnant wages and global competition, opportunity comes to be seen as a zero sum game, in which your dreams come at my expense. So when they are told to bus their children to a school across town; when they hear an African American is getting an advantage in landing a good job or a spot in a good college because of an injustice that they themselves never committed; when they're told that their fears about crime in urban neighbourhoods are somehow prejudiced, resentment builds over time.

Like the anger within the black community, these resentments aren't always expressed in polite company. But they have helped shape the political landscape for at least a generation. Anger over welfare and affirmative action helped forge the Reagan Coalition. Politicians routinely exploited fears of crime for their own electoral ends. Talk show hosts and conservative commentators built entire careers unmasking bogus claims of racism while dismissing legitimate discussions of racial injustice and inequality as mere political correctness or reverse racism.

Just as black anger often proved counterproductive, so have these white resentments distracted attention from the real culprits of the middle-class squeeze—a corporate culture rife with inside dealing, questionable accounting practices and short-term greed; a Washington dominated by lobbyists and special interests; economic policies that favour the few over the many. And yet, to wish away the resentments of white Americans, to label them as misguided or even racist, without recognizing they are grounded in legitimate concerns—this too widens the racial divide and blocks the path to understanding.

This is where we are right now. It's a racial stalemate we've been stuck in for years. Contrary to the claims of some of my critics, black and white, I have never been so naïve as to believe that we can get beyond our racial divisions in a single election cycle, or with a single candidacy—particularly a candidacy as imperfect as my own.

But I have asserted a firm conviction—a conviction rooted in my faith in God and my faith in the American people— that, working together, we can move beyond some of our old racial wounds, and that in fact we have no choice if we are to continue on the path of a more perfect union.

For the African American community, that path means embracing the burdens of our past without becoming victims of our past. It means continuing to insist on a full measure of justice in every aspect of American life. But it also means binding our particular grievances—for better healthcare and better schools and better jobs—to the larger aspirations of all Americans: the white woman struggling to break the glass ceiling, the white man who has been laid off, the immigrant trying to feed his family. And it means taking full responsibility of our own lives—by demanding more from our fathers, and spending more time with our children, and reading to them, and teaching them that while they may face challenges and discrimination in their own lives, they must never succumb to despair or cynicism; they must always believe that they can write their own destiny.

Ironically, this quintessentially American—and yes, conservative—notion of self-help found frequent expression in Reverend Wright's sermons. But what my former pastor too often failed to understand is that embarking on a programme of self-help also requires a belief that society can change.

The profound mistake of Reverend Wright's sermons is not that he spoke about racism in our society. It's that he spoke as if our society was static; as if no progress had been made; as if this country—a country that has made it possible for one of his own members to run for the highest office in the land and build a coalition of white and black, Latino and Asian, rich and poor, young and old—is still irrevocably bound to a tragic past. But what we know—what we have seen—is that America can change. That is the true genius of this nation. What we have already achieved gives us hope—the audacity to hope—for what we can and must achieve tomorrow.

In the white community, the path to a more perfect union means acknowledging that what ails the African American community does not just exist in the minds of black people; that the legacy of discrimination—and current incidents of discrimination, while less overt than in the past—are real and must be addressed, not just with words, but with deeds, by investing in our schools and our communities; by enforcing our civil rights laws and ensuring fairness in our criminal justice system; by providing this generation with ladders of opportunity that were unavailable for previous generations. It requires all Americans to realize that your dreams do not have to come at the expense of my dreams; that investing in the health, welfare and education of black and brown and white children will ultimately help all of America [to] prosper.

In the end, then, what is called for is nothing more and nothing less than what all the world's great religions demand—that we do unto others as we would have them do unto us. Let us be our brother's keeper, scripture tells us. Let us be our sister's keeper. Let us find that common stake we all have in one another, and let our politics reflect that spirit as well.

For we have a choice in this country. We can accept a politics that breeds division and conflict and cynicism. We can tackle race only as spectacle—as we did in the OJ trial[2]—or in the wake of tragedy—as we did in the aftermath of [Hurricane] Katrina—or as fodder for the nightly news. We can play Reverend Wright's sermons on every channel, every day and talk about them from now until the election, and make the only question in this campaign whether or not the American people think that I somehow believe or sympathize with his most offensive words. We can pounce on some gaffe by a Hillary [Clinton] supporter as evidence that she's playing the race card, or we can speculate on whether white men will

---

[2]O.J. Simpson was a famous black football player. His trial on the murder of his ex-wife in 1995 (he had retired by then) was one of the most televised and scrutinized criminal trial in American history.

all flock to John McCain[3] in the general election regardless of his policies.

We can do that.

But if we do, I can tell you that in the next election, we'll be talking about some other distraction. And then another one. And then another one. And nothing will change.

That is one option. Or, at this moment, in this election, we can come together and say, 'Not this time.' This time, we want to talk about the crumbling schools that are stealing the future of black children and white children and Asian children and Hispanic children and Native American children. This time, we want to reject the cynicism that tells us that these kids can't learn; that those kids who don't look like us are somebody else's problem. The children of America are not those kids, they are our kids, and we will not let them fall behind in a twenty-first century economy. Not this time.

This time we want to talk about how the lines in the emergency room are filled with whites and blacks and Hispanics who do not have healthcare, who don't have the power on their own to overcome the special interests in Washington, but who can take them on if we do it together.

This time, we want to talk about the shuttered mills that once provided a decent life for men and women of every race, and the homes for sale that once belonged to Americans from every religion, every region, every walk of life. This time, we want to talk about the fact that the real problem is not that someone who doesn't look like you might take your job; it's that the corporation you work for will ship it overseas for nothing more than a profit.

---

[3]John McCain is US Senator from Arizona.

This time, we want to talk about the men and women of every colour and creed who serve together and fight together and bleed together under the same proud flag. We want to talk about how to bring them home from a war that should have never been authorized and should have never been waged. And we want to talk about how we'll show our patriotism by caring for them and their families, and giving them the benefits that they have earned.

I would not be running for President if I didn't believe with all my heart that this is what the vast majority of Americans want for this country. This union may never be perfect, but generation after generation has shown that it can always be perfected. And today, whenever I find myself feeling doubtful or cynical about this possibility, what gives me the most hope is the next generation—the young people whose attitudes and beliefs and openness to change have already made history in this election.

There is one story in particular that I'd like to leave you with today—a story I told when I had the great honour of speaking on Dr King's birthday at his home church, Ebenezer Baptist, in Atlanta.

There is a young, 23-year-old white woman named Ashley Baia who organized for our campaign in Florence, S.C. She had been working to organize a mostly African American community since the beginning of this campaign, and one day she was at a round-table discussion where everyone went around telling their story and why they were there.

And Ashley said that when she was 9 years old, her mother got cancer. And because she had to miss days of work, she was let go and lost her healthcare. They had to file for bankruptcy, and that's when Ashley decided that she had to do something to help her mom.

She knew that food was one of their most expensive costs, and so Ashley convinced her mother that what she really liked and really wanted to eat more than anything else was mustard and relish sandwiches—because that was the cheapest way to eat. That's the mind of a 9-year-old.

She did this for a year until her mom got better. So she told everyone at the round table that the reason she joined our campaign was so that she could help the millions of other children in the country who want and need to help their parents, too.

Now, Ashley might have made a different choice. Perhaps somebody told her along the way that the source of her mother's problems were blacks who were on welfare and too lazy to work, or Hispanics who were coming into the country illegally. But she didn't. She sought out allies in her fight against injustice.

Anyway, Ashley finishes her story and then goes around the room and asks everyone else why they're supporting the campaign. They all have different stories and different reasons. Many bring up a specific issue. And finally they come to this elderly black man who's been sitting there quietly the entire time. And Ashley asks him why he's there. And he does not bring up a specific issue. He does not say healthcare or the economy. He does not say education or the war. He does not say that he was there because of Barack Obama. He simply says to everyone in the room, 'I am here because of Ashley.'

'I'm here because of Ashley.' By itself, that single moment of recognition between that young white girl and that old black man is not enough. It is not enough to give healthcare to the sick, or jobs to the jobless, or education to our children.

But it is where we start. It is where our union grows stronger. And as so many generations have come to realize over the course of the 221 years since a band of patriots signed that document right here in Philadelphia, that is where the perfection begins.

◆

These men and women remind us that heroism is found not only on the fields of battle.[*]

Remarks by the President at a memorial service held at the University of Arizona campus for the victims of the shooting in Tucson, Arizona, on 12 January 2011.[1]

Thank you. Thank you very much. Please, please be seated. To the families of those we've lost, to all who called them friends, to the students of this university, the public servants who are gathered here, the people of Tucson and the people of Arizona: I have come here tonight as an American who, like all Americans, kneels to pray with you today and will stand by you tomorrow.

There is nothing I can say that will fill the sudden hole torn in your hearts. But know this: The hopes of a nation are here tonight. We mourn with you for the fallen. We join you in your grief. And we add our faith to yours that Representative

*Source: White House website
[1]On 8 January 2011, a gunman opened fire during a constituent meeting presided by US Representative Gabrielle Giffords, held in a supermarket parking lot in Tucson, Arizona.

Gabrielle Giffords and the other living victims of this tragedy will pull through.

Scripture tells us:

> There is a river whose streams make glad the city of
> God, the holy place where the Most High dwells.
> God is within her, she will not fall;
> God will help her at break of day.

On Saturday morning, Gabby, her staff and many of her constituents gathered outside a supermarket to exercise their right to peaceful assembly and free speech. They were fulfilling a central tenet of the democracy envisioned by our Founders—representatives of the people answering questions to their constituents, so as to carry their concerns back to our nation's capital. Gabby called it 'Congress on Your Corner'—just an updated version of government of and by and for the people.

And that quintessentially American scene, that was the scene that was shattered by a gunman's bullets. And the six people who lost their lives on Saturday—they, too, represented what is best in us, what is best in America.

Judge John Roll served our legal system for nearly forty years. A graduate of this university and a graduate of this law school, Judge Roll was recommended for the federal bench by John McCain twenty years ago, appointed by President George H.W. Bush and rose to become Arizona's chief federal judge.

His colleagues described him as the hardest working judge within the Ninth Circuit. He was on his way back from attending Mass, as he did every day, when he decided to stop by and say hi to his representative. John is survived by his loving wife, Maureen, his three sons and his five beautiful grandchildren.

George and Dorothy Morris—'Dot' to her friends— were high school sweethearts who got married and had two daughters. They did everything together—travelling the open road in their RV, enjoying what their friends called a fifty-year honeymoon. Saturday morning, they went by the Safeway to hear what their congresswoman had to say. When gunfire rang out, George, a former Marine, instinctively tried to shield his wife. Both were shot. Dot passed away.

A New Jersey native, Phyllis Schneck retired to Tucson to beat the snow. But in the summer, she would return East, where her world revolved around her three children, her seven grandchildren and 2-year-old great-granddaughter. A gifted quilter, she'd often work under a favourite tree, or sometimes she'd sew aprons with the logos of the Jets and the Giants to give out at the church where she volunteered. A Republican, she took a liking to Gabby, and wanted to get to know her better.

Dorwan and Mavy Stoddard grew up in Tucson together— about 70 years ago. They moved apart and started their own respective families. But after both were widowed they found their way back here, to, as one of Mavy's daughters put it, 'be boyfriend and girlfriend again.'

When they weren't out on the road in their motor home, you could find them just up the road, helping folks in need at the Mountain Avenue Church of Christ. A retired construction worker, Dorwan spent his spare time fixing up the church along with his dog, Tux. His final act of selflessness was to dive on top of his wife, sacrificing his life for hers.

Everything—everything—Gabe Zimmerman did, he did with passion. But his true passion was helping people. As Gabby's outreach director, he made the cares of thousands of her constituents his own, seeing to it that seniors got the

Medicare benefits that they had earned, that veterans got the medals and the care that they deserved, that government was working for ordinary folks. He died doing what he loved—talking with people and seeing how he could help. And Gabe is survived by his parents, Ross and Emily, his brother, Ben, and his fiancée, Kelly, who he planned to marry next year.

And then there is 9-year-old Christina Taylor Green. Christina was an A student, she was a dancer, she was a gymnast, she was a swimmer. She decided that she wanted to be the first woman to play in the Major Leagues, and as the only girl on her Little League team, no one put it past her.

She showed an appreciation for life uncommon for a girl her age. She'd remind her mother, 'We are so blessed. We have the best life.' And she'd pay those blessings back by participating in a charity that helped children who were less fortunate.

Our hearts are broken by their sudden passing. Our hearts are broken—and yet, our hearts also have reason for fullness. Our hearts are full of hope and thanks for the thirteen Americans who survived the shooting, including the congresswoman many of them went to see on Saturday.

I have just come from the University Medical Center, just a mile from here, where our friend Gabby courageously fights to recover even as we speak. And I want to tell you—her husband Mark is here and he allows me to share this with you—right after we went to visit, a few minutes after we left her room and some of her colleagues in Congress were in the room, Gabby opened her eyes for the first time. Gabby opened her eyes for the first time.

Gabby opened her eyes. Gabby opened her eyes, so I can tell you she knows we are here. She knows we love her. And she knows that we are rooting for her through what is undoubtedly going to be a difficult journey. We are there for her.

Our hearts are full of thanks for that good news, and our hearts are full of gratitude for those who saved others. We are grateful to Daniel Hernandez—a volunteer in Gabby's office.

And, Daniel, I'm sorry, you may deny it, but we've decided you are a hero because you ran through the chaos to minister to your boss, and tended to her wounds and helped keep her alive.

We are grateful to the men who tackled the gunman as he stopped to reload. Right over there. We are grateful for petite Patricia Maisch, who wrestled away the killer's ammunition, and undoubtedly saved some lives. And we are grateful for the doctors and nurses and first responders who worked wonders to heal those who'd been hurt. We are grateful to them.

These men and women remind us that heroism is found not only on the fields of battle. They remind us that heroism does not require special training or physical strength. Heroism is here, in the hearts of so many of our fellow citizens, all around us, just waiting to be summoned—as it was on Saturday morning. Their actions, their selflessness poses a challenge to each of us. It raises a question of what, beyond prayers and expressions of concern, is required of us going forward. How can we honour the fallen? How can we be true to their memory?

You see, when a tragedy like this strikes, it is part of our nature to demand explanations—to try and pose some order on the chaos and make sense out of that which seems senseless. Already we've seen a national conversation commence, not only about the motivations behind these killings, but about everything from the merits of gun safety laws to the adequacy of our mental health system. And much of this process, of debating what might be done to prevent such tragedies in the future, is an essential ingredient in our exercise of self-government.

But at a time when our discourse has become so sharply polarized—at a time when we are far too eager to lay the blame for all that ails the world at the feet of those who happen to think differently than we do—it's important for us to pause for a moment and make sure that we're talking with each other in a way that heals, not in a way that wounds.

Scripture tells us that there is evil in the world, and that terrible things happen for reasons that defy human understanding. In the words of Job, 'When I looked for light, then came darkness.' Bad things happen, and we have to guard against simple explanations in the aftermath.

For the truth is none of us can know exactly what triggered this vicious attack. None of us can know with any certainty what might have stopped these shots from being fired, or what thoughts lurked in the inner recesses of a violent man's mind. Yes, we have to examine all the facts behind this tragedy. We cannot and will not be passive in the face of such violence. We should be willing to challenge old assumptions in order to lessen the prospects of such violence in the future. But what we cannot do is use this tragedy as one more occasion to turn on each other. That we cannot do. That we cannot do.

As we discuss these issues, let each of us do so with a good dose of humility. Rather than pointing fingers or assigning blame, let's use this occasion to expand our moral imaginations, to listen to each other more carefully, to sharpen our instincts for empathy and remind ourselves of all the ways that our hopes and dreams are bound together.

After all, that's what most of us do when we lose somebody in our family—especially if the loss is unexpected. We're shaken out of our routines. We're forced to look inward. We reflect on the past: Did we spend enough time with an aging parent, we wonder. Did we express our gratitude for all the sacrifices that they made for us? Did we tell a spouse just how desperately we loved them, not just once in a while but every single day?

So sudden loss causes us to look backward—but it also forces us to look forward; to reflect on the present and the future, on the manner in which we live our lives and nurture our relationships with those who are still with us.

We may ask ourselves if we've shown enough kindness and generosity and compassion to the people in our lives. Perhaps we question whether we're doing right by our children, or our community, whether our priorities are in order.

We recognize our own mortality, and we are reminded that in the fleeting time we have on this earth, what matters is not wealth, or status, or power, or fame—but rather, how well we have loved and what small part we have played in making the lives of other people better.

And that process—that process of reflection, of making sure we align our values with our actions—that, I believe, is what a tragedy like this requires.

For those who were harmed, those who were killed—they are part of our family, an American family three million strong. We may not have known them personally, but surely we see ourselves in them. In George and Dot, in Dorwan and Mavy, we sense the abiding love we have for our own husbands, our own wives, our own life partners. Phyllis—she's our mom or our grandma, Gabe our brother or son. In Judge Roll, we recognize not only a man who prized his family and doing his job well, but also a man who embodied America's fidelity to the law.

And in Gabby—in Gabby, we see a reflection of our public-spiritedness; that desire to participate in that sometimes frustrating, sometimes contentious, but always necessary and never-ending process to form a more perfect union.

And in Christina—in Christina we see all of our children. So curious, so trusting, so energetic, so full of magic. So deserving of our love. And so deserving of our good example.

If this tragedy prompts reflection and debate—as it should—let's make sure it's worthy of those we have lost. Let's make sure it's not on the usual plane of politics and point-scoring and pettiness that drifts away in the next news cycle.

The loss of these wonderful people should make every one of us strive to be better. To be better in our private lives, to be better friends and neighbours and co-workers and parents. And if, as has been discussed in recent days, their death helps usher in more civility in our public discourse, let us remember it is not because a simple lack of civility caused this tragedy— it did not—but rather because only a more civil and honest public discourse can help us face up to the challenges of our nation in a way that would make them proud.

We should be civil because we want to live up to the example of public servants like John Roll and Gabby Giffords, who knew first and foremost that we are all Americans, and that we can question each other's ideas without questioning each other's love of country and that our task, working together, is to constantly widen the circle of our concern so that we bequeath the American Dream to future generations.

They believed—they believed, and I believe that we can be better. Those who died here, those who saved life here— they help me believe. We may not be able to stop all evil in the world, but I know that how we treat one another, that's entirely up to us.

And I believe that for all our imperfections, we are full of decency and goodness, and that the forces that divide us are not as strong as those that unite us.

That's what I believe, in part because that's what a child like Christina Taylor Green believed.

Imagine—imagine for a moment, here was a young girl who was just becoming aware of our democracy; just beginning to understand the obligations of citizenship; just starting to glimpse the fact that some day she, too, might play a part in shaping her nation's future. She had been elected to her student council. She saw public service as something exciting and hopeful. She was off to meet her congresswoman, someone she was sure was good and important and might be a role model. She saw all this through the eyes of a child, undimmed by the cynicism or vitriol that we adults all too often just take for granted.

I want to live up to her expectations. I want our democracy to be as good as Christina imagined it. I want America to be as good as she imagined it. All of us—we should do everything we can to make sure this country lives up to our children's expectations.

As has already been mentioned, Christina was given to us on September 11th, 2001, one of fifty babies born that day to be pictured in a book called *Faces of Hope*. On either side of her photo in that book were simple wishes for a child's life. 'I hope you help those in need,' read one. 'I hope you know all the words to the National Anthem and sing it with your hand over your heart.' 'I hope you jump in rain puddles.'

If there are rain puddles in heaven, Christina is jumping

in them today. And here on this earth—here on this earth, we place our hands over our hearts, and we commit ourselves as Americans to forging a country that is forever worthy of her gentle, happy spirit.

May God bless and keep those we've lost in restful and eternal peace. May He love and watch over the survivors. And may He bless the United States of America.

◆

We know the march is not yet over. We know the race is not yet won.[*]

Remarks by the President at an event to mark the 50th anniversary of the Marches from Selma to Montgomery[1] on 7 March 2015.

It is a rare honour in this life to follow one of your heroes. And John Lewis is one of my heroes.

Now, I have to imagine that when a younger John Lewis woke up that morning fifty years ago and made his way to Brown Chapel, heroics were not on his mind. A day like this was not on his mind. Young folks with bedrolls and backpacks were milling about. Veterans of the movement trained newcomers in the tactics of non-violence; the right way to protect yourself when attacked. A doctor described what tear gas does to the body, while marchers scribbled

---

*Source: White House website
[1] Led by Martin Luther King Jr., the march from Selma, Alabama, to the state's capital, Montgomery, from March 21–25, 1965, became a landmark event in the American civil rights movement.

down instructions for contacting their loved ones. The air was thick with doubt, anticipation and fear. And they comforted themselves with the final verse of the final hymn they sung:

No matter what may be the test, God will take care of you;
Lean, weary one, upon His breast, God will take care of you.

And then, his knapsack stocked with an apple, a toothbrush and a book on government—all you need for a night behind bars—John Lewis led them out of the church on a mission to change America.

President and Mrs Bush, Governor [Robert] Bentley, Mayor [George] Evans, [Terri] Sewell, Reverend Strong, members of Congress, elected officials, foot soldiers, friends, fellow Americans:

As John noted, there are places and moments in America where this nation's destiny has been decided. Many are sites of war—Concord and Lexington, Appomattox, Gettysburg. Others are sites that symbolize the daring of America's character—Independence Hall and Seneca Falls, Kitty Hawk and Cape Canaveral.

Selma is such a place. In one afternoon fifty years ago, so much of our turbulent history—the stain of slavery and anguish of civil war; the yoke of segregation and tyranny of Jim Crow; the death of four little girls in Birmingham; and the dream of a Baptist preacher—all that history met on this bridge.

It was not a clash of armies, but a clash of wills; a contest to determine the true meaning of America. And because of men and women like John Lewis, Joseph Lowery, Hosea Williams, Amelia Boynton, Diane Nash, Ralph Abernathy, C.T. Vivian, Andrew Young, Fred Shuttlesworth, Dr Martin Luther King, Jr., and so many others, the idea of a just America and a fair America, an inclusive America and a generous America—that idea ultimately triumphed.

As is true across the landscape of American history, we cannot examine this moment in isolation. The march on Selma was part of a broader campaign that spanned generations—the leaders that day part of a long line of heroes.

We gather here to celebrate them. We gather here to honour the courage of ordinary Americans willing to endure billy clubs and the chastening rod, tear gas and the trampling hoof, men and women who despite the gush of blood and splintered bone would stay true to their North Star and keep marching towards justice.

They did as Scripture instructed: 'Rejoice in hope, be patient in tribulation, be constant in prayer.' And in the days to come, they went back again and again. When the trumpet call sounded for more to join, the people came—black and white, young and old, Christian and Jew, waving the American flag and singing the same anthems full of faith and hope. A white newsman, Bill Plante, who covered the marches then and who is with us here today, quipped that the growing number of white people lowered the quality of the singing. To those who marched, though, those old gospel songs must have never sounded so sweet.

In time, their chorus would well up and reach President Johnson[2]. And he would send them protection, and speak to the nation, echoing their call for America and the world to hear: 'We shall overcome.' What enormous faith these men

---

[2]Lyndon B. Johnson served as the 36th President of the United States of America from 1963–69.

and women had. Faith in God, but also faith in America.

The Americans who crossed this bridge, they were not physically imposing. But they gave courage to millions. They held no elected office. But they led a nation. They marched as Americans who had endured hundreds of years of brutal violence, countless daily indignities—but they didn't seek special treatment, just the equal treatment promised to them almost a century before.

What they did here will reverberate through the ages. Not because the change they won was preordained, not because their victory was complete, but because they proved that non-violent change is possible, that love and hope can conquer hate.

As we commemorate their achievement, we are well-served to remember that at the time of the marches, many in power condemned rather than praised them. Back then, they were called Communists, or half-breeds, or outside agitators, sexual and moral degenerates, and worse—they were called everything but the name their parents gave them. Their faith was questioned. Their lives were threatened. Their patriotism challenged.

And yet, what could be more American than what happened in this place? What could more profoundly vindicate the idea of America than plain and humble people—unsung, the downtrodden, the dreamers not of high station, not born to wealth or privilege, not of one religious tradition but many, coming together to shape their country's course?

What greater expression of faith in the American experiment than this, what greater form of patriotism is there than the belief that America is not yet finished, that we are strong enough to be self-critical, that each successive generation can look upon our imperfections and decide that it is in our power to remake this nation to more closely align with our highest ideals?

That's why Selma is not some outlier in the American experience. That's why it's not a museum or a static monument to behold from a distance. It is instead the manifestation of a creed written into our founding documents: 'We the People... in order to form a more perfect union.' 'We hold these truths to be self-evident, that all men are created equal.'

These are not just words. They're a living thing, a call to action, a roadmap for citizenship and an insistence in the capacity of free men and women to shape our own destiny. For Founders like [Benjamin] Franklin and [Thomas] Jefferson, for leaders like [Abraham] Lincoln and FDR[3], the success of our experiment in self-government rested on engaging all of our citizens in this work. And that's what we celebrate here in Selma. That's what this movement was all about, one leg in our long journey towards freedom.

The American instinct that led these young men and women to pick up the torch and cross this bridge, that's the same instinct that moved patriots to choose revolution over tyranny. It's the same instinct that drew immigrants from across oceans and the Rio Grande; the same instinct that led women to reach for the ballot, workers to organize against an unjust status quo; the same instinct that led us to plant a flag at Iwo Jima and on the surface of the moon.

It's the idea held by generations of citizens who believed that America is a constant work in progress; who believed

---

[3]Franklin D. Roosevelt (FDR) served as the 32nd President of the United States of America from 1933–45.

that loving this country requires more than singing its praises or avoiding uncomfortable truths. It requires the occasional disruption, the willingness to speak out for what is right, to shake up the status quo. That's America.

That's what makes us unique. That's what cements our reputation as a beacon of opportunity. Young people behind the Iron Curtain would see Selma and eventually tear down that wall. Young people in Soweto would hear Bobby Kennedy[4] talk about ripples of hope and eventually banish the scourge of apartheid. Young people in Burma went to prison rather than submit to military rule. They saw what John Lewis had done. From the streets of Tunis to the Maidan in Ukraine, this generation of young people can draw strength from this place, where the powerless could change the world's greatest power and push their leaders to expand the boundaries of freedom.

They saw that idea made real right here in Selma, Alabama. They saw that idea manifest itself here in America.

Because of campaigns like this, a Voting Rights Act was passed. Political and economic and social barriers came down. And the change these men and women wrought is visible here today in the presence of African Americans who run boardrooms, who sit on the bench, who serve in elected office from small towns to big cities; from the Congressional Black Caucus all the way to the Oval Office.

Because of what they did, the doors of opportunity swung open not just for black folks, but for every American. Women marched through those doors. Latinos marched through

---

[4]Robert F. Kennedy was the US Attorney General and adviser during the administration of his brother, President John F. Kennedy. He was a US Senator when he was assassinated on 6 June 1968.

those doors. Asian Americans, gay Americans, Americans with disabilities—they all came through those doors. Their endeavours gave the entire South the chance to rise again, not by reasserting the past, but by transcending the past.

What a glorious thing, Dr King might say. And what a solemn debt we owe. Which leads us to ask, just how might we repay that debt?

First and foremost, we have to recognize that one day's commemoration, no matter how special, is not enough. If Selma taught us anything, it's that our work is never done. The American experiment in self-government gives work and purpose to each generation.

Selma teaches us, as well, that action requires that we shed our cynicism. For when it comes to the pursuit of justice, we can afford neither complacency nor despair.

Just this week, I was asked whether I thought the Department of Justice's Ferguson report shows that, with respect to race, little has changed in this country. And I understood the question; the report's narrative was sadly familiar. It evoked the kind of abuse and disregard for citizens that spawned the civil rights movement. But I rejected the notion that nothing's changed. What happened in Ferguson may not be unique, but it's no longer endemic. It's no longer sanctioned by law or by custom. And before the civil rights movement, it most surely was.

We do a disservice to the cause of justice by intimating that bias and discrimination are immutable, that racial division is inherent to America. If you think nothing's changed in the past fifty years, ask somebody who lived through the Selma or Chicago or Los Angeles of the 1950s. Ask the female CEO who once might have been assigned to the secretarial pool if nothing's changed. Ask your gay friend if it's easier to be out and proud in America now than it was thirty years ago. To deny this progress, this hard-won progress—our progress—would be to rob us of our own agency, our own capacity, our responsibility to do what we can to make America better.

Of course, a more common mistake is to suggest that Ferguson[5] is an isolated incident; that racism is banished; that the work that drew men and women to Selma is now complete, and that whatever racial tensions remain are a consequence of those seeking to play the 'race card' for their own purposes. We don't need the Ferguson report to know that's not true. We just need to open our eyes, and our ears, and our hearts to know that this nation's racial history still casts its long shadow upon us.

We know the march is not yet over. We know the race is not yet won. We know that reaching that blessed destination where we are judged, all of us, by the content of our character requires admitting as much, facing up to the truth. 'We are capable of bearing a great burden,' James Baldwin once wrote, 'once we discover that the burden is reality and arrive where reality is.'

There's nothing America can't handle if we actually look squarely at the problem. And this is work for all Americans, not just some. Not just whites. Not just blacks. If we want to honour the courage of those who marched that day, then all of us are called to possess their moral imagination. All of us will need to feel as they did the fierce urgency of now. All of

---

[5]Reference to shooting of 18-year-old Michael Brown in Ferguson, Missouri, on 9 August 2014. The black teen, who was a suspect of a convenience store robbery, was fatally shot by a white police officer.

us need to recognize as they did that change depends on our actions, on our attitudes, the things we teach our children. And if we make such an effort, no matter how hard it may sometimes seem, laws can be passed, and consciences can be stirred, and consensus can be built.

With such an effort, we can make sure our criminal justice system serves all and not just some. Together, we can raise the level of mutual trust that policing is built on—the idea that police officers are members of the community they risk their lives to protect, and citizens in Ferguson and New York and Cleveland, they just want the same thing young people here marched for fifty years ago—the protection of the law. Together we can address unfair sentencing and overcrowded prisons, and the stunted circumstances that rob too many boys of the chance to become men, and rob the nation of too many men who could be good dads, and good workers and good neighbours.

With effort, we can roll back poverty and the roadblocks to opportunity. Americans don't accept a free ride for anybody, nor do we believe in equality of outcomes. But we do expect equal opportunity. And if we really mean it, if we're not just giving lip service to it, but if we really mean it and are willing to sacrifice for it, then, yes, we can make sure every child gets an education suitable to this new century, one that expands imaginations and lifts sights and gives those children the skills they need. We can make sure every person willing to work has the dignity of a job, and a fair wage, and a real voice, and sturdier rungs on that ladder into the middle-class.

And with effort, we can protect the foundation stone of our democracy for which so many marched across this bridge—and that is the right to vote. Right now, in 2015, fifty years after Selma, there are laws across this country designed to make it harder for people to vote. As we speak, more of such laws are being proposed. Meanwhile, the Voting Rights Act, the culmination of so much blood, so much sweat and tears, the product of so much sacrifice in the face of wanton violence, the Voting Rights Act stands weakened, its future subject to political rancour.

How can that be? The Voting Rights Act was one of the crowning achievements of our democracy, the result of Republican and Democratic efforts. President [Ronald] Reagan[6] signed its renewal when he was in office. President George W. Bush signed its renewal when he was in office. One hundred members of Congress have come here today to honour people who were willing to die for the right to protect it. If we want to honour this day, let that hundred go back to Washington and gather four hundred more, and together, pledge to make it their mission to restore that law this year. That's how we honour those on this bridge.

Of course, our democracy is not the task of Congress alone, or the courts alone, or even the President alone. If every new voter-suppression law was struck down today, we would still have, here in America, one of the lowest voting rates among free peoples. Fifty years ago, registering to vote here in Selma and much of the South meant guessing the number of jellybeans in a jar, the number of bubbles on a bar of soap. It meant risking your dignity, and, sometimes, your life.

What's our excuse today for not voting? How do we so casually discard the right for which so many fought? How

---

[6]Ronald Reagan served as the 40th President of the United States of America from 1981–89.

do we so fully give away our power, our voice, in shaping America's future? Why are we pointing to somebody else when we could take the time just to go to the polling places? We give away our power.

Fellow marchers, so much has changed in fifty years. We have endured war and we've fashioned peace. We've seen technological wonders that touch every aspect of our lives. We take for granted conveniences that our parents could have scarcely imagined. But what has not changed is the imperative of citizenship; that willingness of a 26-year-old deacon, or a Unitarian minister, or a young mother of five to decide they loved this country so much that they'd risk everything to realize its promise.

That's what it means to love America. That's what it means to believe in America. That's what it means when we say America is exceptional.

For we were born of change. We broke the old aristocracies, declaring ourselves entitled not by bloodline, but endowed by our Creator with certain inalienable rights. We secure our rights and responsibilities through a system of self-government, of and by and for the people. That's why we argue and fight with so much passion and conviction—because we know our efforts matter. We know America is what we make of it.

Look at our history. We are Lewis and Clark and Sacajawea, pioneers who braved the unfamiliar, followed by a stampede of farmers and miners, and entrepreneurs and hucksters. That's our spirit. That's who we are.

We are Sojourner Truth and Fannie Lou Hamer, women who could do as much as any man and then some. And we're Susan B. Anthony,[7] who shook the system until the law reflected that truth. That is our character.

We're the immigrants who stowed away on ships to reach these shores, the huddled masses yearning to breathe free— Holocaust survivors, Soviet defectors, the Lost Boys of Sudan. We're the hopeful strivers who cross the Rio Grande because we want our kids to know a better life. That's how we came to be.

We're the slaves who built the White House and the economy of the South. We're the ranch hands and cowboys who opened up the West, and countless labourers who laid rail, and raised skyscrapers, and organized for workers' rights.

We're the fresh-faced GIs who fought to liberate a continent. And we're the Tuskegee Airmen, and the Navajo code talkers and the Japanese Americans who fought for this country even as their own liberty had been denied.

We're the firefighters who rushed into those buildings on 9/11, the volunteers who signed up to fight in Afghanistan and Iraq. We're the gay Americans whose blood ran in the streets of San Francisco and New York, just as blood ran down this bridge.

We are storytellers, writers, poets, artists who abhor unfairness, and despise hypocrisy, and give voice to the voiceless, and tell truths that need to be told.

We're the inventors of gospel and jazz and blues, bluegrass and country, and hip-hop and rock and roll, and our very own sound with all the sweet sorrow and reckless joy of freedom.

We are Jackie Robinson, enduring scorn and spiked cleats and pitches coming straight to his head and stealing home in

---

[7]Sojourner Truth, Fannie Lou Hamer and Susan B. Anthony were American voting and women's rights activists.

the World Series anyway.

We are the people Langston Hughes wrote of who 'build our temples for tomorrow, strong as we know how'. We are the people [Ralph Waldo] Emerson wrote of, 'who for truth and honour's sake stand fast and suffer long', who are 'never tired, so long as we can see far enough'.

That's what America is. Not stock photos or airbrushed history, or feeble attempts to define some of us as more American than others. We respect the past, but we don't pine for the past. We don't fear the future; we grab for it. America is not some fragile thing. We are large, in the words of Whitman, containing multitudes. We are boisterous and diverse and full of energy, perpetually young in spirit. That's why someone like John Lewis at the ripe old age of 25 could lead a mighty march.

And that's what the young people here today and listening all across the country must take away from this day. You are America. Unconstrained by habit and convention. Unencumbered by what is, because you're ready to seize what ought to be.

For everywhere in this country, there are first steps to be taken, there's new ground to cover, there are more bridges to be crossed. And it is you, the young and fearless at heart, the most diverse and educated generation in our history, who the nation is waiting to follow.

Because Selma shows us that America is not the project of any one person. Because the single-most powerful word in our democracy is the word 'We'. 'We The People'. 'We Shall Overcome'. 'Yes We Can'. That word is owned by no one. It belongs to everyone. Oh, what a glorious task we are given, to continually try to improve this great nation of ours.

Fifty years from Bloody Sunday, our march is not yet finished, but we're getting closer. Two hundred and thirty-nine years after this nation's founding our union is not yet perfect, but we are getting closer. Our job's easier because somebody already got us through that first mile. Somebody already got us over that bridge. When it feels the road is too hard, when the torch we've been passed feels too heavy, we will remember these early travellers, and draw strength from their example, and hold firmly the words of the prophet Isaiah:

Those who hope in the Lord will renew their strength. They will soar on [the] wings like eagles. They will run and not grow weary. They will walk and not be faint.

We honour those who walked so we could run. We must run so our children soar. And we will not grow weary. For we believe in the power of an awesome God, and we believe in this country's sacred promise.

May He bless those warriors of justice no longer with us, and bless the United States of America. Thank you, everybody.

◆

4

Hillary Clinton
67th United States Secretary of State (2009–2013)
under President Barack Obama

The only thing we have to fear is fear itself.[*]

The following speech was given by Hillary Clinton during an address to the Democratic National Convention in Philadelphia on 28 July 2016.

Thank you! Thank you for that amazing welcome.

And Chelsea, thank you. I'm so proud to be your mother and so proud of the woman you've become. Thanks for bringing Marc into our family, and Charlotte and Aidan into the world.

And Bill, that conversation we started in the law library forty-five years ago is still going strong. It's lasted through

---

*Source: Hillary Clinton

good times that filled us with joy, and hard times that tested us. And I've even gotten a few words in along the way. On Tuesday night, I was so happy to see that my Explainer-in-Chief is still on the job.

I'm also grateful to the rest of my family and the friends of a lifetime.

To all of you whose hard work brought us here tonight. And to those of you who joined our campaign this week. And what a remarkable week it's been.

We heard the man from Hope, Bill Clinton. And the man of Hope, Barack Obama. America is stronger because of President Obama's leadership, and I'm better because of his friendship. We heard from our terrific Vice President, the one-and-only Joe Biden, who spoke from his big heart about our party's commitment to working people. First Lady Michelle Obama reminded us that our children are watching, and the President we elect is going to be their President, too.

And for those of you out there who are just getting to know Tim Kaine—you're soon going to understand why the people of Virginia keep promoting him: from City Council and mayor, to Governor and now Senator. He'll make the whole country proud as our Vice President.

And...I want to thank Bernie Sanders; Bernie, your campaign inspired millions of Americans, particularly the young people who threw their hearts and souls into our primary. You've put economic and social justice issues front and centre—where they belong. And to all of your supporters here and around the country: I want you to know, I've heard you; your cause is our cause. Our country needs your ideas, energy and passion. That's the only way we can turn our progressive platform into real change for America. We wrote it together—now let's go out there and make it happen together.

My friends, we've come to Philadelphia—the birthplace of our nation—because what happened in this city 240 years ago still has something to teach us today. We all know the story; but we usually focus on how it turned out—and not enough on how close that story came to never being written at all.

When representatives from thirteen unruly colonies met just down the road from here, some wanted to stick with the king, some wanted to stick it to the king and go their own way. The revolution hung in the balance. Then somehow they began listening to each other…compromising…finding common purpose. And by the time they left Philadelphia, they had begun to see themselves as one nation. That's what made it possible to stand up to a king. That took courage; they had courage. Our Founders embraced the enduring truth—that we are stronger together.

America is once again at a moment of reckoning. Powerful forces are threatening to pull us apart; bonds of trust and respect are fraying. And just as with our Founders, there are no guarantees. It truly is up to us—we have to decide whether we all will work together so we all can rise together.

Our country's motto is e pluribus unum—out of many, we are one. Will we stay true to that motto?

Well, we heard Donald Trump's answer last week at his convention. He wants to divide us—from the rest of the world, and from each other. He's betting that the perils of today's world will blind us to its unlimited promise. He's taken the Republican Party a long way…from 'morning in America' to 'midnight in America'. He wants us to fear the future and fear each other. Well, a great Democratic President, Franklin

Delano Roosevelt, came up with the perfect rebuke to Trump more than eighty years ago, during a much more perilous time.

'The only thing we have to fear is fear itself.'

Now we are clear-eyed about what our country is up against. But we are not afraid. We will rise to the challenge, just as we always have. We will not build a wall. Instead, we will build an economy where everyone who wants a good paying job can get one. And we'll build a path to citizenship for millions of immigrants who are already contributing to our economy! We will not ban a religion. We will work with all Americans and our allies to fight terrorism.

There's a lot of work to do. Too many people haven't had a pay raise since the crash. There's too much inequality. Too little social mobility. Too much paralysis in Washington. Too many threats at home and abroad.

But just look at the strengths we bring to meet these challenges. We have the most dynamic and diverse people in the world. We have the most tolerant and generous young people we've ever had. We have the most powerful military. The most innovative entrepreneurs. The most enduring values. Freedom and equality, justice and opportunity. We should be so proud that these words are associated with us. That when people hear them, they hear—America.

So don't let anyone tell you that our country is weak. We're not. Don't let anyone tell you we don't have what it takes. We do. And most of all, don't believe anyone who says: 'I alone can fix it.' Those were actually Donald Trump's words in Cleveland. And they should set off alarm bells for all of us.

Really? I alone can fix it? Isn't he forgetting? Troops on the front lines. Police officers and firefighters who run towards danger. Doctors and nurses who care for us. Teachers who change lives. Entrepreneurs who see possibilities in every problem. Mothers who lost children to violence and are building a movement to keep other kids safe. He's forgetting every last one of us. Americans don't say: 'I alone can fix it.'

We say: 'We'll fix it together.'

Remember: Our Founders fought a revolution and wrote a Constitution so America would never be a nation where one person had all the power. Two hundred and forty years later, we still put our faith in each other. Look at what happened in Dallas after the assassinations of five brave police officers. Chief David Brown asked the community to support his force, maybe even join them. And you know how the community responded? Nearly five hundred people applied in just twelve days. That's how Americans answer when the call for help goes out.

Twenty years ago I wrote a book called *It Takes a Village*. A lot of people looked at the title and asked, what the heck do you mean by that? This is what I mean. None of us can raise a family, build a business, heal a community or lift a country totally alone. America needs every one of us to lend our energy, our talents, our ambition to making our nation better and stronger. I believe that with all my heart.

That's why 'Stronger Together' is not just a lesson from our history. It's not just a slogan for our campaign. It's a guiding principle for the country we've always been and the future we're going to build. A country where the economy works for everyone, not just those at the top. Where you can get a good job and send your kids to a good school, no matter what ZIP code you live in. A country where all our children can dream, and those dreams are within reach. Where families are strong...communities are safe. And yes, love trumps hate.

That's the country we're fighting for. That's the future we're working towards.

And so it is with humility…determination…and boundless confidence in America's promise…that I accept your nomination for President of the United States!

Now, sometimes the people at this podium are new to the national stage. As you know, I'm not one of those people. I've been your First Lady, served eight years as a Senator from the great State of New York. I ran for President and lost. Then I represented all of you as Secretary of State. But my job titles only tell you what I've done. They don't tell you why. The truth is, through all these years of public service, the 'service' part has always come easier to me than the 'public' part.

I get it that some people just don't know what to make of me. So let me tell you. The family I'm from…well, no one had their name on big buildings. My family were builders of a different kind. Builders in the way most American families are. They used whatever tools they had—whatever God gave them—and whatever life in America provided—and built better lives and better futures for their kids. My grandfather worked in the same Scranton lace mill for fifty years. Because he believed that if he gave everything he had, his children would have a better life than he did. And he was right. My dad, Hugh, made it to college. He played football at Penn State and enlisted in the Navy after Pearl Harbor[1]. When the war was over he started his own small business, printing fabric for draperies. I remember watching him stand for hours over silk

---

[1]The surprise aerial attack on the US naval base at Pearl Harbor on Oahu Island, Hawaii, by the Japanese on 7 December 1941 precipitated the entry of the United States into World War II.

screens. He wanted to give my brothers and me opportunities he never had. And he did.

My mother, Dorothy, was abandoned by her parents as a young girl. She ended up on her own at 14, working as a housemaid. She was saved by the kindness of others. Her first grade teacher saw she had nothing to eat at lunch, and brought extra food to share. The lesson she passed on to me years later stuck with me: No one gets through life alone. We have to look out for each other and lift each other up. She made sure I learned the words of our Methodist faith: 'Do all the good you can, for all the people you can, in all the ways you can, as long as ever you can.'

I went to work for the Children's Defense Fund, going door-to-door in New Bedford, Massachusetts, on behalf of children with disabilities who were denied the chance to go to school. I remember meeting a young girl in a wheelchair on the small back porch of her house. She told me how badly she wanted to go to school—it just didn't seem possible. And I couldn't stop thinking of my mother and what she went through as a child. It became clear to me that simply caring is not enough. To drive real progress, you have to change both hearts and laws. You need both understanding and action.

So we gathered facts. We built a coalition. And our work helped convince Congress to ensure access to education for all students with disabilities. It's a big idea, isn't it? Every kid with a disability has the right to go to school. But how do you make an idea like that real? You do it step-by-step, year-by-year...sometimes even door-by-door.

And my heart just swelled when I saw Anastasia Somoza on this stage, representing millions of young people who—because of those changes to our laws—are able to get an education. It's true...I sweat the details of policy—whether we're talking about the exact level of lead in the drinking water in Flint, Michigan, the number of mental health facilities in Iowa, or the cost of your prescription drugs. Because it's not just a detail if it's your kid—if it's your family. It's a big deal. And it should be a big deal to your President.

Over the last three days, you've seen some of the people who've inspired me. People who let me into their lives, and became a part of mine. People like Ryan Moore and Lauren Manning. They told their stories Tuesday night. I first met Ryan as a 7-year old. He was wearing a full-body brace that must have weighed 40 pounds. Children like Ryan kept me going when our plan for universal healthcare failed...and kept me working with leaders of both parties to help create the Children's Health Insurance Program that covers eight million kids every year.

Lauren was gravely injured on 9/11. It was the thought of her, and Debbie St. John, and John Dolan and Joe Sweeney, and all the victims and survivors, that kept me working as hard as I could in the Senate on behalf of 9/11 families, and our first responders who got sick from their time at ground zero. I was still thinking of Lauren, Debbie and all the others ten years later in the White House Situation Room when President Obama made the courageous decision that finally brought Osama bin Laden to justice[2].

In this campaign, I've met so many people who motivate me to keep fighting for change. And, with your help, I will carry all of your voices and stories with me to the White House. I will

---

[2]On 2 May 2011, the Al-qaeda chief was killed when US forces raided the compound in Pakistan where he had been hiding.

be a President for Democrats, Republicans and Independents. For the struggling, the striving and the successful. For those who vote for me and those who don't. For all Americans.

Tonight, we've reached a milestone in our nation's march towards a more perfect union: the first time that a major party has nominated a woman for President. Standing here as my mother's daughter, and my daughter's mother, I'm so happy this day has come. Happy for grandmothers and little girls and everyone in between. Happy for boys and men, too—because when any barrier falls in America, for anyone, it clears the way for everyone. When there are no ceilings, the sky's the limit.

So let's keep going, until every one of the 161 million women and girls across America has the opportunity she deserves. Because even more important than the history we make tonight, is the history we will write together in the years ahead. Let's begin with what we're going to do to help working people in our country get ahead and stay ahead.

Now, I don't think President Obama and Vice President Biden get the credit they deserve for saving us from the worst economic crisis of our lifetimes. Our economy is so much stronger than when they took office. Nearly fifteen million new private sector jobs. Twenty million more Americans with health insurance. And an auto industry that just had its best year ever. That's real progress.

But none of us can be satisfied with the status quo. Not by a long shot. We're still facing deep-seated problems that developed long before the recession and have stayed with us through the recovery. I've gone around our country talking to working families. And I've heard from so many of you who feel like the economy just isn't working. Some of you are frustrated—even furious.

And you know what? You're right. It's not yet working the way it should. Americans are willing to work—and work hard. But right now, an awful lot of people feel there is less and less respect for the work they do. And less respect for them, period.

Democrats are the party of working people. But we haven't done a good enough job showing that we get what you're going through, and that we're going to do something about it. So I want to tell you tonight how we will empower Americans to live better lives.

My primary mission as President will be to create more opportunity and more good jobs with rising wages right here in the United States. From my first day in office to my last! Especially in places that for too long have been left out and left behind. From our inner cities to our small towns, from Indian Country to Coal Country. From communities ravaged by addiction to regions hollowed out by plant closures.

And here's what I believe. I believe America thrives when the middle-class thrives. I believe that our economy isn't working the way it should because our democracy isn't working the way it should. That's why we need to appoint Supreme Court justices who will get money out of politics and expand voting rights, not restrict them. And we'll pass a constitutional amendment to overturn Citizens United!

I believe American corporations that have gotten so much from our country should be just as patriotic in return. Many of them are. But too many aren't. It's wrong to take tax breaks with one hand and give out pink slips with the other. And I believe Wall Street can never, ever be allowed to wreck Main Street again.

I believe in science. I believe that climate change is real

and that we can save our planet while creating millions of good-paying clean energy jobs.

I believe that when we have millions of hard-working immigrants contributing to our economy, it would be self-defeating and inhumane to kick them out. Comprehensive immigration reform will grow our economy and keep families together—and it's the right thing to do. Whatever party you belong to, or if you belong to no party at all, if you share these beliefs, this is your campaign.

If you believe that companies should share profits with their workers, not pad executive bonuses, join us.

If you believe the minimum wage should be a living wage...and no one working full-time should have to raise their children in poverty...join us.

If you believe that every man, woman and child in America has the right to affordable healthcare...join us.

If you believe that we should say 'no' to unfair trade deals...that we should stand up to China...that we should support our steelworkers and autoworkers and homegrown manufacturers...join us.

If you believe we should expand Social Security and protect a woman's right to make her own healthcare decisions...join us.

And yes, if you believe that your working mother, wife, sister or daughter deserves equal pay...join us. Let's make sure this economy works for everyone, not just those at the top.

Now, you didn't hear any of this from Donald Trump at his convention. He spoke for seventy odd minutes—and I do mean odd. And he offered zero solutions. But we already know he doesn't believe these things. No wonder he doesn't like talking about his plans. You might have noticed, I love talking about mine.

In my first hundred days, we will work with both parties to pass the biggest investment in new, good-paying jobs since World War II. Jobs in manufacturing, clean energy, technology and innovation, small business and infrastructure. If we invest in infrastructure now, we'll not only create jobs today, but lay the foundation for the jobs of the future. And we will transform the way we prepare our young people for those jobs.

Bernie Sanders and I will work together to make college tuition-free for the middle-class and debt-free for all! We will also liberate millions of people who already have student debt. It's just not right that Donald Trump can ignore his debts, but students and families can't refinance theirs. And here's something we don't say often enough: College is crucial, but a four-year degree should not be the only path to a good job. We're going to help more people learn a skill or practice a trade and make a good living doing it.

We're going to give small businesses a boost. Make it easier to get credit. Way too many dreams die in the parking lots of banks. In America, if you can dream it, you should be able to build it.

We're going to help you balance family and work. And you know what, if fighting for affordable childcare and paid family leave is playing the 'woman card', then Deal Me In!

Oh, you've heard that one?

Now, here's the thing, we're not only going to make all these investments, we're going to pay for every single one of them. And here's how: Wall Street, corporations and the super-rich are going to start paying their fair share of taxes. Not because we resent success. Because when more than 90 per cent of the gains have gone to the top 1 per cent, that's where the money is. And if companies take tax breaks and then ship jobs overseas, we'll make them pay us back. And we'll put that money to work where it belongs…creating jobs here at home!

Now I know some of you are sitting at home thinking, well that all sounds pretty good. But how are you going to get it done? How are you going to break through the gridlock in Washington? Look at my record. I've worked across the aisle to pass laws and treaties and to launch new programmes that help millions of people. And if you give me the chance, that's what I'll do as President.

But Trump, he's a businessman. He must know something about the economy. Well, let's take a closer look. In Atlantic City, 60 miles from here, you'll find contractors and small businesses who lost everything because Donald Trump refused to pay his bills. People who did the work and needed the money, and didn't get it—not because he couldn't pay them, but because he wouldn't pay them. That sales pitch he's making to be your President? Put your faith in him—and you'll win big? That's the same sales pitch he made to all those small businesses. Then Trump walked away, and left working people holding the bag.

He also talks a big game about putting America First. Please explain to me what part of America First leads him to make Trump ties in China, not Colorado. Trump suits in Mexico, not Michigan. Trump furniture in Turkey, not Ohio. Trump picture frames in India, not Wisconsin. Donald Trump says he wants to make America great again—well, he could start by actually making things in America again.

The choice we face is just as stark when it comes to our national security. Anyone reading the news can see the threats and turbulence we face. From Baghdad and Kabul, to

Nice and Paris and Brussels, to San Bernardino and Orlando, we're dealing with determined enemies that must be defeated. No wonder people are anxious and looking for reassurance. Looking for steady leadership.

You want a leader who understands we are stronger when we work with our allies around the world and care for our veterans here at home. Keeping our nation safe and honouring the people who do it will be my highest priority.

I'm proud that we put a lid on Iran's nuclear programme without firing a single shot—now we have to enforce it, and keep supporting Israel's security. I'm proud that we shaped a global climate agreement—now we have to hold every country accountable to their commitments, including ourselves. I'm proud to stand by our allies in NATO against any threat they face, including from Russia.

I've laid out my strategy for defeating ISIS. We will strike their sanctuaries from the air, and support local forces taking them out on the ground. We will surge our intelligence so that we detect and prevent attacks before they happen. We will disrupt their efforts online to reach and radicalize young people in our country. It won't be easy or quick, but make no mistake—we will prevail.

Now Donald Trump says, and this is a quote, 'I know more about ISIS than the generals do.'

No, Donald, you don't.

He thinks that he knows more than our military because he claimed our armed forces are 'a disaster.' Well, I've had the privilege to work closely with our troops and our veterans for many years, including as a Senator on the Armed Services Committee. I know how wrong he is. Our military is a national treasure. We entrust our Commander-in-Chief to make the hardest decisions our nation faces. Decisions about war and peace. Life and death. A President should respect the men and women who risk their lives to serve our country—including the sons of Tim Kaine and Mike Pence, both marines.

Ask yourself: Does Donald Trump have the temperament to be Commander-in-Chief? Donald Trump can't even handle the rough-and-tumble of a presidential campaign. He loses his cool at the slightest provocation. When he's gotten a tough question from a reporter. When he's challenged in a debate. When he sees a protester at a rally. Imagine him in the Oval Office facing a real crisis. A man you can bait with a tweet is not a man we can trust with nuclear weapons.

I can't put it any better than Jackie Kennedy[3] did after the Cuban Missile Crisis. She said that what worried President Kennedy during that very dangerous time was that a war might be started not by big men with self-control and restraint, but by little men—the ones moved by fear and pride.

America's strength doesn't come from lashing out. Strength relies on smarts, judgement, cool resolve and the precise and strategic application of power. That's the kind of Commander-in-Chief I pledge to be.

And if we're serious about keeping our country safe, we also can't afford to have a President who's in the pocket of the gun lobby. I'm not here to repeal the Second Amendment. I'm not here to take away your guns. I just don't want you to be shot by someone who shouldn't have a gun in the first place. We should be working with responsible gun owners to pass common-sense reforms and keep guns out of the hands

---

[3]Jacqueline Kennedy was the wife of John F. Kennedy, the 35th President of the United States of America from 1961–63.

of criminals, terrorists and all others who would do us harm.

For decades, people have said this issue was too hard to solve and the politics were too hot to touch. But I ask you: How can we just stand by and do nothing? You heard, you saw family members of people killed by gun violence. You heard, you saw family members of police officers killed in the line of duty because they were outgunned by criminals. I refuse to believe we can't find common ground here. We have to heal the divides in our country. Not just on guns. But on race. Immigration. And more.

That starts with listening to each other. Hearing each other. Trying, as best we can, to walk in each other's shoes. So let's put ourselves in the shoes of young black and Latino men and women who face the effects of systemic racism, and are made to feel like their lives are disposable. Let's put ourselves in the shoes of police officers, kissing their kids and spouses goodbye every day and heading off to do a dangerous and necessary job.

We will reform our criminal justice system from end-to-end, and rebuild trust between law enforcement and the communities they serve. We will defend all our rights—civil rights, human rights and voting rights...women's rights and workers' rights...LGBT rights and the rights of people with disabilities!

And we will stand up against mean and divisive rhetoric wherever it comes from. For the past year, many people made the mistake of laughing off Donald Trump's comments— excusing him as an entertainer just putting on a show. They think he couldn't possibly mean all the horrible things he says, like when he called women 'pigs'. Or said that an American judge couldn't be fair because of his Mexican heritage. Or when he mocks and mimics a reporter with a disability. Or insults prisoners of war like John McCain—a true hero and patriot who deserves our respect.

At first, I admit, I couldn't believe he meant it either. It was just too hard to fathom—that someone who wants to lead our nation could say those things. Could be like that. But here's the sad truth: There is no other Donald Trump—This is it.

And in the end, it comes down to what Donald Trump doesn't get: that America is great—because America is good.

So enough with the bigotry and bombast. Donald Trump's not offering real change. He's offering empty promises. What are we offering? A bold agenda to improve the lives of people across our country—to keep you safe, to get you good jobs, and to give your kids the opportunities they deserve.

The choice is clear.

Every generation of Americans has come together to make our country freer, fairer, and stronger. None of us can do it alone. I know that at a time when so much seems to be pulling us apart, it can be hard to imagine how we'll ever pull together again. But I'm here to tell you tonight—progress is possible.

I know because I've seen it in the lives of people across America who get knocked down and get right back up. And I know it from my own life. More than a few times, I've had to pick myself up and get back in the game. Like so much else, I got this from my mother. She never let me back down from any challenge. When I tried to hide from a neighbourhood bully, she literally blocked the door. 'Go back out there,' she said.

And she was right. You have to stand up to bullies. You have to keep working to make things better, even when the odds are long and the opposition is fierce. We lost my mother a few years ago. I miss her every day. And I still hear her voice urging me to keep working, keep fighting for right, no matter what.

That's what we need to do together as a nation. Though 'we may not live to see the glory', as the song from the musical Hamilton goes, 'let us gladly join the fight'.

Let our legacy be about 'planting seeds in a garden you never get to see'. That's why we're here…not just in this hall, but on this earth. The Founders showed us that. And so have many others since. They were drawn together by love of country, and the selfless passion to build something better for all who follow.

That is the story of America. And we begin a new chapter tonight.

Yes, the world is watching what we do.

Yes, America's destiny is ours to choose.

So let's be stronger together. Looking to the future with courage and confidence. Building a better tomorrow for our beloved children and our beloved country. When we do, America will be greater than ever.

Thank you and may God bless the United States of America!

◆

We have seen that our nation is more deeply divided than we thought. But I still believe in America and I always will.[*]

This speech was delivered by Hillary Clinton on 9 November 2016, conceding her defeat to President-elect Donald Trump. Hillary was presidential candidate for the Democrats and her percentage of votes was more than that of Donald Trump.

Thank you. Thank you all. Thank you.

Thank you all very much. Thank you. Thank you. Thank you so much.

Very rowdy group. Thank you, my friends. Thank you. Thank you, thank you so very much for being here and I love you all, too.

Last night, I congratulated Donald Trump and offered to work with him on behalf of our country, I hope that he will be a successful President for all Americans. This is not the outcome we wanted or we worked so hard for and I'm sorry that we did not win this election for the values we share and the vision we hold for our country.

But I feel pride and gratitude for this wonderful campaign that we built together, this vast, diverse, creative, unruly, energized campaign. You represent the best of America and being your candidate has been one of the greatest honours of my life.

I know how disappointed you feel because I feel it too, and so do tens of millions of Americans who invested their hopes and dreams in this effort. This is painful and it will

---

*Source: Hillary Clinton

be for a long time, but I want you to remember this. Our campaign was never about one person or even one election, it was about the country we love and about building an America that's hopeful, inclusive and big-hearted.

We have seen that our nation is more deeply divided than we thought. But I still believe in America and I always will. And if you do, then we must accept this result and then look to the future. Donald Trump is going to be our President. We owe him an open mind and the chance to lead.

Our constitutional democracy enshrines the peaceful transfer of power and we don't just respect that, we cherish it. It also enshrines other things—the rule of law, the principle that we are all equal in rights and dignity, freedom of worship and expression. We respect and cherish these values too and we must defend them.

Now, and let me add, our constitutional democracy demands our participation, not just every four years but all the time. So let's do all we can to keep advancing the causes and values we all hold dear, making our economy work for everyone not just those at the top, protecting our country and protecting our planet and breaking down all the barriers that hold any American back from achieving their dreams.

We've spent a year and a half bringing together millions of people from every corner of our country to say with one voice that we believe that the American dream is big enough for everyone—for people of all races and religions, for men and women, for immigrants, for LGBT people and people with disabilities. For everyone.

So now, our responsibility as citizens is to keep doing our part to build that better, stronger, fairer America we seek. And I know you will.

I am so grateful to stand with all of you. I want to thank Tim Kaine and Anne Holton for being our partners on this journey. It has been a joy getting to know them better, and it gives me great hope and comfort to know that Tim will remain on the front lines of our democracy representing Virginia in the Senate.

To Barack and Michelle Obama, our country owes you an enormous debt of gratitude. We...we thank you for your graceful, determined leadership that has meant so much to so many Americans and people across the world.

And to Bill and Chelsea, Marc, Charlotte, Aidan, our brothers and our entire family, my love for you means more than I can ever express. You criss-crossed this country on our behalf and lifted me up when I needed it most—even 4-month-old Aidan who travelled with his mom.

I will always be grateful to the creative, talented, dedicated men and women at our headquarters in Brooklyn and across our country. You poured your hearts into this campaign. For some of you who are veterans, it was a campaign after you had done other campaigns. Some of you, it was your first campaign. I want each of you to know that you were the best campaign anybody could have ever expected or wanted.

And to the millions of volunteers, community leaders, activists and union organizers who knocked on doors, talked to neighbours, posted on Facebook, even in secret, private Facebook sites... I want everybody coming out from behind that and make sure your voices are heard going forward.

To everyone who sent in contributions as small at $5 and kept us going, thank you. Thank you from all of us.

And to the young people in particular, I hope you will hear this. I have, as Tim said, spent my entire adult life fighting for what I believe in. I've had successes and I've had setbacks. Sometimes, really painful ones. Many of you are at the beginning of your professional, public and political careers. You will have successes and setbacks, too.

This loss hurts, but please never stop believing that fighting for what's right is worth it. It is—it is worth it. And so we need—we need you to keep up these fights now and for the rest of your lives.

And to all the women, and especially the young women, who put their faith in this campaign and in me, I want you to know that nothing has made me prouder than to be your champion. Now, I...I know...I know we have still not shattered that highest and hardest glass ceiling, but some day someone will and hopefully sooner than we might think right now.

And, and to all the little girls who are watching this, never doubt that you are valuable and powerful and deserving of every chance and opportunity in the world to pursue and achieve your own dreams.

Finally... Finally, I am so grateful for our country and for all it has given to me. I count my blessings every single day that I am an American. And I still believe as deeply as I ever have that if we stand together and work together with respect for our differences, strength in our convictions and love for this nation, our best days are still ahead of us.

Because, you know...you know, I believe we are stronger together and we will go forward together. And you should never, ever regret fighting for that. You know, scripture tells us, 'Let us not grow weary in doing good, for in due season, we shall reap if we do not lose heart.'

So my friends, let us have faith in each other, let us not

grow weary, let us not lose heart, for there are more seasons to come. And there is more work to do.

I am incredibly honoured and grateful to have had this chance to represent all of you in this consequential election.

May God bless you and may God bless the United States of America.

◆

5

Angela Merkel
German Federal Chancellor

I want to state explicitly that the European Union also has a responsibility—to take in refugees, to address the reasons why people flee and to help people in need properly.[*]

This speech was delivered on 18 February 2017 during the 53rd Munich Security Conference.

Mr Ischinger[1], esteemed colleagues, distinguished participants of this year's Munich Security Conference,

The Internationale Wehrkundetagung in 1963 marked the start of an annual free and frank discussion—an event that has had a significant impact each year and remains a forum

---

[*]Source: Federal Government of Germany
[1]Wolfgang Ischinger is the Chairman of the Munich Security Conference.

for discussion on a wide range of topics in the form of the Munich Security Conference. People from 125 countries are attending this year's event. And as Chancellor of the Federal Republic of Germany, I would like to welcome them all warmly to Munich. The Minister President of Bavaria will of course also welcome the guests because Bavaria is something very special in Germany, but as Federal Chancellor, I also wish to do so.

Until 1990, this conference was dominated by the Cold War and the uncompromising confrontation between two blocs, as well as by nuclear deterrence. Thanks to the western partners' cohesion and strength, we were able to experience the end of the Cold War and the achievement of the goals of values based cooperation, particularly those of transatlantic cooperation, in 1990.

This is why I would like to bid a very warm welcome once again to the delegation of the United States of America, and of course especially to the Vice President and to all those who have travelled from the United States. A very warm welcome to you!

Since then, the world has changed dramatically. Today, over a quarter of a century later, we no longer have two blocs. There is a new type of order. There is a new balance of power. The structure has become far more multilateral, but we still have a super power—the United States of America—and we still have a transatlantic link. We have a united Europe with twenty-eight members. We have seen the rise of emerging economies, particularly in Asia.

To spell this out even more clearly, I looked at how gross world product has developed when I was preparing for this conference. We can say that it more or less tripled in the twenty-five years between 1990 and 2015. The United States's

GDP (Gross Domestic Product) has also tripled. The European Union's GDP has only doubled as regards the twenty-eight member states. China's GDP has increased twenty-eight fold. This means the EU now has a share of 22 per cent of gross world product compared with its previous share of 31 per cent. The United States of America has been able to maintain its share of one quarter, with a slight decrease from 26 to 25 per cent. And China's share has increased from 2 to 15 per cent. That is an example of the shifts we are witnessing.

We are facing asymmetrical threats, particularly that of Islamist terrorism, starting on 11 September 2001. There are new conflicts as a result of civil wars, population growth and climate change. There is growing interdependence as a result of globalization and the spread of digital technology. This means we do not have a fixed international order. Despite the end of the Cold War, relations with Russia remain on shaky ground—I say that now from a European perspective.

I firmly believe that the challenges of today's world cannot be overcome by any one country alone. These challenges require joint efforts. This is why I believe we need multilateral international structures, which we must strengthen and make more efficient. This goes for the European Union, NATO and the United Nations. And it goes for a forum for which Germany is responsible this year, that is, the G20, whose presidency Germany currently holds. This group was set up at the level of heads of state and government in 2008 in response to the international financial crisis. Prior to that, it had only existed at Finance Minister level. At the time, we were only able to resolve this far-reaching global crisis by working together. This was a good example of how we can also take multilateral action. That is why we chose the motto, 'shaping an interconnected world', for the G20 Presidency—in the firm belief that joint action strengthens everyone.

However, we now need to acknowledge that multilateral structures are not efficient enough in many areas, with the result that members of the public in almost all of our countries are asking if the multilateral approach is really the right one as regards solving problems or if there is a way to withdraw into protectionism and isolation. I firmly believe that it is worth fighting for joint international multilateral structures. However, we need to improve them in many ways.

In this regard, I would like to start with what we need to improve at home, that is, in the European Union. The European Union is in an exceptionally difficult phase. The outcome of the UK referendum means that we will no longer have twenty-eight member states in the future, but rather only twenty-seven. In my opinion, this is unfortunate—but it is a fact. The twenty-seven member states must ask themselves all the more how they can make their European Union a success. There are many things with which we cannot be satisfied.

First and foremost, the single market is the hallmark of the European Union. This single market, which also needs to be further expanded in response to the challenges of digital technology, must be of benefit. This means jobs, competitiveness and prosperity for the people. The social market economy in Germany was always a sound guiding principle for society as it led to prosperity for all. And this is also what people expect of the European Union.

Secondly, we need to strengthen our single currency. We have already experienced two profound crises in the European Union from which we have not yet fully recovered. One reason for this is that after we decided to introduce a single currency, the euro, we were not sufficiently prepared for crises and only put security mechanisms in place afterwards in order to safeguard the euro. We will need to continue working on this.

We have now also experienced the same thing as regards freedom of movement. You can move freely and without border controls in most EU member states. But we were not prepared for the fact that pressure could arise at our external borders, for example as a result of refugee flows, and we had to take steps after this situation arose—through joint border police and many other measures—in order to safeguard this freedom of movement within the Union. We will also need to keep working on this.

The European Union thus needs to learn to concentrate more on the truly important challenges, that is, on competitiveness, jobs, internal security and international security. We will also need to think more in the coming years about where we have superfluous regulations that make our lives difficult and curtail our competitiveness. It cannot be the case that once we have reached an acquis communautaire, as we love to call it, that this is the last word. We must also allow amendments to be made.

Naturally, we want to maintain our friendly relations with the UK. We will also do more in the field of defence policy. The Treaty of Lisbon provides for structured cooperation between the EU member states. The German and French Defence Ministers have taken the initiative to do more in this area. I think I am right in saying that almost all member states say that, yes, if we want to be a security union, then we need to do more as regards defence policy. The EU is currently conducting sixteen military operations and missions around the world. It covers over a third of the costs of UN peace missions. It is the largest provider of humanitarian aid in both Syria and Afghanistan.

But we need to do more to join up military capabilities. Our Defence Minister spoke about this in detail yesterday. We need leadership within the European Union to allow us to design a joined up approach that can include development policy and good governance, not only military capabilities. This will also enable us to make progress on an area that is particularly important to us in our relations with African countries, namely training and equipping soldiers locally. That is also important.

I firmly believe that European defence capability can never be seen as an alternative to NATO, but must always fit in with NATO's capabilities. We also share this view.

Particularly when it comes to defence cooperation, Franco-German initiatives have frequently played a major role. The Franco-German Brigade was founded in 1989 and comprises 6,000 soldiers. We are now working on joint procurement projects. This is great progress. Apart from military cooperation, Germany and France have extremely close ties in other activities, such as internal security. When it comes to protecting the external borders, there are many Franco-German initiatives, which will also become initiatives at European level.

As Mr Ischinger just mentioned, we took the initiative on an essential issue by establishing the Normandy format to address the conflict between Ukraine and Russia. I know that further talks will take place on the margins of this conference. Unfortunately, Mr Ischinger, I am unable to report that we have already met all the points in the Minsk agreement. But this agreement remains the basis for further endeavours. We need to continue working not only to further the political process, but also to finally ensure a lasting ceasefire, as people are profoundly unsettled when this does not exist.

The situation in Ukraine leads me on to NATO, the second major topic I wish to address. NATO became even more important for what I would describe as a very sad reason—that is because of the annexation of Crimea and the conflict in eastern Ukraine, where Russia is supporting the separatists. Why is this such a great concern? Why has it led to so much uncertainty? It has led to so much uncertainty—and we must repeatedly remind ourselves about this—because it violated the principle that brought us peace and security in Europe after the Second World War, namely the principle of territorial integrity. This principle is something on which the European peaceful order has been based since the Second World War. That is why we need to be so strict on this issue. If this principle no longer exists, the entire European order will be destabilized.

That is why we—the NATO Secretary General is also here with us—saw the need to strengthen the eastern flank. Germany is taking on responsibility for this in Lithuania; the United Kingdom is doing so in Estonia; and Canada and the United States of America are taking on responsibility in Latvia and Poland, respectively. We are doing this in the spirit of Article 5 and assuring each other of our joint capacities and our support.

NATO has also been active in Afghanistan since 2001. This was where the fight against terrorism really began following the attacks on 11 September 2001. Germany is still active, including within NATO, along with twenty other nations in northern Afghanistan. I spoke with the Afghan President yesterday. We also need continued military support here. But we also need a political settlement in order to ensure a peaceful future for Afghanistan.

When we speak about NATO, these days the talk quickly turns to the financial contributions made by each member. I do not want to steer clear of this topic. Like all other countries at the NATO Summit in Wales—that was in 2014—Germany made a commitment to reach the 2 per cent target within ten years. I join the Defence Minister in saying that we will do our utmost to achieve this and that we feel committed to this target. However, I would also like to add that NATO is profoundly in Europe's interest, in Germany's interest and, I believe, also in the United States's interest. It is a strong alliance of us all. That is why we will work hard and that is why we count on NATO being and remaining a project of joint interest.

Thirdly, ladies and gentlemen, there is a great threat. With regard to the NATO mission in Afghanistan, I mentioned the threat of Islamist terrorism, which has constantly grown since then through IS and other organizations such as Boko Haram. A Counter ISIL Coalition is now responding to this threat. In my view, it is active far beyond the NATO member countries, naturally in Iraq and Syria. Germany is also involved in this coalition. I just spoke with the Turkish Prime Minister. We know how Turkey, in particular as a NATO partner, is adversely affected by the challenges of Islamist terrorism, by Daesh and of course equally by PKK terrorism. I want to say very clearly here that Europeans cannot win the fight against Islamist terrorism on their own. We need the military strength of the United States of America. I say this because Islamist terrorism is also being perpetrated very close to the European Union's external borders and thus has a strong impact on Europe. This is another reason why cooperation with the United States of

America is of course very important for us.

But it is equally important to me that we included Islamic, Muslim countries in this coalition, as I believe that these countries in particular must play their part in spelling out that the cause of terrorism is not 'Islam', but rather a misguided form of Islam. That is why I also expect—and I have said this on various occasions—the Islamic religious authorities to speak out clearly about the difference between peaceful Islam and terrorism in the name of Islam. We, who are not Muslims, cannot do this in the same way the Islamic authorities can.

Ladies and gentlemen, terrorism has a wide-ranging impact. It leads to forced migration. I want to underline here what countries around Syria and, for example, near Iraq have done to help. Turkey has taken in almost three million refugees. Jordan and Lebanon have reached the limits of what is feasible. That is why we have a joint responsibility here; I want to state explicitly that the European Union also has a responsibility—to take in refugees, to address the reasons why people flee and to help people in need properly. We in Germany have taken on this responsibility along with a few European member states. Unfortunately, we do not have a joint position on this issue within the European Union. But when you recall that Cyprus is one of Syria's neighbouring countries, then you see that our external borders also run directly alongside Syria's. This is why we cannot simply opt out of the question of how people who have been forced to flee are faring. We need to deal with this issue.

I would like to make a further remark on the fight against Islamist terrorism. At the start of my speech, I said that we unfortunately—this is my own point of view—have not been able to establish stable and permanently good relations with Russia in the past twenty-five years. But Russia is also a neighbouring country of the European Union. Russia is situated at our external border and is a neighbour of ours. That is why I will continue to advocate working towards good relations with Russia, despite our having different opinions on many issues.

For me, this means continuing to stand by the NATO Russia Founding Act and not abandoning it even if times are hard—I would like to thank the NATO Secretary General for repeatedly holding meetings between Russia and NATO—and it means looking for common ground in the fight against Islamist terrorism. I believe that we share the exact same interests here and can also work together.

As a final point, I would like to speak about the role of multilateral institutions, particularly that of the United Nations. The contribution made by the United Nations's work to overall security in the world, as well as the fact that the UN Secretary General is here with us today, is very good and important. After all, this conference now focuses on a very wide-ranging definition of security that involves far more than the issue of defence cooperation. And I think this is right.

Secretary General [António] Guterres has put crisis prevention at the very top of the agenda of the United Nations's future work. I can only support that. Every crisis and conflict that can be prevented and does not take place means we do not have to spend money on defence, but instead have a chance to foster development. Africa is an important neighbouring region of the European Union. That is why we need to put our heads together and think about how we can finally bring about dynamic development in Africa like that in Asia in recent decades, alongside classical development aid. This will also be a topic of our G20 Presidency. We have not come as far as I would like, but this is so important. Thanks to smartphones and the spread of digital technology, people now know what life is like in other places. The pressure caused by forced migration will only be overcome when there is development everywhere.

Ladies and gentlemen, we will address many of these topics during our G20 Presidency—the question of forced migration, the question of addressing the reasons why people flee and the questions of global health and education, particularly the education of girls and women, so that they can live independent lives. I would therefore like to invite all of you to support us in various ways in shaping the G20 Presidency.

Thank you for your attention. It was an honour and a pleasure to give this speech today—in a year in which we all feel incredibly challenged and as if something is at stake. Will we continue being able to take joint action or will we revert to our individual roles? I call on us to find joint positions and I hope we will do so. Let us work together to make the world a better place. It will then be a better place for each and every one of us. Thank you very much indeed.

◆

6

Vladimir Putin
President of Russian Federation

**Gentlemen, the people you are dealing with are cruel but they are not dumb.
They are as smart as you are.**[*]

This speech was delivered at the 70th Session of the UN General Assembly on 28 September 2015.

Mr Secretary General, distinguished heads of state and government, ladies and gentlemen,

The 70th anniversary of the United Nations is a good occasion to both take stock of history and talk about our common future. In 1945, the countries that defeated Nazism joined their efforts to lay a solid foundation for the post-war world order. Let me remind you that key decisions on the

---

[*]Source: President of Russia website

principles defining interaction between states, as well as the decision to establish the UN, were made in our country, at the Yalta Conference of the leaders of the anti-Hitler coalition.

The Yalta system was truly born in travail. It was born at the cost of tens of millions of lives and two world wars that swept through the planet in the twentieth century. Let's be fair, it helped humankind pass through turbulent, and at times dramatic, events of the last seven decades. It saved the world from large-scale upheavals.

The United Nations is unique in terms of legitimacy, representation and universality. True, the UN has been criticized lately for being inefficient or for the fact that decision-making on fundamental issues stalls due to insurmountable differences, especially among Security Council members.

However, I'd like to point out that there have always been differences in the UN throughout the seventy years of its history, and that the veto right has been regularly used by the United States, the United Kingdom, France, China and the Soviet Union, and later Russia. It is only natural for such a diverse and representative organization. When the UN was first established, nobody expected that there would always be unanimity. The mission of the organization is to seek and reach compromises, and its strength comes from taking different views and opinions into consideration. The decisions debated within the UN are either taken in the form of resolutions or not. As diplomats say, they either pass or they don't. Any action taken by circumventing this procedure is illegitimate and constitutes a violation of the UN Charter and contemporary international law.

We all know that after the end of the Cold War the world was left with one centre of dominance, and those who found themselves at the top of the pyramid were tempted to think that, since they are so powerful and exceptional, they know best what needs to be done and thus they don't need to reckon with the UN, which, instead of rubber-stamping the decisions they need, often stands in their way.

That's why they say that the UN has run its course and is now obsolete and outdated. Of course, the world changes, and the UN should also undergo natural transformation. Russia is ready to work together with its partners to develop the UN further on the basis of a broad consensus, but we consider any attempts to undermine the legitimacy of the United Nations as extremely dangerous. They may result in the collapse of the entire architecture of international relations, and then indeed there will be no rules left except for the rule of force. The world will be dominated by selfishness rather than collective effort, by dictate rather than equality and liberty, and instead of truly independent states we will have protectorates controlled from outside.

What is the meaning of state sovereignty, the term which has been mentioned by our colleagues here? It basically means freedom, every person and every state being free to choose their future.

By the way, this brings us to the issue of the so-called legitimacy of state authorities. You shouldn't play with words and manipulate them. In international law, international affairs, every term has to be clearly defined, transparent and interpreted the same way by one and all.

We are all different, and we should respect that. Nations shouldn't be forced to all conform to the same development model that somebody has declared the only appropriate one.

We should all remember the lessons of the past. For example, we remember examples from our Soviet past, when the Soviet Union exported social experiments, pushing for changes in other countries for ideological reasons, and this often led to tragic consequences and caused degradation instead of progress.

It seems, however, that instead of learning from other people's mistakes, some prefer to repeat them and continue to export revolutions, only now these are 'democratic' revolutions. Just look at the situation in the Middle East and Northern Africa already mentioned by the previous speaker. Of course, political and social problems have been piling up for a long time in this region, and people there wanted change. But what was the actual outcome? Instead of bringing about reforms, aggressive intervention rashly destroyed government institutions and the local way of life. Instead of democracy and progress, there is now violence, poverty, social disasters and total disregard for human rights, including even the right to life.

I'm urged to ask those who created this situation: Do you at least realize now what you've done? But I'm afraid that this question will remain unanswered, because they have never abandoned their policy, which is based on arrogance, exceptionalism and impunity.

Power vacuum in some countries in the Middle East and Northern Africa obviously resulted in the emergence of areas of anarchy, which were quickly filled with extremists and terrorists. The so-called Islamic State has tens of thousands of militants fighting for it, including former Iraqi soldiers who were left on the street after the 2003 invasion. Many recruits come from Libya whose statehood was destroyed as a result of a gross violation of UN Security Council Resolution 1973. And now radical groups are joined by members of the so-called 'moderate' Syrian opposition backed by the West. They get weapons and training, and then they defect and join the so-called Islamic State.

In fact, the Islamic State itself did not come out of nowhere. It was initially developed as a weapon against undesirable secular regimes. Having established control over parts of Syria and Iraq, Islamic State now aggressively expands into other regions. It seeks dominance in the Muslim world and beyond. Their plans go further.

The situation is extremely dangerous. In these circumstances, it is hypocritical and irresponsible to make declarations about the threat of terrorism and at the same time turn a blind eye to the channels used to finance and support terrorists, including revenues from drug trafficking, the illegal oil trade and the arms trade.

It is equally irresponsible to manipulate extremist groups and use them to achieve your political goals, hoping that later you'll find a way to get rid of them or somehow eliminate them.

I'd like to tell those who engage in this: Gentlemen, the people you are dealing with are cruel but they are not dumb. They are as smart as you are. So, it's a big question: Who's playing who here? The recent incident where the most 'moderate' opposition group handed over their weapons to terrorists is a vivid example of that.

We consider that any attempts to flirt with terrorists, let alone arm them, are short-sighted and extremely dangerous. This may make the global terrorist threat much worse, spreading it to new regions around the globe, especially since there are fighters from many different countries, including European ones, gaining combat experience with Islamic State. Unfortunately, Russia is no exception.

Now that those thugs have tasted blood, we can't allow

them to return home and continue with their criminal activities. Nobody wants that, right?

Russia has consistently opposed terrorism in all its forms. Today, we provide military–technical assistance to Iraq, Syria and other regional countries fighting terrorist groups. We think it's a big mistake to refuse to cooperate with the Syrian authorities and government forces who valiantly fight terrorists on the ground.

We should finally admit that President [Bashar] Assad's government forces and the Kurdish militia are the only forces really fighting terrorists in Syria. Yes, we are aware of all the problems and conflicts in the region, but we definitely have to consider the actual situation on the ground.

Dear colleagues, I must note that such an honest and frank approach on Russia's part has been recently used as a pretext for accusing it of its growing ambitions—as if those who say that have no ambitions at all. However, it is not about Russia's ambitions, dear colleagues, but about the recognition of the fact that we can no longer tolerate the current state of affairs in the world.

What we actually propose is to be guided by common values and common interests rather than by ambitions. Relying on international law, we must join efforts to address the problems that all of us are facing, and create a genuinely broad international coalition against terrorism. Similar to the anti-Hitler coalition, it could unite a broad range of parties willing to stand firm against those who, just like the Nazis, sow evil and hatred of humankind. And of course, Muslim nations should play a key role in such a coalition, since Islamic State not only poses a direct threat to them, but also tarnishes one of the greatest world religions with its atrocities. The ideologues of these extremists make a mockery of Islam and subvert its true humanist values.

I would also like to address Muslim spiritual leaders: Your authority and your guidance are of great importance right now. It is essential to prevent people targeted for recruitment by extremists from making hasty decisions, and those who have already been deceived and, due to various circumstances, found themselves among terrorists, must be assisted in finding a way back to normal life, laying down arms and putting an end to fratricide.

In the days to come, Russia, as the current President of the UN Security Council, will convene a ministerial meeting to carry out a comprehensive analysis of the threats in the Middle East. First of all, we propose exploring opportunities for adopting a resolution that would serve to coordinate the efforts of all parties that oppose Islamic State and other terrorist groups. Once again, such coordination should be based upon the principles of the UN Charter.

We hope that the international community will be able to develop a comprehensive strategy of political stabilization, as well as social and economic recovery in the Middle East. Then, dear friends, there would be no need for setting up more refugee camps. Today, the flow of people forced to leave their native land has literally engulfed, first, the neighbouring countries, and then Europe. There are hundreds of thousands of them now, and before long, there might be millions. It is, essentially, a new, tragic Migration Period, and a harsh lesson for all of us, including Europe.

I would like to stress that refugees undoubtedly need our compassion and support. However, the only way to solve this problem for good is to restore statehood where it has been destroyed; to strengthen government institutions where they still exist, or are being re-established; to provide comprehensive military, economic and material assistance to countries in a difficult situation; and certainly to people who, despite all their ordeals, did not abandon their homes. Of course, any assistance to sovereign nations can, and should, be offered rather than imposed, in strict compliance with the UN Charter. In other words, our organization should support any measures that have been, or will be, taken in this regard in accordance with international law, and reject any actions that are in breach of the UN Charter. Above all, I believe it is of utmost importance to help restore government institutions in Libya, support the new government of Iraq and provide comprehensive assistance to the legitimate government of Syria.

Dear colleagues, ensuring peace and global and regional stability remains a key task for the international community guided by the United Nations. We believe this means creating an equal and indivisible security environment that would not serve a privileged few, but everyone. Indeed, it is a challenging, complicated and time-consuming task, but there is simply no alternative.

Sadly, some of our counterparts are still dominated by their Cold War-era bloc mentality and the ambition to conquer new geopolitical areas. First, they continued their policy of expanding NATO—one should wonder why, considering that the Warsaw Pact had ceased to exist and the Soviet Union had disintegrated.

Nevertheless, NATO has kept on expanding, together with its military infrastructure. Next, the post-Soviet states were forced to face a false choice between joining the West and carrying on with the East. Sooner or later, this logic of confrontation was bound to spark off a major geopolitical crisis. And that is exactly what happened in Ukraine, where the people's widespread frustration with the government was used for instigating a coup d'état from abroad.

This has triggered a civil war. We are convinced that the only way out of this dead end lies through comprehensive and diligent implementation of the Minsk agreements of February 12th, 2015. Ukraine's territorial integrity cannot be secured through the use of threats or military force, but it must be secured. The people of Donbas should have their rights and interests genuinely considered, and their choice respected; they should be engaged in devising the key elements of the country's political system, in line with the provisions of the Minsk agreements. Such steps would guarantee that Ukraine will develop as a civilized state, and a vital link in creating a common space of security and economic cooperation, both in Europe and in Eurasia.

Ladies and gentlemen, I have deliberately mentioned a common space for economic cooperation. Until quite recently, it seemed that we would learn to do without dividing lines in the area of the economy with its objective market laws, and act based on transparent and jointly formulated rules, including the WTO principles, which embrace free trade and investment and fair competition. However, unilaterally imposed sanctions circumventing the UN Charter have all but become commonplace today. They not only serve political objectives, but are also used for eliminating market competition.

I would like to note one more sign of rising economic selfishness. A number of nations have chosen to create exclusive economic associations, with their establishment being negotiated behind closed doors, secretly from those very nations' own public and business communities, as well as from the rest of the world. Other states, whose interests may be affected, have not been informed of anything, either. It seems that someone would like to impose upon us some new game rules, deliberately tailored to accommodate the interests of a privileged few, with the WTO having no say in it. This is fraught with utterly unbalancing global trade and splitting up the global economic space.

These issues affect the interests of all nations and influence the future of the entire global economy. That is why we propose discussing those issues within the framework of the United Nations, the WTO and the G20. Contrary to the policy of exclusion, Russia advocates harmonizing regional economic projects. I am referring to the so-called 'integration of integrations' based on the universal and transparent rules of international trade. As an example, I would like to cite our plans to interconnect the Eurasian Economic Union with China's initiative for creating a Silk Road economic belt. We continue to see great promise in harmonizing the integration vehicles between the Eurasian Economic Union and the European Union.

Ladies and gentlemen, one more issue that shall affect the future of the entire humankind is climate change. It is in our interest to ensure that the coming UN Climate Change Conference that will take place in Paris in December this year should deliver some feasible results. As part of our national contribution, we plan to limit greenhouse gas emissions to 70–75 per cent of the 1990 levels by the year 2030.

However, I suggest that we take a broader look at the issue. Admittedly, we may be able to defuse it for a while by introducing emission quotas and using other tactical measures, but we certainly will not solve it for good that way. What we need is an essentially different approach, one that would involve introducing new, groundbreaking, nature-like technologies that would not damage the environment, but rather work in harmony with it, enabling us to restore the balance between the biosphere and technology upset by human activities.

It is indeed a challenge of global proportions. And I am confident that humanity does have the necessary intellectual capacity to respond to it. We need to join our efforts, primarily engaging countries that possess strong research and development capabilities, and have made significant advances in fundamental research. We propose convening a special forum under the auspices of the UN to comprehensively address issues related to the depletion of natural resources, habitat destruction and climate change. Russia is willing to co-sponsor such a forum.

Ladies and gentlemen, dear colleagues. On January 10th, 1946, the UN General Assembly convened for its first meeting in London. Chairman of the Preparatory Commission, Dr Zuleta Angel, a Colombian diplomat, opened the session by offering what I see as a very concise definition of the principles that the United Nations should be based upon, which are goodwill, disdain for scheming and trickery and a spirit of cooperation. Today, his words sound like guidance for all of us.

Russia is confident of the United Nations's enormous potential, which should help us avoid a new confrontation and embrace a strategy of cooperation. Hand in hand with other nations, we will consistently work to strengthen the UN's central, coordinating role. I am convinced that by working together, we will make the world stable and safe, and provide an enabling environment for the development of all nations and peoples.

7

Theresa May
Prime Minister of the United Kingdom

It means we believe in a Union, not just between the nations of the United Kingdom, but between all of our citizens, whoever we are, and wherever we're from.[*]

This was Theresa May's first speech as Prime Minister, delivered from 10 Downing Street on 13 July 2016.

I have just been to Buckingham Palace, where Her Majesty The Queen has asked me to form a new government, and I accepted.

In David Cameron[1], I follow in the footsteps of a great, modern Prime Minister. Under David's leadership, the

---

[*]Source: UK Government website
[1]David Cameron served as Prime Minister of the United Kingdom from 2010–16.

government stabilized the economy, reduced the budget deficit and helped more people into work than ever before.

But David's true legacy is not about the economy but about social justice. From the introduction of same-sex marriage, to taking people on low wages out of income tax altogether, David Cameron has led a one-nation government, and it is in that spirit that I also plan to lead.

Because not everybody knows this, but the full title of my party is the Conservative and Unionist Party, and that word 'unionist' is very important to me.

It means we believe in the Union—the precious, precious bond between England, Scotland, Wales and Northern Ireland. But it means something else that is just as important; it means we believe in a union not just between the nations of the United Kingdom but between all of our citizens, every one of us, whoever we are and wherever we're from.

That means fighting against the burning injustice that, if you're born poor, you will die on average nine years earlier than others. If you're black, you're treated more harshly by the criminal justice system than if you're white. If you're a white, working-class boy, you're less likely than anybody else in Britain to go to university. If you're at a state school, you're less likely to reach the top professions than if you're educated privately. If you're a woman, you will earn less than a man. If you suffer from mental health problems, there's not enough help to hand. If you're young, you'll find it harder than ever before to own your own home.

But the mission to make Britain a country that works for everyone means more than fighting these injustices. If you're from an ordinary working-class family, life is much harder than many people in Westminster realize. You have a job but you don't always have job security. You have your own home, but you worry about paying a mortgage. You can just about manage but you worry about the cost of living and getting your kids into a good school.

If you're one of those families, if you're just managing, I want to address you directly.

I know you're working around the clock, I know you're doing your best and I know that sometimes life can be a struggle. The government I lead will be driven not by the interests of the privileged few, but by yours.

We will do everything we can to give you more control over your lives. When we take the big calls, we'll think not of the powerful, but you. When we pass new laws, we'll listen not to the mighty but to you. When it comes to taxes, we'll prioritize not the wealthy, but you. When it comes to opportunity, we won't entrench the advantages of the fortunate few. We will do everything we can to help anybody, whatever your background, to go as far as your talents will take you.

We are living through an important moment in our country's history. Following the referendum, we face a time of great national change.

And I know because we're Great Britain, that we will rise to the challenge. As we leave the European Union, we will forge a bold new positive role for ourselves in the world, and we will make Britain a country that works not for a privileged few, but for every one of us.

That will be the mission of the government I lead, and together we will build a better Britain.

◆

The British people have decided to leave the EU; and to be a global, free-trading nation, able to chart our own way in the world.*

Speech on Brexit[1] in Florence, Italy, on 22 September 2017, laying out her offer to introduce a transition period after the UK formally leaves the European Union in March 2019.

It's good to be here in this great city of Florence today at a critical time in the evolution of the relationship between the United Kingdom and the European Union.

It was here, more than anywhere else, that the Renaissance began—a period of history that inspired centuries of creativity and critical thought across our continent and which in many ways defined what it meant to be European. A period of history whose example shaped the modern world. A period of history that teaches us that when we come together in a spirit of ambition and innovation, we have it within ourselves to do great things.

That shows us that if we open our minds to new thinking and new possibilities, we can forge a better, brighter future for all our peoples.

And that is what I want to focus on today; for we are moving through a new and critical period in the history of the United Kingdom's relationship with the European Union.

The British people have decided to leave the EU; and to

---

*Source: UK Government website
[1]Britain's Exit or 'Brexit' for short; on 23 June 2016, the United Kingdom voted in a referendum to withdraw from the European Union.

be a global, free-trading nation, able to chart our own way in the world.

For many, this is an exciting time, full of promise; for others it is a worrying one. I look ahead with optimism, believing that if we use this moment to change not just our relationship with Europe, but also the way we do things at home, this will be a defining moment in the history of our nation.

And it is an exciting time for many in Europe too. The European Union is beginning a new chapter in the story of its development. Just last week, President Juncker[2] set out his ambitions for the future of the European Union. There is a vibrant debate going on about the shape of the EU's institutions and the direction of the Union in the years ahead. We don't want to stand in the way of that.

Indeed, we want to be your strongest friend and partner as the EU and the UK thrive side by side.

And that partnership is important. For as we look ahead, we see shared challenges and opportunities in common.

Here in Italy today, our two countries are working together to tackle some of the greatest challenges of our time; challenges where all too often geography has put Italy on the front line.

As I speak, Britain's Royal Navy, National Crime Agency and Border Force are working alongside their Italian partners to save lives in the Mediterranean and crack down on the evil traffickers who are exploiting desperate men, women and children who seek a better life.

Our two countries are also working together in the fight against terrorism—from our positions at the forefront of the international coalition against Daesh to our work to disrupt

---

[2]Jean-Claude Juncker is President of the European Commission.

the networks terrorist groups use to finance their operations and recruit to their ranks.

And earlier this week, I was delighted that Prime Minister Gentiloni[3] was able to join President Macron[4] and myself in convening the first ever UN summit of government and industry to move further and faster in preventing terrorist use of the Internet.

Mass migration and terrorism are but two examples of the challenges to our shared European interests and values that we can only solve in partnership.

The weakening growth of global trade; the loss of popular support for the forces of liberalism and free trade that is driving moves towards protectionism; the threat of climate change depleting and degrading the planet we leave for future generations; and most recently, the outrageous proliferation of nuclear weapons by North Korea with a threat to use them.

Here on our own continent, we see territorial aggression to the east; and from the south threats from instability and civil war; terrorism, crime and other challenges which respect no borders.

The only way for us to respond to this vast array of challenges is for like-minded nations and peoples to come together and defend the international order that we have worked so hard to create—and the values of liberty, democracy, human rights and the rule of law by which we stand.

Britain has always—and will always—stand with its friends and allies in defence of these values.

Our decision to leave the European Union is in no way a repudiation of this long-standing commitment. We may be

---

[3]Paolo Gentiloni is the Prime Minister of Italy.
[4]Emmanuel Macron is the President of France.

leaving the European Union, but we are not leaving Europe.

Our resolve to draw on the full weight of our military, intelligence, diplomatic and development resources to lead international action, with our partners, on the issues that affect the security and prosperity of our peoples is unchanged.

Our commitment to the defence—and indeed the advance—of our shared values is undimmed.

Our determination to defend the stability, security and prosperity of our European neighbours and friends remains steadfast.

And we will do all this as a sovereign nation in which the British people are in control. Their decision to leave the institution of the European Union was an expression of that desire—a statement about how they want their democracy to work. They want more direct control of decisions that affect their daily lives; and that means those decisions being made in Britain by people directly accountable to them.

The strength of feeling that the British people have about this need for control and the direct accountability of their politicians is one reason why, throughout its membership, the United Kingdom has never totally felt at home being in the European Union. And perhaps because of our history and geography, the European Union never felt to us like an integral part of our national story in the way it does to so many elsewhere in Europe.

It is a matter of choices. The profound pooling of sovereignty that is a crucial feature of the European Union permits unprecedentedly deep cooperation, which brings benefits.

But it also means that when countries are in the minority they must sometimes accept decisions they do not want, even affecting domestic matters with no market implications beyond their borders. And when such decisions are taken, they can be very hard to change.

So the British electorate made a choice. They chose the power of domestic democratic control over pooling that control, strengthening the role of the UK Parliament and the devolved Scottish Parliament, Welsh and Northern Ireland Assemblies in deciding our laws.

That is our choice. It does not mean we are no longer a proud member of the family of European nations. And it does not mean we are turning our back on Europe; or worse that we do not wish the EU to succeed. The success of the EU is profoundly in our national interest and that of the wider world.

But having made this choice, the question now is whether we—the leaders of Britain, and of the EU's member states and institutions—can demonstrate that creativity, that innovation, that ambition that we need to shape a new partnership to the benefit of all our people.

I believe we must. And I believe we can.

For while the UK's departure from the EU is inevitably a difficult process, it is in all of our interests for our negotiations to succeed. If we were to fail, or be divided, the only beneficiaries would be those who reject our values and oppose our interests.

So I believe we share a profound sense of responsibility to make this change work smoothly and sensibly, not just for people today but for the next generation who will inherit the world we leave them.

The eyes of the world are on us, but if we can be imaginative and creative about the way we establish this new relationship, if we can proceed on the basis of trust in each other, I believe we can be optimistic about the future we can build for the United Kingdom and for the European Union.

In my speech at Lancaster House earlier this year, I set out the UK's negotiating objectives.

Those still stand today. Since that speech and the triggering of Article 50 in March, the UK has published fourteen papers to address the current issues in the talks and set out the building blocks of the relationship we would like to see with the EU, both as we leave, and into the future.

We have now conducted three rounds of negotiations. And while, at times, these negotiations have been tough, it is clear that, thanks to the professionalism and diligence of David Davis and Michel Barnier[5], we have made concrete progress on many important issues.

For example, we have recognized from the outset there are unique issues to consider when it comes to Northern Ireland.

The UK Government, the Irish Government and the EU as a whole have been clear that through the process of our withdrawal we will protect progress made in Northern Ireland over recent years—and the lives and livelihoods that depend on this progress.

As part of this, we and the EU have committed to protecting the Belfast Agreement and the Common Travel Area and, looking ahead, we have both stated explicitly that we will not accept any physical infrastructure at the border. We owe it to the people of Northern Ireland—and indeed to everyone on the island of Ireland—to see through these commitments.

---

[5]David Davis is the UK's Brexit Secretary; Michel Barnier is the EU's chief Brexit negotiator.

We have also made significant progress on how we look after European nationals living in the UK and British nationals living in the twenty member states of the EU. I know this whole process has been a cause of great worry and anxiety for them and their loved ones.

But I want to repeat to the 6,00,000 Italians in the UK—and indeed to all EU citizens who have made their lives in our country—that we want you to stay; we value you; and we thank you for your contribution to our national life—and it has been, and remains, one of my first goals in this negotiation to ensure that you can carry on living your lives as before.

I am clear that the guarantee I am giving on your rights is real. And I doubt anyone with real experience of the UK would doubt the independence of our courts or of the rigour with which they will uphold people's legal rights.

But I know there are concerns that over time the rights of EU citizens in the UK and UK citizens overseas will diverge. I want to incorporate our agreement fully into UK law and make sure the UK courts can refer directly to it.

Where there is uncertainty around underlying EU law, I want the UK courts to be able to take into account the judgements of the European Court of Justice with a view to ensuring consistent interpretation. On this basis, I hope our teams can reach firm agreement quickly.

At the moment, the negotiations are focused on the arrangements for the UK's withdrawal from the EU. But we need to move on to talk about our future relationship.

Of course we recognize that we can't leave the EU and have everything stay the same. Life for us will be different. But what we do want—and what we hope that you, our European friends, want too—is to stay as partners who carry on working together for our mutual benefit.

In short, we want to work hand in hand with the European Union, rather than as part of the European Union.

That is why in my speech at Lancaster House I said that the United Kingdom would seek to secure a new, deep and special partnership with the European Union. And this should span both a new economic relationship and a new relationship on security.

So let me set out what each of these relationships could look like—before turning to the question of how we get there.

Let me start with the economic partnership.

The United Kingdom is leaving the European Union. We will no longer be members of its single market or its customs union. For we understand that the single market's four freedoms are indivisible for our European friends.

We recognize that the single market is built on a balance of rights and obligations. And we do not pretend that you can have all the benefits of membership of the single market without its obligations.

So our task is to find a new framework that allows for a close economic partnership but holds those rights and obligations in a new and different balance.

But as we work out together how to do so, we do not start with a blank sheet of paper, like other external partners negotiating a free trade deal from scratch have done. In fact, we start from an unprecedented position. For we have the same rules and regulations as the EU—and our EU Withdrawal bill will ensure they are carried over into our domestic law at the moment we leave the EU.

So the question for us now in building a new economic partnership is not how we bring our rules and regulations closer together, but what we do when one of us wants to make changes.

One way of approaching this question is to put forward a stark and unimaginative choice between two models: either something based on European Economic Area membership, or a traditional Free Trade Agreement, such as that the EU has recently negotiated with Canada.

I don't believe either of these options would be best for the UK or best for the European Union.

European Economic Area membership would mean the UK having to adopt at home—automatically and in their entirety—new EU rules. Rules over which, in future, we will have little influence and no vote.

Such a loss of democratic control could not work for the British people. I fear it would inevitably lead to friction and then a damaging reopening of the nature of our relationship in the near future: the very last thing that anyone on either side of the Channel wants.

As for a Canadian-style free trade agreement, we should recognize that this is the most advanced free trade agreement the EU has yet concluded and a breakthrough in trade between Canada and the EU. But compared with what exists between Britain and the EU today, it would nevertheless represent such a restriction on our mutual market access that it would benefit neither of our economies.

Not only that, it would start from the false premise that there is no pre-existing regulatory relationship between us. And precedent suggests that it could take years to negotiate.

We can do so much better than this.

As I said at Lancaster House, let us not seek merely to adopt a model already enjoyed by other countries. Instead, let us be creative as well as practical in designing an ambitious economic partnership which respects the freedoms and principles of the EU, and the wishes of the British people.

I believe there are good reasons for this level of optimism and ambition.

First of all, the UK is the EU's largest trading partner, one of the largest economies in the world, and a market of considerable importance for many businesses and jobs across the continent. And the EU is our largest trading partner, so it is in all our interests to find a creative solution.

The European Union has shown in the past that creative arrangements can be agreed in other areas. For example, it has developed a diverse array of arrangements with neighbouring countries outside the EU, both in economic relations and in justice and home affairs.

Furthermore, we share the same set of fundamental beliefs—a belief in free trade, rigorous and fair competition, strong consumer rights and that trying to beat other countries' industries by unfairly subsidizing one's own is a serious mistake. So there is no need to impose tariffs where we have none now, and I don't think anyone sensible is contemplating this.

And as we have set out in a future partnership paper, when it comes to trade in goods, we will do everything we can to avoid friction at the border. But of course the regulatory issues are crucial.

We share a commitment to high regulatory standards.

People in Britain do not want shoddy goods, shoddy services, a poor environment or exploitative working practices and I can never imagine them thinking those things to be acceptable. The government I lead is committed not only to protecting high standards, but strengthening them.

So I am optimistic about what we can achieve by finding a creative solution to a new economic relationship that can support prosperity for all our peoples.

Now in any trading relationship, both sides have to agree on a set of rules which govern how each side behaves.

So we will need to discuss with our European partners new ways of managing our interdependence and our differences, in the context of our shared values. There will be areas of policy and regulation which are outside the scope of our trade and economic relations where this should be straightforward.

There will be areas which do affect our economic relations where we and our European friends may have different goals, or where we share the same goals but want to achieve them through different means. And there will be areas where we want to achieve the same goals in the same ways, because it makes sense for our economies.

And because rights and obligations must be held in balance, the decisions we both take will have consequences for the UK's access to European markets and vice versa.

To make this partnership work, because disagreements inevitably arise, we will need a strong and appropriate dispute resolution mechanism.

It is, of course, vital that any agreement reached—its specific terms and the principles on which it is based—are interpreted in the same way by the European Union and the United Kingdom and we want to discuss how we do that.

This could not mean the European Court of Justice—or indeed UK courts—being the arbiter of disputes about the implementation of the agreement between the UK and the EU however. It wouldn't be right for one party's court to have jurisdiction over the other. But I am confident we can find an appropriate mechanism for resolving disputes.

So this new economic partnership would be comprehensive and ambitious. It would be underpinned by high standards, and a practical approach to regulation that enables us to continue to work together in bringing shared prosperity to our peoples for generations to come.

Let me turn to the new security relationship that we want to see.

To keep our people safe and to secure our values and interests, I believe it is essential that, although the UK is leaving the EU, the quality of our cooperation on security is maintained.

We believe we should be as open-minded as possible about how we continue to work together on what can be life and death matters.

Our security cooperation is not just vital because our people face the same threats, but also because we share a deep, historic belief in the same values—the values of peace, democracy, human rights and the rule of law.

Of course, there is no pre-existing model for cooperation between the EU and external partners which replicates the full scale and depth of the collaboration that currently exists between the EU and the UK on security, law enforcement and criminal justice.

But as the threats we face evolve faster than ever, I believe it is vital that we work together to design new, dynamic arrangements that go beyond the existing arrangements that the EU has in this area—and draw on the legal models the EU has previously used to structure cooperation with external partners in other fields such as trade.

So we are proposing a bold new strategic agreement that

provides a comprehensive framework for future security, law enforcement and criminal justice cooperation: a treaty between the UK and the EU. This would complement the extensive and mature bilateral relationships that we already have with European friends to promote our common security.

Our ambition would be to build a model that is underpinned by our shared principles, including high standards of data protection and human rights. It would be kept sufficiently versatile and dynamic to respond to the ever-evolving threats that we face. And it would create an ongoing dialogue in which law enforcement and criminal justice priorities can be shared and—where appropriate—tackled jointly.

We are also proposing a far-reaching partnership on how we protect Europe together from the threats we face in the world today, how we work together to promote our shared values and interests abroad—whether security, spreading the rule of law, dealing with emerging threats, handling the migration crisis or helping countries out of poverty.

The United Kingdom has outstanding capabilities. We have the biggest defence budget in Europe and one of the largest development budgets in the world. We have a far-reaching diplomatic network, and world-class security, intelligence and law enforcement services.

So what we are offering will be unprecedented in its breadth, taking in cooperation on diplomacy, defence and security and development. And it will be unprecedented in its depth, in terms of the degree of engagement that we would aim to deliver.

It is our ambition to work as closely as possible together with the EU, protecting our people, promoting our values and ensuring the future security of our continent.

The United Kingdom is unconditionally committed to maintaining Europe's security. And the UK will continue to offer aid and assistance to EU member states that are the victims of armed aggression, terrorism and natural or man-made disasters.

Taken as a whole, this bold new security partnership will not only reflect our history and the practical benefits of cooperation in tackling shared threats, but also demonstrate the UK's genuine commitment to promoting our shared values across the world and to maintaining a secure and prosperous Europe.

That is the partnership I want Britain and the European Union to have in the future.

None of its goals should be controversial. Everything I have said is about creating a long-term relationship through which the nations of the European Union and the United Kingdom can work together for the mutual benefit of all our people.

If we adopt this vision of a deep and special partnership, the question is then how we get there—how we build a bridge from where we are now to where we want to be.

The United Kingdom will cease to be a member of the European Union on 29th March 2019.

We will no longer sit at the European Council table or in the Council of Ministers, and we will no longer have Members of the European Parliament. Our relations with countries outside the EU can be developed in new ways, including through our own trade negotiations, because we will no longer be an EU country, and we will no longer directly benefit from the EU's future trade negotiations.

But the fact is that, at that point, neither the UK—nor the EU and its members states—will be in a position to implement smoothly many of the detailed arrangements that will underpin this new relationship we seek.

Neither is the European Union legally able to conclude an agreement with the UK as an external partner while it is itself still part of the European Union. And such an agreement on the future partnership will require the appropriate legal ratification, which would take time.

It is also the case that people and businesses—both in the UK and in the EU—would benefit from a period to adjust to the new arrangements in a smooth and orderly way.

As I said in my speech at Lancaster House a period of implementation would be in our mutual interest. That is why I am proposing that there should be such a period after the UK leaves the EU.

Clearly, people, businesses and public services should only have to plan for one set of changes in the relationship between the UK and the EU. So during the implementation period, access to one another's markets should continue on current terms and Britain also should continue to take part in existing security measures. And I know businesses, in particular, would welcome the certainty this would provide.

The framework for this strictly time-limited period, which can be agreed under Article 50, would be the existing structure of EU rules and regulations.

How long the period is should be determined simply by how long it will take to prepare and implement the new processes and new systems that will underpin that future partnership.

For example, it will take time to put in place the new immigration system required to retake control of the UK's borders. So during the implementation period, people will continue to be able to come and live and work in the UK; but there will be a registration system—an essential preparation for the new regime.

As of today, these considerations point to an implementation period of around two years.

But because I don't believe that either the EU or the British people will want the UK to stay longer in the existing structures than is necessary, we could also agree to bring forward aspects of that future framework, such as new dispute resolution mechanisms, more quickly if this can be done smoothly.

It is clear that what would be most helpful to people and businesses on both sides, who want this process to be smooth and orderly, is for us to agree the detailed arrangements for this implementation period as early as possible. Although we recognize that the EU institutions will need to adopt a formal position.

And at the heart of these arrangements, there should be a clear double lock—a guarantee that there will be a period of implementation giving businesses and people alike the certainty that they will be able to prepare for the change; and a guarantee that this implementation period will be time-limited, giving everyone the certainty that this will not go on forever.

These arrangements will create valuable certainty.

But in this context I am conscious that our departure causes another type of uncertainty for the remaining member states and their taxpayers over the EU budget.

Some of the claims made on this issue are exaggerated and unhelpful and we can only resolve this as part of the settlement of all the issues I have been talking about today.

Still, I do not want our partners to fear that they will need to pay more or receive less over the remainder of the current budget plan as a result of our decision to leave. The UK will honour commitments we have made during the period of our membership.

And as we move forward, we will also want to continue working together in ways that promote the long-term economic development of our continent. This includes continuing to take part in those specific policies and programmes which are greatly to the UK and the EU's joint advantage, such as those that promote science, education and culture, and those that promote our mutual security. And as I set out in my speech at Lancaster House, in doing so, we would want to make an ongoing contribution to cover our fair share of the costs involved.

Then at the end of this process we will find that we are able to resolve the issues where we disagree respectfully and quickly.

And if we can do that, then when this chapter of our European history is written, it will be remembered not for the differences we faced but for the vision we showed; not for the challenges we endured but for the creativity we used to overcome them; not for a relationship that ended but a new partnership that began.

A partnership of interests, a partnership of values; a partnership of ambition for a shared future: the UK and the EU side by side delivering prosperity and opportunity for all our people.

This is the future within our grasp—so, together, let us seize it.

◆

8

Shinzo Abe
Prime Minister of Japan

We must never repeat the horrors of war again.*

The following speech was made during Shinzo Abe's symbolic visit to Pearl Harbor, Hawai, on 27 December 2016, with US President Barack Obama commemorating the victims of Japan's World War II attack.

President Obama, Commander [Harry B.] Harris, ladies and gentlemen, and all American citizens:

I stand here at Pearl Harbor as the Prime Minister of Japan.

If we listen closely we can make out the sound of restless waves, breaking and then retreating again. The calm inlet of brilliant blue is radiant with the gentle sparkle of the warm sun.

Behind me, a striking white form atop the azure, is the USS Arizona Memorial.

---

*Source: Official website of the Prime Minister of Japan

Together with President Obama, I paid a visit to that memorial, the resting place for many souls.

It was a place which brought utter silence to me.

Inscribed there are the names of the servicemen who lost their lives. Sailors and marines hailing from California and New York, Michigan and Texas and various other places, serving to uphold their noble duty of protecting the homeland they loved, lost their lives amidst searing flames that day, when aerial bombing tore the USS Arizona in two.

Even seventy-five years later, the USS Arizona, now at rest atop the seabed, is the final resting place for a tremendous number of sailors and marines.

Listening again as I focus my senses, alongside the song of the breeze and the rumble of the rolling waves, I can almost discern the voices of those crewmen.

Voices of lively conversations, upbeat and at ease, on that day, on a Sunday morning. Voices of young servicemen talking to each other about their futures and dreams. Voices calling out the names of loved ones in their very final moments. Voices praying for the happiness of children still unborn.

Each and every one of those servicemen had a mother and a father anxious about his safety. Many had wives and girlfriends they loved. And many must have had children they would have loved to watch grow up.

All of that was brought to an end. When I contemplate that solemn reality, I am rendered entirely speechless.

Rest in peace, precious souls of the fallen.

With that sentiment, I cast flowers on behalf of Japanese people, upon the waters where those sailors and marines sleep.

President Obama, the people of the United States of America, and the people around the world,

As the Prime Minister of Japan, I offer my sincere and everlasting condolences to the souls of those who lost their lives here, as well as to the spirits of all the brave men and women whose lives were taken by a war that commenced in this very place, and also to the souls of the countless innocent people who became victims of the war.

We must never repeat the horrors of war again.

This is the solemn vow we, the people of Japan, have taken. And since the war, we have created a free and democratic country that values the rule of law and has resolutely upheld our vow never again to wage war.

We, the people of Japan, will continue to uphold this unwavering principle, while harbouring quiet pride in the path we have walked as a peace-loving nation over these seventy years since the war ended.

To the souls of the servicemen who lie in eternal rest aboard the USS Arizona, to the American people and to all peoples around the world, I pledge that unwavering vow here as the Prime Minister of Japan.

Yesterday, at the Marine Corps Base Hawaii in Kaneohe Bay, I visited the memorial marker for an Imperial Japanese Navy officer. He was a fighter pilot by the name of Commander Fusata Iida who was hit during the attack on Pearl Harbor and gave up on returning to his aircraft carrier. He went back instead and died.

It was not [the] Japanese who erected a marker at the site that Iida's fighter plane crashed. It was US servicemen who had been on the receiving end of his attack. Applauding the bravery of the dead pilot, they erected this stone marker.

On the marker, his rank at that time is inscribed, 'Lieutenant, Imperial Japanese Navy', showing their respect towards a serviceman who gave his life for his country.

'The brave respect the brave.' So wrote Ambrose Bierce in a famous poem. Showing respect even to an enemy they fought against; trying to understand even an enemy that they hated—therein lies the spirit of tolerance embraced by the American people.

When the war ended and Japan was a nation in burnt-out ruins as far as the eye could see, suffering under abject poverty, it was the United States, and its good people, that unstintingly sent us food to eat and clothes to wear. The Japanese people managed to survive and make their way towards the future thanks to the sweaters and milk sent by the American people.

And it was the United States that opened up the path for Japan to return to the international community once more after the war. Under the leadership of the United States, we, as a member of the free world, were able to enjoy peace and prosperity.

The goodwill and assistance you extended to us Japanese, the enemy you had fought so fiercely, together with the tremendous spirit of tolerance were etched deeply into the hearts and minds of our grandfathers and mothers. We also remember them. Our children and grandchildren will also continue to pass these memories down and never forget what you did for us.

The words pass through my mind; those words inscribed on the wall at the Lincoln Memorial in Washington D.C., where I visited with President Obama: 'With malice toward none, with charity for all…let us strive on…to do all which may achieve and cherish a…lasting peace among ourselves and with all nations.'

These are the words of President Abraham Lincoln[1].

On behalf of the Japanese people, I hereby wish to express once again my heartfelt gratitude to the United States and to the world for the tolerance extended to Japan.

It has now been seventy-five years since that 'Pearl Harbor'. Japan and the United States, which fought a fierce war that will go down in the annals of human history, have become allies with deep and strong ties rarely found anywhere in history. We are allies that will tackle together, to an even greater degree than ever before, the many challenges covering the globe.

Ours is an 'alliance of hope' that will lead us to the future.

What has bonded us together is the power of reconciliation, made possible through the spirit of tolerance. What I want to appeal to the people of the world, here at Pearl Harbor, together with President Obama, is this power of reconciliation.

Even today, the horrors of war have not been eradicated from the surface of the world. There is no end to the spiral where hatred creates hatred.

The world needs the spirit of tolerance and the power of reconciliation now—and especially now.

Japan and the United States, which have eradicated hatred and cultivated friendship and trust on the basis of common values, are now, and especially now, taking responsibility for appealing to the world about the importance of tolerance and the power of reconciliation.

That is precisely why the Japan–US alliance is 'an alliance of hope'.

The inlet gazing at us is tranquil as far as the eye can see.

---

[1]Abraham Lincoln served as the 16th President of the United States of America from 1861–65.

Pearl Harbor.

It is precisely this beautiful inlet, shimmering like pearls, that is a symbol of tolerance and reconciliation.

It is my wish that our Japanese children, and President Obama, your American children, and indeed their children and grandchildren, and people all around the world, will continue to remember Pearl Harbor as the symbol of reconciliation.

We will spare no efforts to continue our endeavours to make that wish a reality. Together with President Obama, I hereby make my steadfast pledge.

Thank you very much.

◆

9

Malala Yousafzai
Pakistani activist for female education

They thought that the bullets will silence us.
But they failed.[*]

Yousafzai gained global attention when she survived an assassination attempt by the Taliban at age 15. On her sixteenth birthday—12 July 2013—she delivered the following speech at the United Nations General Assembly. Yousafzai is also the youngest recipient of the Nobel Peace Prize (2014).

Honourable UN Secretary General Mr Ban Ki-moon; respected President of the General Assembly, Vuk Jeremic; honourable UN envoy for global education, Mr Gordon Brown; respected elders and my dear brothers and sisters— Assalamu alaikum.

---

*With special permission from Ziauddin Yousafzai and Malala Yousafzai.

Today, it is an honour for me to be speaking again after a long time. Being here with such honourable people is a great moment in my life and it is an honour for me that today I am wearing a shawl of the late Benazir Bhutto[1].

I don't know where to begin my speech. I don't know what people would be expecting me to say, but first of all thank you to God for whom we all are equal and thank you to every person who has prayed for my fast recovery and new life. I cannot believe how much love people have shown me. I have received thousands of good-wish cards and gifts from all over the world. Thank you to all of them. Thank you to the children whose innocent words encouraged me. Thank you to my elders whose prayers strengthened me. I would like to thank my nurses, doctors and the staff of the hospitals in Pakistan and the UK and the UAE Government who have helped me to get better and recover my strength.

I fully support UN Secretary General Ban Ki-moon in his Global Education First Initiative and the work of UN Special Envoy for Global Education, Gordon Brown, and the respectful president of the UN General Assembly, Vuk Jeremic. I thank them for the leadership they continue to give. They continue to inspire all of us to action.

Dear brothers and sisters, do remember one thing: Malala Day is not my day. Today is the day of every woman, every boy and every girl who have raised their voice for their rights. There are hundreds of human rights activists and social workers who are not only speaking for their rights, but who are struggling to achieve their goal of peace, education and equality. Thousands

---

[1]Pakistani politician Benazir Bhutto served as Prime Minister in 1988–90 and 1993–96.

of people have been killed by the terrorists and millions have been injured. I am just one of them.

So here I stand, one girl among many.

I speak not for myself, but so [that] those without a voice can be heard. Those who have fought for their rights. Their right to live in peace. Their right to be treated with dignity. Their right to equality of opportunity. Their right to be educated.

Dear friends, on 9 October 2012, the Taliban shot me on the left side of my forehead. They shot my friends, too. They thought that the bullets would silence us, but they failed. And out of that silence came thousands of voices. The terrorists thought they would change my aims and stop my ambitions. But nothing changed in my life except this: weakness, fear and hopelessness died. Strength, power and courage was born. I am the same Malala. My ambitions are the same. My hopes are the same. And my dreams are the same.

Dear sisters and brothers, I am not against anyone. Neither am I here to speak in terms of personal revenge against the Taliban or any other terrorist group. I am here to speak for the right of education for every child. I want education for the sons and daughters of the Taliban and all the terrorists and extremists. I do not even hate the Talib who shot me.

Even if there was a gun in my hand and he was standing in front of me, I would not shoot him. This is the compassion I have learned from Mohammed, the prophet of mercy, Jesus Christ and Lord Buddha. This is the legacy of change I have inherited from Martin Luther King, Nelson Mandela and Mohammed Ali Jinnah.

This is the philosophy of non-violence that I have learned from Gandhi, Bacha Khan and Mother Teresa. And this is the forgiveness that I have learned from my father and from my mother. This is what my soul is telling me: be peaceful and love everyone.

Dear sisters and brothers, we realize the importance of light when we see darkness. We realize the importance of our voice when we are silenced. In the same way, when we were in Swat, the north of Pakistan, we realized the importance of pens and books when we saw the guns. The wise saying—'The pen is mightier than the sword'—it is true. The extremists are afraid of books and pens. The power of education frightens them. They are afraid of women. The power of the voice of women frightens them. This is why they killed fourteen innocent students in the recent attack in Quetta. And that is why they kill female teachers. That is why they are blasting schools every day because they were and they are afraid of change and equality that we will bring to our society. And I remember that there was a boy in our school who was asked by a journalist: 'Why are the Taliban against education?' He answered very simply by pointing to his book, he said: 'A Talib doesn't know what is written inside this book.'

They think that God is a tiny, little conservative being who would point guns at people's heads just for going to school. These terrorists are misusing the name of Islam for their own personal benefit. Pakistan is a peace-loving, democratic country. Pashtuns want education for their daughters and sons. Islam is a religion of peace, humanity and brotherhood. It is the duty and responsibility to get education for each child, that is what it says. Peace is a necessity for education. In many parts of the world, especially Pakistan and Afghanistan, terrorism, war and conflicts stop children from going to schools. We are really tired of these wars. Women and children are suffering in many ways in many parts of the world.

In India, innocent and poor children are victims of child labour. Many schools have been destroyed in Nigeria. People in Afghanistan have been affected by extremism. Young girls have to do domestic child labour and are forced to get married at an early age. Poverty, ignorance, injustice, racism and the deprivation of basic rights are the main problems faced by both men and women.

Today, I am focusing on women's rights and girls' education because they are suffering the most. There was a time when women activists asked men to stand up for their rights. But this time we will do it by ourselves. I am not telling men to step away from speaking for women's rights, but I am focusing on women to be independent and fight for themselves.

So dear sisters and brothers, now it's time to speak up. So today, we call upon the world leaders to change their strategic policies in favour of peace and prosperity. We call upon the world leaders that all of these deals must protect women and children's rights. A deal that goes against the rights of women is unacceptable.

We call upon all governments to ensure free, compulsory education all over the world for every child. We call upon all the governments to fight against terrorism and violence. To protect children from brutality and harm. We call upon the developed nations to support the expansion of education opportunities for girls in the developing world. We call upon all communities to be tolerant, to reject prejudice based on caste, creed, sect, colour, religion or agenda to ensure freedom and equality for women so they can flourish. We cannot all succeed when half of us are held back. We call upon our sisters around the world to be brave, to embrace the strength within themselves and realize their full potential.

Dear brothers and sisters, we want schools and education for every child's bright future. We will continue our journey to our destination of peace and education. No one can stop us. We will speak up for our rights and we will bring change to our voice. We believe in the power and the strength of our words. Our words can change the whole world because we are all together, united for the cause of education. And if we want to achieve our goal, then let us empower ourselves with the weapon of knowledge and let us shield ourselves with unity and togetherness.

Dear brothers and sisters, we must not forget that millions of people are suffering from poverty and injustice and ignorance. We must not forget that millions of children are out of their schools. We must not forget that our sisters and brothers are waiting for a bright, peaceful future.

So let us wage a glorious struggle against illiteracy, poverty and terrorism; let us pick up our books and our pens, they are the most powerful weapons. One child, one teacher, one book and one pen can change the world. Education is the only solution. Education first.

Thank you.

◆

10

Aung San Suu Kyi
Politician and Nobel Peace Prize winner from Myanmar

The peace of our world is indivisible. As long as negative forces are getting the better of positive forces anywhere, we are all at risk.[*]

Remarks from her Nobel Lecture in Oslo, Norway, on 16 June 2012.

Your Majesties, Your Royal Highness, Excellencies, distinguished members of the Norwegian Nobel Committee, dear friends,

Long years ago, sometimes it seems many lives ago, I was at Oxford listening to the radio programme *Desert*

Island Discs with my young son Alexander. It was a well-known programme—for all I know it still continues—on which famous people from all walks of life were invited to talk about the eight discs, the one book beside the Bible and the complete works of Shakespeare and the one luxury item they would wish to have with them were they to be marooned on a desert island. At the end of the programme, which we had both enjoyed, Alexander asked me if I thought I might ever be invited to speak on *Desert Island Discs*. 'Why not?' I responded lightly. Since he knew that in general only celebrities took part in the programme he proceeded to ask, with genuine interest, for what reason I thought I might be invited. I considered this for a moment and then answered: 'Perhaps because I'd have won the Nobel Prize for literature,' and we both laughed. The prospect seemed pleasant but hardly probable.

I cannot now remember why I gave that answer, perhaps because I had recently read a book by a Nobel laureate or perhaps because the *Desert Island* celebrity of that day had been a famous writer.

In 1989, when my late husband, Michael Aris, came to see me during my first term of house arrest, he told me that a friend, John Finnis, had nominated me for the Nobel Peace Prize. This time also I laughed. For an instant Michael looked amazed, then he realized why I was amused. The Nobel Peace Prize? A pleasant prospect, but quite improbable! So how did I feel when I was actually awarded the Nobel Prize for Peace? The question has been put to me many times and this is surely the most appropriate occasion on which to examine what the Nobel Prize means to me and what peace means to me.

As I have said repeatedly in many an interview, I heard the news that I had been awarded the Nobel Peace Prize on the radio one evening. It did not altogether come as a surprise because I had been mentioned as one of the front runners for the prize in a number of broadcasts during the previous week. While drafting this lecture, I have tried very hard to remember what my immediate reaction to the announcement of the award had been. I think, I can no longer be sure, it was something like, 'Oh, so they've decided to give it to me.' It did not seem quite real because in a sense I did not feel myself to be quite real at that time.

Often during my days of house arrest it felt as though I were no longer a part of the real world. There was the house which was my world, there was the world of others who also were not free but who were together in prison as a community and there was the world of the free—each was a different planet pursuing its own separate course in an indifferent universe.

What the Nobel Peace Prize did was to draw me once again into the world of other human beings outside the isolated area in which I lived, to restore a sense of reality to me. This did not happen instantly, of course, but as the days and months went by and news of reactions to the award came over the airwaves, I began to understand the significance of the Nobel Prize. It had made me real once again; it had drawn me back into the wider human community. And what was more important, the Nobel Prize had drawn the attention of the world to the struggle for democracy and human rights in Burma. We were not going to be forgotten.

To be forgotten. The French say that to part is to die a little. To be forgotten too is to die a little. It is to lose some of the links that anchor us to the rest of humanity. When I met Burmese migrant workers and refugees during my recent visit to Thailand, many cried out: 'Don't forget us!' They meant: 'Don't forget our plight, don't forget to do what you can to help us, don't forget we also belong to your world.'

When the Nobel Committee awarded the Peace Prize to me they were recognizing that the oppressed and the isolated in Burma were also a part of the world, they were recognizing the oneness of humanity. So for me, receiving the Nobel Peace Prize means personally extending my concerns for democracy and human rights beyond national borders. The Nobel Peace Prize opened up a door in my heart.

The Burmese concept of peace can be explained as the happiness arising from the cessation of factors that militate against the harmonious and the wholesome. The word 'nyein-chan' translates literally as the beneficial coolness that comes when a fire is extinguished. Fires of suffering and strife are raging around the world. In my own country, hostilities have not ceased in the far north; to the west, communal violence resulting in arson and murder were taking place just several days before I started out on the journey that has brought me here today.

News of atrocities in other reaches of the earth abound. Reports of hunger, disease, displacement, joblessness, poverty, injustice, discrimination, prejudice, bigotry; these are our daily fare. Everywhere, there are negative forces eating away at the foundations of peace. Everywhere can be found thoughtless dissipation of material and human resources that are necessary for the conservation of harmony and happiness in our world.

The First World War represented a terrifying waste of youth and potential, a cruel squandering of the positive forces of our planet. The poetry of that era has a special significance for me because I first read it at a time when I was the same age as many of those young men who had to face the prospect of withering before they had barely blossomed. A young American fighting with the French Foreign Legion wrote before he was killed in action in 1916 that he would meet his death 'at some disputed barricade', 'on some scarred slope of battered hill', 'at midnight in some flaming town'. Youth and love and life perishing forever in senseless attempts to capture nameless, unremembered places. And for what? Nearly a century on, we have yet to find a satisfactory answer.

Are we not still guilty, if to a less violent degree, of recklessness, of improvidence with regard to our future and our humanity? War is not the only arena where peace is done to death. Wherever suffering is ignored, there will be the seeds of conflict, for suffering degrades and embitters and enrages.

A positive aspect of living in isolation was that I had ample time in which to ruminate over the meaning of words and precepts that I had known and accepted all my life. As a Buddhist, I had heard about 'dukha', generally translated as suffering, since I was a small child. Almost on a daily basis, elderly, and sometimes not so elderly, people around me would murmur 'dukha, dukha' when they suffered from aches and pains or when they met with some small, annoying mishaps. However, it was only during my years of house arrest that I got around to investigating the nature of the six great dukha. These are: to be conceived, to age, to sicken, to die, to be parted from those one loves, to be forced to live in propinquity with those one does not love.

I examined each of the six great sufferings, not in a religious context but in the context of our ordinary, everyday lives. If suffering were an unavoidable part of our existence, we should try to alleviate it as far as possible in practical, earthly ways. I mulled over the effectiveness of ante- and post-natal programmes and mother and childcare; of adequate facilities for the aging population; of comprehensive health services; of compassionate nursing and hospices. I was particularly intrigued by the last two kinds of suffering: to be parted from those one loves and to be forced to live in propinquity with those one does not love. What experiences might our Lord Buddha have undergone in his own life that he had included these two states among the great sufferings? I thought of prisoners and refugees, of migrant workers and victims of human trafficking, of that great mass of the uprooted of the earth who have been torn away from their homes, parted from families and friends, forced to live out their lives among strangers who are not always welcoming.

We are fortunate to be living in an age when social welfare and humanitarian assistance are recognized not only as desirable but necessary. I am fortunate to be living in an age when the fate of prisoners of conscience anywhere has become the concern of peoples everywhere, an age when democracy and human rights are widely, even if not universally, accepted as the birthright of all. How often during my years under house arrest have I drawn strength from my favourite passages in the preamble to the Universal Declaration of Human Rights:

'...disregard and contempt for human rights have resulted in barbarous acts which have outraged the conscience of mankind, and the advent of a world in which human beings shall enjoy freedom of speech and belief and freedom from fear and want has been proclaimed as the highest aspirations of the common people...'

'...it is essential, if man is not to be compelled to have recourse, as a last resort, to rebellion against tyranny and oppression, that human rights should be protected by the rule of law...'

If I am asked why I am fighting for human rights in Burma, the above passages will provide the answer. If I am asked why I am fighting for democracy in Burma, it is because I believe that democratic institutions and practices are necessary for the guarantee of human rights.

Over the past year, there have been signs that the endeavours of those who believe in democracy and human rights are beginning to bear fruit in Burma. There have been changes in a positive direction; steps towards democratization have been taken.

If I advocate cautious optimism it is not because I do not have faith in the future but because I do not want to encourage blind faith. Without faith in the future, without the conviction that democratic values and fundamental human rights are not only necessary but possible for our society, our movement could not have been sustained throughout the destroying years. Some of our warriors fell at their post, some deserted us, but a dedicated core remained strong and committed. At times when I think of the years that have passed, I am amazed that so many remained staunch under the most trying circumstances. Their faith in our cause is not blind; it is based on a clear-eyed assessment of their own powers of endurance and a profound respect for the aspirations of our people.

It is because of recent changes in my country that I am with you today; and these changes have come about because of you and other lovers of freedom and justice who contributed towards a global awareness of our situation. Before continuing to speak of my country, may I speak out for our prisoners of conscience. There still remain such prisoners in Burma. It is to be feared that because the best known detainees have been released, the remainder, the unknown ones, will be forgotten. I am standing here because I was once a prisoner of conscience. As you look at me and listen to me, please remember the often repeated truth that one prisoner of conscience is one too many. Those who have not yet been freed, those who have not yet been given access to the benefits of justice in my country number much more than one. Please remember them and do whatever is possible to effect their earliest, unconditional release.

Burma is a country of many ethnic nationalities, and faith in its future can be founded only on a true spirit of union. Since we achieved independence in 1948, there never has been a time when we could claim the whole country was at peace. We have not been able to develop the trust and understanding necessary to remove causes of conflict.

Hopes were raised by ceasefires that were maintained from the early 1990s until 2010 when these broke down over the course of a few months. One unconsidered move can be enough to remove long-standing ceasefires. In recent months, negotiations between the government and ethnic nationality forces have been making progress. We hope that ceasefire agreements will lead to political settlements founded on the aspirations of the peoples, and the spirit of union.

My party, the National League for Democracy, and I stand ready and willing to play any role in the process of national reconciliation. The reform measures that were put into motion by President U Thein Sein's government[1] can be sustained only with the intelligent cooperation of all internal forces—the military, our ethnic nationalities, political parties,

---

[1] U Thein Sein served as Myanmar's President from 2011–16.

the media, civil society organizations, the business community and, most important of all, the general public.

We can say that reform is effective only if the lives of the people are improved and in this regard, the international community has a vital role to play. Development and humanitarian aid, bilateral agreements and investments should be coordinated and calibrated to ensure that these will promote social, political and economic growth that is balanced and sustainable. The potential of our country is enormous. This should be nurtured and developed to create not just a more prosperous but also a more harmonious, democratic society where our people can live in peace, security and freedom.

The peace of our world is indivisible. As long as negative forces are getting the better of positive forces anywhere, we are all at risk. It may be questioned whether all negative forces could ever be removed. The simple answer is: 'No!'

It is in human nature to contain both the positive and the negative. However, it is also within human capability to work to reinforce the positive and to minimize or neutralize the negative. Absolute peace in our world is an unattainable goal. But it is one towards which we must continue to journey, our eyes fixed on it as a traveller in a desert fixes his eyes on the one guiding star that will lead him to salvation. Even if we do not achieve perfect peace on earth, because perfect peace is not of this earth, common endeavours to gain peace will unite individuals and nations in trust and friendship and help to make our human community safer and kinder.

I used the word 'kinder' after careful deliberation; I might say the careful deliberation of many years. Of the sweets of adversity—and let me say that these are not numerous—I have found the sweetest, the most precious of all, is the lesson I learnt on the value of kindness. Every kindness I received, small or big, convinced me that there could never be enough of it in our world. To be kind is to respond with sensitivity and human warmth to the hopes and needs of others. Even the briefest touch of kindness can lighten a heavy heart. Kindness can change the lives of people.

Norway has shown exemplary kindness in providing a home for the displaced of the earth, offering sanctuary to those who have been cut loose from the moorings of security and freedom in their native lands.

There are refugees in all parts of the world. When I was at the Maela refugee camp in Thailand recently, I met dedicated people who were striving daily to make the lives of the inmates as free from hardship as possible. They spoke of their concern over 'donor fatigue', which could also translate as 'compassion fatigue'. 'Donor fatigue' expresses itself precisely in the reduction of funding. 'Compassion fatigue' expresses itself less obviously in the reduction of concern. One is the consequence of the other. Can we afford to indulge in compassion fatigue? Is the cost of meeting the needs of refugees greater than the cost that would be consequent on turning an indifferent, if not a blind, eye on their suffering? I appeal to donors the world over to fulfil the needs of these people who are in search, often it must seem to them a vain search, of refuge.

At Maela, I had valuable discussions with Thai officials responsible for the administration of Tak province where this and several other camps are situated. They acquainted me with some of the more serious problems related to refugee camps— violation of forestry laws, illegal drug use, home-brewed spirits, the problems of controlling malaria, tuberculosis, dengue fever and cholera. The concerns of the administration are as legitimate as the concerns of the refugees. Host countries also deserve consideration and practical help in coping with the difficulties related to their responsibilities.

Ultimately, our aim should be to create a world free from the displaced, the homeless and the hopeless, a world of which each and every corner is a true sanctuary where the inhabitants will have the freedom and the capacity to live in peace. Every thought, every word and every action that adds to the positive and the wholesome is a contribution to peace. Each and every one of us is capable of making such a contribution. Let us join hands to try to create a peaceful world where we can sleep in security and wake in happiness.

The Nobel Committee concluded its statement of 14 October 1991 with the words: 'In awarding the Nobel Peace Prize...to Aung San Suu Kyi, the Norwegian Nobel Committee wishes to honour this woman for her unflagging efforts and to show its support for the many people throughout the world who are striving to attain democracy, human rights and ethnic conciliation by peaceful means.'

When I joined the democracy movement in Burma it never occurred to me that I might ever be the recipient of any prize or honour. The prize we were working for was a free, secure and just society where our people might be able to realize their full potential. The honour lay in our endeavour. History had given us the opportunity to give our best for a cause in which we believed. When the Nobel Committee chose to honour me, the road I had chosen of my own free will became a less lonely path to follow. For this I thank the Committee, the people of Norway and peoples all over the world whose support has strengthened my faith in the common quest for peace.

Thank you.

11

António Guterres
Secretary General, United Nations

The Holocaust was an incomparable tragedy and an incomparable crime in human history.[*]

This speech was delivered at the Museum of the Jewish People in Tel Aviv, Israel, on 30 August 2017.

Dear Prime Minister, Ambassador, Excellencies, ladies and gentlemen, dear friends,

I am honoured to speak to you today after visiting the Museum of the Jewish People, which tells a story stretching over millennia and to all corners of the world.

This remarkably rich mosaic is a Jewish legacy. But it is also an important part of the collective heritage of humanity, a showcase of its highest summits and its lowest depths.

---

*Reprinted with permission of the United Nations

One cannot escape the fact that so many communities, where Jews lived and thrived for centuries, no longer exist because of countless waves of persecution and genocide.

Ladies and gentlemen, for one of my first speeches as Secretary General, I took part in the International Holocaust Remembrance Day ceremony in the UN General Assembly Hall.

The Holocaust was an incomparable tragedy and an incomparable crime in human history. The world has a duty to remember that the Holocaust was a systematic attempt to eliminate the Jewish people, together with some others. Let us also recognize that the Holocaust was the culmination of thousands of years of hatred and discrimination targeting the Jews—what we now call anti-Semitism.

I am ashamed that my own country, Portugal, is marred by this history, and I was deeply moved by the eloquent testimony in the museum about the history of Portuguese Jews, their predicament and their success around the world.

The persecution reached its height with the order by King Manuel I in the sixteenth century, expelling all Jews who refused to convert. This was a hideous crime that caused tremendous suffering.

But it was also a colossally stupid act that deprived Portugal of much of the country's dynamism and led to prolonged periods of cultural and economic stagnation.

Many Portuguese Jews went to the Netherlands, and we have seen a model of that wonderful building, the Portuguese Synagogue of Amsterdam, and they helped that country become one of the seventeenth century's leading economies and innovators.

When I became Prime Minister in 1995, I felt it was my

duty to demonstrate my country's remorse for the Portuguese Inquisition and centuries of merciless attacks against the Jews. In 1996, the Parliament revoked the letter of expulsion. This was an admittedly symbolic act, but the spirit of repentance was genuine. Several descendants of expelled families have now exercised their right to regain Portuguese nationality.

And I then was able to visit the Portuguese Synagogue in Amsterdam to formally present a copy of that decree and apologize on behalf of my country. I was impressed, as everybody can be, looking at the model right here, by the beauty of that synagogue, and moved by what I learned about the vibrancy of Jewish life in the years before the Second World War. But sadly, in the Netherlands too, the Jewish community was almost completely destroyed by the Holocaust. As we have seen again and again, anti-Semitism tends to come back.

After the Holocaust, the founding of the United Nations generated hope that the world could avoid such hatred and violence and would work together to advance equality and human rights for all.

Yet, anti-Semitism and intolerance remain disturbingly widespread.

There are still people who, despite the facts, deny the Holocaust or diminish its scope. There is even a tendency in some countries to rewrite the history around the Second World War and to rehabilitate some of the figures that were themselves involved in the crimes and the tragedy of the Holocaust.

The Internet and social media are filled with hate speech and anti-Semitic imagery. We hear on the streets of democratic societies the repeating of some of the most vile Nazi chants and charges, just a few weeks ago, 'blood and soil' or 'the Jews will not replace us'.

Today, anti-Semitism, along with racism, xenophobia, anti-Muslim hatred and other forms of intolerance, are being triggered by populism and by political figures who exploit fear to win votes. Immigrants, refugees and minorities across the world are also among the most frequent targets of this animus.

Let me stress that when I talk about anti-Semitism, I include calls for the destruction of Israel. Israel is a member state of the United Nations. It bears all the responsibilities and enjoys all the rights of every other member state and, therefore, it must be treated as such.

As Secretary General of the United Nations, I am determined to do everything I can to stand against anti-Semitism and to all other forms of bigotry and discrimination.

Ladies and gentlemen, three months from now, we will mark the 70th anniversary of the vote at the General Assembly on the 'Partition Plan' that led to the creation of the state of Israel. Seventy years later, however, the promise of peace has not yet been delivered. Decades of conflict have cost thousands of lives and left deep scars in virtually every Palestinian and Israeli family.

The United Nations remains committed to providing Israelis and Palestinians with all possible assistance and support to reach the goal of a comprehensive two-state solution. I have observed this process over the years with great concern, as someone who cares deeply about this land and its people.

As Prime Minister of Portugal and in other political capacities, I worked with Israeli and Palestinian leaders and was impressed by the genuine desire they have shown to provide a secure and dignified future for their peoples, hoping to see a negotiated solution of two states based on relevant UN resolutions. Like many here and around the world, I have gone from great hopes about the peace process, to frustration over its stagnation.

It is my deep belief that a two-state solution is the only way forward—the only path towards the historic compromise that can settle this conflict and lead to a better future for all. That is why I have been, and will continue to be, expressing my disagreement when it's the case, with unilateral measures and facts on the ground that can or could undermine that solution—including settlement activities—but also continued violence, terror and incitement.

I am well aware of the suspicious polarization and despair that have kept each side from seeing the other as a partner. I am equally cognizant of the political difficulties faced by each side's political leaders. Yet I believe there is no alternative to a negotiated solution between the two parties.

It is equally clear that we in the international community cannot simply turn away and allow the situation to deteriorate. We have a role and a responsibility to support the parties in resolving this conflict.

The basic premise has not changed—this land is the ancestral homeland of two peoples. Both have an undeniable historic and religious bond with it; both have a right to live on it independently and as a free people, as masters of their own fate.

Anyone visiting Israel is left with no doubt that it has fulfilled the rights and national aspirations of Jews throughout generations. Your country has become renowned worldwide for its great cultural, scientific, technological and scholarly achievements.

We had the opportunity just two days ago to see some remarkable examples of innovation that can be of extreme utility for humankind all over the world in fighting climate change or in accomplishing the Sustainable Development Goals. You have succeeded in protecting your security against many threats, and signing peace treaties with Egypt and Jordan, and building successful international alliances.

Most importantly, you have created, for the first time in 2,000 years, a home for your people.

It is now overdue that the Palestinians also fulfil their legitimate rights and national aspirations. I am deeply convinced that, when they do, when they are citizens of their own state, living side by side in peace and security with Israel, Jews will enjoy greater security—as it needs to be guaranteed, prosperity and recognition, and it will be an even greater source of pride for Israelis and for Jews around the world.

I know that many in Israel share this conviction.

Young men and women, including many of you here today, have the power to challenge physical and psychological barriers and seek to build a common future.

Allow me to pay tribute to Palestinians and Israelis who are taking positive actions in their daily lives, often very quietly, to promote tolerance, cooperation and understanding between the two peoples.

I was deeply moved this morning. We visited Nahal Oz, a kibbutz close to the Gaza Strip, that has been bombarded several times and in which one child has been killed by a rocket. I had the enormous pleasure, when talking to the families of the kibbutzim, to note that instead of what would be natural—a feeling of anger in relation to what is an attack on civilians and a violation of international humanitarian law—I have seen from them an extraordinary message of peace and reconciliation, asking us to help the Palestinians in Gaza to overcome their tragic humanitarian problems and being themselves ready to help and to provide support to the Palestinian community in Gaza.

It was a fantastic example of solidarity, of humanity, of tolerance, that I want to pay tribute here publicly today.

The voices of these true peacemakers must not be drowned out by the strident voices and violent actions of the far fewer agents of hate and division.

Let us not forget that those individual peace-builders represent the best faces of their communities and serve as the human foundation so essential for a lasting peace, here and everywhere.

Thank you very much.

◆

12

Nelson Mandela
Former President of South Africa and anti-apartheid revolutionary

On this day of my release.*

Address to a rally in Cape Town on his release from prison on 11 February 1990 after twenty-seven and a half years in prison, the event that much of South Africa and the rest of the world had been waiting for decades. The release, at 5 p.m., was an hour late. Mandela was last seen in public almost three decades back, in 1962. This was fourteen years before South Africa got television. The 40-mile journey to downtown Cape Town was stopped multiple times so that Mandela could get out and speak to ordinary South Africans along the route. There are two versions of this historic speech—verbatim and prepared. We have used the verbatim version.

---

*Source: Taken with permission from the Nelson Mandela Foundation.

Slogan: Amandla! Amandla! iAfrika! Mayibuye!

Friends, comrades and fellow South Africans, I greet you all in the name of peace, democracy, and freedom for all. I stand here before you not as a prophet but as a humble servant of you, the people.

Your tireless and heroic sacrifices have made it possible for me to be here today. I, therefore, place the remaining years of my life in your hands.

On this day of my release, I extend my sincere and warmest gratitude to the millions of my compatriots and those in every corner of the globe who have campaigned tirelessly for my release.

I extend special greetings to the people of Cape Town. This city to which, which has been my home for three decades. Your mass marches, and other forms of struggle, have served as a constant source of strength to all political prisoners.

I salute the African National Congress. It has fulfilled our every expectation in its role as leader of the great march to freedom.

I salute our President, comrade Oliver Tambo[1], for leading the ANC even under the most difficult circumstances. I salute the rank and file members of the ANC. You have sacrificed life and limb in the pursuit of the noble cause of our struggle.

I salute combatants of Umkhonto we Sizwe[2], like Solomon Mahlangu and Ashley Kriel, who have paid the ultimate price for the freedom of all South Africans.

I salute the South African Communist Party for its steady

---

[1] Oliver Tambo was President of South Africa's black nationalist party, African National Congress (ANC), from 1967–91.
[2] ANC's military organization.

contribution to the struggle for democracy. You have survived forty years of unrelenting persecution. The memory of great communists, like Moses Kotane, Yusuf Dadoo, Bram Fischer and Moses Mabhida, will be cherished for generations to come. I salute General Secretary Joe Slovo[3], one of our finest patriots. We are heartened by the fact that the alliance between ourselves and the Party remains as strong as it always was.

I salute the United Democratic Front, the National Education Crisis Committee, the South African Youth Congress, the Transvaal and Natal Indian Congresses and COSATU[4], and the many other formations of the Mass Democratic Movement.

I also salute the Black Sash and the National Union of South African Students. We note, with pride, that you have acted as the conscience of white South Africans. Even during the darkest days of the history of our struggle you held the flag of liberty high. The large-scale mass mobilization of the past few years is one of the key factors which led to the opening of the final chapter of our struggle.

I extend my greetings to the working class of our country. Your organized strength is the pride of our movement. You remain the most dependable force in the struggle to end exploitation and oppression.

I pay tribute, I pay tribute to the many religious communities who carried the campaign for justice forward when the organizations of our people were silenced.

I greet the traditional leaders of our country. Many among

---

[3]Lawyer and activist Joe Slovo was the chief white leader in the struggle against apartheid in South Africa.
[4]Congress of South African Trade Unions

you continue to walk in the footsteps of great heroes, like Hintsa and Sekhukhune.

I pay tribute to the endless heroism of the youth. You, the young lions, you, the young lions, have energized our entire struggle.

I pay tribute to the mothers and wives and sisters of our nation. You are the rock-hard foundation of our struggle. Apartheid has inflicted more pain on you than on anyone else.

On this occasion, we thank the world, we thank the world community for their great contribution to the anti-apartheid struggle. Without your support, our struggle would not have reached this advanced stage. The sacrifice of the front line states will be remembered by South Africans forever.

My salutations will be incomplete without expressing my deep appreciation for the strength given to me during my long and lonely years in prison by my beloved wife and family. I am convinced that your pain and suffering was far greater than my own.

Before I go any further, I wish to make the point that I intend making only a few preliminary comments at this stage. I will make a more complete statement only after I have had the opportunity to consult with my comrades.

Today, the majority of South Africans, black and white, recognize that apartheid has no future. It has to be ended by our own decisive mass action in order to build peace and security. The mass campaigns of defiance, and other actions of our organizations and people, can only culminate in the establishment of democracy.

The apartheid destruction on our subcontinent is incalculable. The fabric of family life of millions of my people has been shattered. Millions are homeless and unemployed.

Our economy, our economy lies in ruins and our people are embroiled in political strife.

Our resort to the armed struggle in 1960, with the formation of the military wing of the ANC, Umkhonto we Sizwe, was a purely defensive action against the violence of apartheid.

The factors which necessitated the armed struggle still exist today. We have no option but to continue. We express the hope that a climate conducive to a negotiated settlement would be created soon so that there may no longer be the need for the armed struggle.

I am a loyal and disciplined member of the African National Congress, I am therefore, in full agreement with all of its objectives, strategies and tactics. The need to unite the people of our country is as important a task now as it always has been. No individual leader is able to take on these enormous tasks on his own.

It is our task as leaders to place our views before our organization and to allow the democratic structures to decide on the way forward. On the question of democratic practice, I feel duty-bound to make the point that a leader of the movement is the person who has been democratically elected at a national conference. This is the principle which must be upheld without any exception.

Today, I wish to report to you that my talks with the government have been aimed at normalizing the political situation in the country. We have not as yet begun discussing the basic demands of the struggle. I wish to stress that I myself have at no time entered into negotiations about the future of our country, except to insist on a meeting between the ANC and the government.

Mr De Klerk[5] has gone further than any other Nationalist President in taking real steps to normalize the situation.

However, there are further steps as outlined in the Harare Declaration that have to be met before negotiations on the basic demands of our people can begin.

I reiterate our call for inter alia, the immediate ending of the state of emergency and the freeing of all, and not only some, political prisoners.

Only such a normalized situation which allows for free political activities can allow us to consult our people in order to obtain a mandate.

The people need to be consulted on who will negotiate and on the content of such negotiations. Negotiations cannot take place above the heads or behind the backs of our people.

It is our belief that the future of our country can only be determined by a body which is democratically elected on a non-racial basis.

Negotiations on the dismantling of apartheid will have to address the overwhelming demands of our people for a democratic, non-racial and unitary South Africa. There must be an end to white monopoly on political power, and a fundamental restructuring of our political and economic systems to ensure that the inequalities of apartheid are addressed and our society thoroughly democratized.

It must be added that Mr De Klerk himself is a man of integrity, who is acutely aware of the dangers of a public figure not honouring his undertakings.

But as an organization, we based our policy and strategy on the harsh reality we are faced with. And this reality is

---

[5] F.W. de Klerk served as the President of South Africa from 1989–94.

that we are still suffering under the policies of the Nationalist government. Our struggle has reached a decisive moment. We call on our people to seize this moment so that the process towards democracy is rapid and uninterrupted.

We have waited too long for our freedom. We can no longer wait. Now is the time to intensify the struggle on all fronts. To relax our efforts now would be a mistake which generations to come will not be able to forgive.

The sight of freedom looming on the horizon should encourage us to redouble our efforts. It is only through disciplined mass action that our victory can be assured.

We call on our white compatriots to join us in the shaping of a new South Africa. The freedom movement is a political home for you too. We call on the international community to continue the campaign to isolate the apartheid regime.

To lift sanctions now would be to run the risk of aborting the process towards the complete eradication of apartheid. Our march to freedom is irreversible. We must not allow fear to stand in our way.

Universal suffrage on a common voters' role in united, democratic and non-racial South Africa is the only way to peace and racial harmony.

In conclusion, I wish to quote my own words during my trial in 1964. They are as true today as they were then. I quote:

> I have fought against white domination and I have fought against black domination. I have cherished the ideal of a democratic and free society in which all persons live together in harmony and with equal opportunities. It is an ideal which I hope to live for and to achieve. But, if needs be, it is an ideal for which I am prepared to die.

13

Tony Blair
Prime Minister of the United Kingdom (1997–2007)

So I do not claim Britain is transformed. I do say the foundations of a New Britain are being laid.[*]

This speech was delivered on 28 September 1999 during the Labour Party Conference.

Today at the frontier of the new millennium I set out for you how, as a nation, we renew British strength and confidence for the twenty-first century; and how, as a Party reborn, we make it a century of progressive politics after one dominated by Conservatives.

A New Britain where the extraordinary talent of the British people is liberated from the forces of conservatism that so long have held them back, to create a model twenty-first-century nation, based not on privilege, class or background, but on

---

*Source: UK Government website

the equal worth of all.

And New Labour, confident at having modernized itself, now the new progressive force in British politics which can modernize the nation, sweep away those forces of conservatism to set the people free.

Hundred years in existence, twenty-two in power, we have never, ever won a full second term. That is our unfinished business. Let us now finish it and with it finish the Tory Party's chances of doing as much damage in the next century as they've done in this one.

Today's Tory Party—the party of fox hunting, Pinochet and hereditary peers: the uneatable, the unspeakable and the unelectable.

There's only one thing you need to know about today's Tory Party.

[Kenneth] Clarke and [Michael] Heseltine: outcasts.

[William] Hague, [Ann] Widdecombe, [John] Redwood and [Michael] Portillo in charge.

The only Party that spent two years in hibernation in search of a new image and came back as the Addams family.

Under John Major, it was weak, weak, weak.

Under William Hague, it's weird, weird, weird.

Far right, far out.

But not far enough for some. Like the letter I got last week from a man who said did I know the Tories had been listening to Britain. They can't have been listening too hard, he said. They're still here.

The more useless they get, the more extreme they get.

In the last few months alone, I've been compared to Hitler, Mussolini and [Slobodan] Milošević. Maybe they think I should be indicted for war crimes—the crime of leading the Labour Party into government, and disturbing the natural order of things.

By convention, prime ministers start with all the good things their government has done. I want to start where the British people start—with all we have still to do.

More than one million still unemployed. Schools and hospitals still needing investment. Pensioners still living in hardship. People still petrified by crime and drugs. Three million children still in poverty.

A century of decline, twenty years of Conservative Government still not put to rights. Do you think I don't feel this, in every fibre of my being?

The frustration, the impatience, the urgency, the anger at the waste of lives unfulfilled, hopes never achieved, dreams never realized. And whilst there is one child still in poverty in Britain today, one pensioner in poverty, one person denied their chance in life, there is one Prime Minister and one Party that will have no rest, no vanity in achievement, no sense of mission completed, until they too are free.

So I do not claim Britain is transformed. I do say the foundations of a New Britain are being laid.

After decades of Tory boom and bust, it is New Labour which is the party of economic competence today and for that we can be proud; and proud of our Chancellor too.

Indeed, I can stand here today, leader of the Labour Party, Prime Minister, and say to the British people: you have never had it so...prudent.

As we think back to 1985, and to Neil Kinnock[1], wasn't it brilliant yesterday, in this hall of all places, to see a Labour

---

[1]Neil Kinnock was leader of the Labour Party from 1983–92.

Chancellor, 'scuttling' back from Washington to hand out the best economic news in a generation, to his own party's Conference.

Six hundred and fifty thousand more jobs in the economy, long-term youth unemployment halved and—here's one for us to put back down a few Tory throats—fewer days lost in strikes than any of the eighteen years of Tory Government. Who says Labour's not working now?

All employees with the right to a paid holiday.

Leave for parents to take time off work for a family crisis.

And after hundred years of trying, the right for union members to have their union recognized, not on the whim of an employer, but as a democratic right in a fair and free society.

Maternity grant doubled.

Seven million families with the largest ever rise in Child Benefit Britain has seen.

And I say to Britain's pensioners: I know when you get an extra £100 for every pensioner household this November—not just those on benefits, everyone—it's not the end of your worries, but it's £100 more than you got under any Conservative Government; and they'd take the £100 back off you if they were ever elected again.

Halfway through one Parliament. Nothing like halfway towards meeting all our goals.

And all around us the challenge of change.

A spectre haunts the world—technological revolution.

Ten years ago, a 15-year-old probably couldn't work a computer. Now he's in danger of living on it.

Over a trillion dollars traded every day in currency markets and with them the fate of nations.

Global finance and communications and media; electronic

commerce; the Internet; the science of genetics—every year a new revolution scattering in its wake, security, and ways of living for millions of people.

These forces of change driving the future: Don't stop at national boundaries; don't respect tradition; they wait for no one and no nation. They are universal.

We know what a twenty-first-century nation needs.

A knowledge-based economy. A strong civic society. A confident place in the world.

Do that and a nation masters the future. Fail and it is the future's victim.

The challenge is how? The answer is people. The future is people.

The liberation of human potential, not just as workers but as citizens.

Not power to the people but power to each person to make the most of what is within them. People are born with talent and everywhere it is in chains.

Look at Britain. Great strengths. Great history. English, the language of the new technology. The national creative genius of the British people. But wasted.

The country run for far too long on the talents of the few, when the genius of the many lies uncared for, and ignored.

Fail to develop the talents of any one person, we fail Britain. Talent is twenty-first-century wealth. Every person liberated to fulfil their potential adds to our wealth. Every person denied opportunity takes our wealth away.

In the eighteenth century, land was our resource. In the nineteenth and twentieth [centuries] it was plant and capital. Today it is people.

The cause we have fought for these hundred years is no

longer simply our cause of social justice. It is the nation's only hope of salvation.

For how do you develop the talent of all, unless in a society that treats us all equally, where the closed doors of snobbery and prejudice, ignorance and poverty, fear and injustice no longer bar our way to fulfilment.

Not equal incomes. Not uniform lifestyles or taste or culture. But true equality—equal worth, an equal chance of fulfilment, equal access to knowledge and opportunity.

Equal rights. Equal responsibilities.

The class war is over. But the struggle for true equality has only just begun.

To the child who goes to school hungry for food, but thirsting for knowledge, I know the talent you were born with, and the frustration you feel that it's trapped inside. We will set your potential free.

To the women free to work, but because they are also mothers, carers, helpers barely know how to get through the day, we will give you the support to set your potential free.

To the 45-year-old who came to my surgery a few months ago, scared he'll never work again, I say: You didn't become useless at 45. You deserve the chance to start afresh and we will set your potential free.

And to those who have wealth, but who say that none of it means anything if my children can't play in the park, and my mother daren't go out at night. We share your belief in a strong community. We will set your potential free.

And it is us, the new radicals, the Labour Party modernized, that must undertake this historic mission. To liberate Britain from the old class divisions, old structures, old prejudices, old ways of working and of doing things, that will not do in this world of change. To be the progressive force that defeats the forces of conservatism.

For the twenty-first century will not be about the battle between capitalism and socialism but between the forces of progress and the forces of conservatism.

They are what hold our nation back. Not just in the Conservative Party but within us, within our nation. The forces that do not understand that creating a new Britain of true equality is no more a betrayal of Britain's history than New Labour is of Labour's values.

The old prejudices, where foreign means bad. Where multiculturalism is not something to celebrate, but a left-wing conspiracy to destroy their way of life. Where women shouldn't work and those who do are responsible for the breakdown of the family.

The old elites, establishments that have run our professions and our country too long. Who have kept women and black and Asian talent out of our top jobs and senior parts of government and the services. Who keep our bright inner city kids from our best universities. And who still think the House of Lords should be run by hereditary peers in the interests of the Tory Party.

The old order, those forces of conservatism, for all their language about promoting the individual, and freedom and liberty, they held people back. They kept people down. They stunted people's potential. Year after year. Decade after decade.

Think back on some of the great achievements of this century.

To us today, it almost defies belief that people had to die to win the fight for the vote for women. But they did. That battle was a massive, heroic struggle. But why did it need such a fight? Because Tory MPs stood up in the House of Commons and said, 'Voting is a man's business'. And that is why we can be so proud that it is this Labour Party that has more women MPs and more women ministers than any government before us until our record is bettered by a future Labour Government.

Look at this Party's greatest achievement. The forces of conservatism, and the force of the Conservative Party, pulled every trick in the book—voting fifty-one times, yes fifty-one times, against the creation of the NHS[2]. One leading Tory, Mr Henry Willink, said at the time that the NHS 'will destroy so much in this country that we value', when we knew human potential can never be realized when whether you are well or ill depends on wealth not need.

The forces of conservatism allied to racism are why one of the heroes of the twentieth century, Martin Luther King, is dead. It's why another, Nelson Mandela, spent the best years of his life in a cell the size of a bed.

And though the fact that Mandela is alive, free and became President, is a sign of the progress we have made. The fact that Stephen Lawrence[3] is dead, for no other reason than he was born black, is a sign of how far we still have to go.

And they still keep opposing progress and justice.

What did they say about the minimum wage? The same as they said right through this century.

They tried the employment argument—it would cost jobs.

They tried the business argument—it would make them bankrupt.

---

[2]The National Health System (NHS) provides medical care throughout the United Kingdom. Most services are free of charge.
[3]On 22 April 1993, 18-year-old Stephen Lawrence was murdered in a racially motivated attack in London.

They then used the economic argument—it would cause inflation.

They then resorted to the selfish argument—businesses wouldn't want to pay it.

Well, businesses are paying it. Inflation is low. Unemployment is falling. There are one million job vacancies in the country.

And two million people have had a pay rise because we believe they are worth more than poverty pay.

These forces of conservatism chain us not only to an outdated view of our people's potential but of our nation's potential. What threatens the nation state today is not change, but the refusal to change in a world opening up, becoming ever more interdependent.

The old air of superiority based on past glory must give way to the ambition to succeed, based on the merit of what Britain stands for today.

For the last half century, we have been torn between Europe and the United States, searching for our identity in the post-Empire world. I pose this simple question: Is our destiny with Europe or not?

If the answer is no, then we should leave. But we would leave an economic union in which 50 per cent of our trade is done, on which millions of British jobs depend. Our economic future would be uncertain.

But what is certain is that we would not be a power. Britain would no longer play a determining part in the future of the continent to which we belong. That would be the real end of one thousand years of history.

We can choose this destiny. But we should do it with our eyes open and our senses alert, not blindfold and dulled by the incessant propaganda of Europhobes.

The single currency is, of course, a decision that must be dependent on the economic conditions; and on the consent of the British people in a referendum.

If we believe our destiny is with Europe, then let us leave behind the muddling through, the hesitation, the half-heartedness, which has characterized British relations with Europe for forty years, and play our part with confidence and pride giving us the chance to defeat the forces of conservatism, economic and political, that hold Europe back too.

There is no choice between Europe and America.

Britain is stronger with the US today because we are strong in Europe. Britain has the potential to be the bridge between Europe and America and for the twenty-first century the narrow-minded isolationism of right-wing Tories should not block our path to fulfilling it.

The nation state is changing.

The Tory policy on devolution left them without a single seat anywhere in Scotland and Wales. Delivering our promise of a Scottish Parliament and Welsh Assembly has strengthened the UK not weakened it, and now having defeated the force of conservatism in granting devolution, let us continue to defeat the separatism which is just the forces of conservatism by another name.

And don't let the forces of conservatism stop devolution in Northern Ireland too. Those who are addicted to violence, those who confuse any progress with selling out, they shouldn't determine Northern Ireland's future. Walk through Belfast, no armed soldiers. Drive through it, no roadblocks.

In the last year, the first time in thirty years, not a single member of the security forces killed. [In] 1996, 8,000 plastic bullets fired; this year ninety-nine.

Yes, there is violence and any violence is unacceptable. But don't throw away all that has been achieved.

And I ask the Conservative Party: We supported you when you were in government; don't make our task harder now because that would be the real betrayal of the children of Northern Ireland.

It would be comforting to think the forces of conservatism were only Tories. But wrong. There were forces of conservatism who said changing Clause 4 would destroy the Labour Party, when in truth it was critical to our renewal.

Who said a referendum on devolution was a ploy to stop it happening, when I knew it was the only way to make it happen. Who said that making young people take a job that was offered to them was a denial of social justice, when our attack on youth unemployment is the route to social justice.

The Third Way is not a new way between progressive and conservative politics. It is progressive politics distinguishing itself from conservatism of left or right.

New Labour must be the new radicals who take on both of them, not just on election day but every day.

People say in our first two years we ran a Tory economic policy. Nonsense. If we had run a Tory economic policy, Britain would be in recession by now which is no doubt why they predicted it.

We gave the Bank of England independence. We cut the borrowing. We cut unemployment. We are at long last reforming welfare, making work pay more than benefit for hard-working families through the Working Families Tax Credit.

They would scrap each and every one of these reforms.

Slowly, the Tory general election strategy is emerging.

To two million people given a pay rise through the minimum wage. Tory pledge one: We'll cut it.

To 1.5 million families helped by the working families tax credit. Tory pledge two: We'll scrap it.

To 2,50,000 young people getting through the New Deal, Tory pledge three: You'll go back on the dole.

I say: Roll on the next general election.

Our reforms are why we are spending £4 billion less on interest payments this year. Saving £2 billion by cutting unemployment. Why, thanks to economic growth, billions of pounds of wealth has been created, not lost in Tory boom and bust.

And as a result, the next three years show the biggest ever investment in schools and hospitals. Not just one year. But the year after and the year after that.

And, if we carry on running this New Labour economic policy, I can tell you today we will continue to get more money into schools and hospitals in a way we can sustain year on year on year. We are rewriting some of the traditional rules of politics.

Now after a century of antagonism, economic efficiency and social justice are finally working in partnership together. We are demonstrating that it is possible to cut poverty and run the economy well. At last our historic reputation for compassion is being matched with a hard-won reputation for economic competence. From now on, people will vote Labour with their head as well as their heart.

The political landscape of Britain has changed forever. That's why Prudence's chastity belt stays on, even for the Liberal Democrats.

And then we open up the UK economy. Open it up to

electronic commerce, so we cut the cost of buying and selling. Open it up to competition so we can stop the consumer being ripped off.

And private capital alongside public investment. In transport, to read some of the papers, you would think John Prescott[4] had created Britain's transport problems. Thanks to him, and the new Strategic Rail Authority, the next ten years will see the largest investment in the railways for hundred years. Let's be honest. When it comes to transport we are all the forces of conservatism. But the real anti-car policy is staying as we are.

Let us take on the forces of conservatism in education too, the greatest liberator of human potential there is: No more nursery vouchers; no return to 11+; no freeze on student numbers in our universities; no more Assisted Places Scheme; not the right, but not the old left either—no tolerance of failing LEAs[5]; no truce on failing schools; no pupils condemned to failure.

We owe it to every child to unleash their potential. They are of equal worth. They deserve an equal chance. A failed education is a life sentence on a child.

If we are to succeed in the knowledge economy, we need—as parents, as teachers, as a country—to get a whole new attitude to learning.

What other country in the world sees being 'too clever by half' as a fault? In today's world, there is no such thing as too clever. The more you know, the further you'll go.

---

[4]Labour Party leader John Prescott served as the Deputy Prime Minister of the United Kingdom from 1997–2007.
[5]Local Education Authorities

The forces of conservatism, the elite, have held us back for too long.

Why is it only now that we are getting nursery places for all 3- and 4-year-olds? Why has it taken this government to realize that 5-, 6- and 7-year-olds need that extra attention that smaller classes give them?

Why, when we have known all our lives the importance of the 3'R's[6], is it only now that we have put in place the literacy and numeracy strategies to get those basics taught properly? And look at the results for 11-year-olds: maths up 10 per cent, reading up 5 per cent, a tribute to our children, to their teachers and to David Blunkett[7].

Why has it taken this government to set about ending the culture of failure in our inner city comprehensives? Doubling the number of specialist schools; creating 1,000 beacon schools; every run-down school getting help with buildings, equipment, facilities from the £5 billion modernization programme: LEAs with a track record of failure taken over and run by people with a track record of success.

Why is it only now, we have lifted the cap on student numbers and 1,00,000 more will go to university in the next two years, 7,00,000 more to further education. So today I set a target of 50 per cent of young adults going into higher education in the next century.

Why if education is the key to success do we allow so many children to leave school at 16 when we should be doing all we can to get them to stay on. Today we are announcing a

---

[6]The three basic subjects: Reading, Writing and Arithmetic.
[7]Labour Party politician David Blunkett was the Education Secretary (1997–2001) and introduced several reforms.

smart card to offer all 16–18-year-olds who stay in education cut price deals at shops, in theatres and cinemas and on trains and buses.

Only now can this happen because there is a Labour Government that cares about educating the many and a Labour Party with the courage to reform the system to do it.

And critical to reform are our teachers. I appeal to them.

You do a great job in our schools. We know how important it is for you to work as a team. But if we are to get the real-step change in your pay you and we both want, we have to link it to performance. We have to raise standards and we have to remove those who really cannot do the job.

And if a Head Teacher transforms a school and so transforms the life chances of our children, aren't they worth as much as a good doctor, banker or lawyer?

In ten years we will have transformed our schools. And our NHS too. And I know the impatience here is at its highest. After all, we created the NHS. It has to be us that rebuilds it.

And yes, it needs money. And yes, the first two years were tough. But the money is now starting. And money is not all it needs.

A predecessor of mine famously said she wanted to be able to go into the hospital of her choice 'on the day I want, at the time I want, with the doctor I want'.

That was Margaret Thatcher's[8] argument for going private.

I want to go to the hospital of my choice, on the day I want, at the time I want. And I want it on the NHS.

---

[8]Margaret Thatcher served as Prime Minister of the United Kingdom from 1979–90.

I say in all frankness to the BMA[9]. You want our reforms to slow down. I want them to speed up.

Already: 4,000 more student nurses and midwives; 4,000 more nurses returning to nursing; twenty-seven new hospitals being built; twenty million people now covered by NHS Direct; and the dreaded Tory internal market finally banished for good.

And over the next three years: There will be 7,000 more doctors, 15,000 more nurses, thirty-seven hospitals built; the whole country covered by NHS Direct; every casualty department that needs it refurbished; and waiting times and waiting lists lower at the end of our time in government than at the beginning.

And will that be enough?

No. But in time, if we are returned to power: We will have booked appointments for everyone; walk-in NHS centres in all our major towns and cities; primary care surgeries that offer you all services on one site; and everyone with the chance to go back on the NHS to see their dentist.

And just to show you it's not impossible. Today I can tell you: We will start next year with booked appointments for cancer and cataract patients.

And working with the British Dental Association, everyone within the next two years will be able once again to see an NHS dentist just by phoning NHS Direct.

So much more to do. But it will be done.

We aren't just workers. We are citizens proud to say there is such a thing as society and proud to be part of it.

Yet, today, we feel our social fabric torn. Respect for law and order broken.

---

[9]British Medical Association

My grandfather's generation was strong on values. Respect for people. Good manners. Horror of crime. But it was a generation also of deference and of prejudices—racial, sexual, social.

The modern world is different. There is less prejudice, less deference, but also less respect.

It is time to move beyond the social indifference of right and left, libertarian nonsense masquerading as freedom. This generation wants a society free from prejudice, but not from rules, from order.

A common duty to provide opportunity for all. An individual duty to be responsible towards all.

There will be a new crime bill in the Queen's Speech.

With the new DNA technology we have the chance to match any DNA at any scene of crime with those on police records. Already thousands of criminals are being caught that way. But less than a fifth are on record. I can announce we will provide the extra resources for a database where every known offender will have their DNA recorded, and evidence from any scene of crime will be matched with it.

And I saw that we said on drugs and new powers was attacked by civil liberties groups.

I believe in civil liberties too: The liberty of parents to drop their kids off at school, without worrying they're dropping them straight into the arms of drug dealers; the liberty of pensioners to live without fear of getting their door kicked in by someone thieving to pay for their habit; the liberty of young people to live a full life, not die young, the victim of the most chilling, evil industry the world has to confront.

Civil liberty to me means just that—the liberty to live in a civil society founded on rights and responsibilities, and in dealing with the drugs menace, that is the society we can help to build.

So when I speak of the need for a new moral purpose and some on the right and left rise up and say this is nothing to do with politics, leave it all to the bishops, I tell you these people know exactly what I'm talking about.

That's what I mean by fulfilling our potential as citizens as well as workers.

We don't live by material goods alone.

That's why today we set out more plans to boost arts, culture, competitive sports in schools. It's why John Prescott puts his heart and soul in the battle to protect our environment, so we leave to our children a safer, healthier planet than the one into which they were born.

Yes we are three times richer than our grandparents. But are we three times happier?

Ours is a moral cause, best expressed through how we see our families and our children.

To our children, we are irreplaceable. If anything happened to me, you'd soon find a new leader. But my kids wouldn't find a new Dad.

There is no more powerful symbol of our politics than the experience of being on a maternity ward. Seeing two babies side by side. Delivered by the same doctors and midwives. Yet two totally different lives ahead of them.

One returns with his mother to a bed and breakfast that is cold, damp, cramped. A mother who has no job, no family to support her, sadder still—no one to share the joy and triumph of the new baby...a father nowhere to be seen. That mother loves her child like any other mother. But her life and her baby's life is a long, hard struggle. For this child, individual potential hangs by a thread.

The second child returns to a prosperous home, grandparents desperate to share the caring and a father with a decent income and an even larger sense of pride. They're already thinking about schools, friends she can make, new toys they can buy. Expectations are sky-high, opportunities truly limitless.

A child is a vulnerable witness on life. A child sees her father hit her mother. A child runs away from home. A child takes drugs. A child gives birth at 12.

If we are in politics for one thing—it is to make sure that all children are given the best chance in life. That the moment they are born, their potential and individuality can sparkle. That every child can grow up with high hopes, certainty, love, security and the attention of their parents.

Strong families cherished by a strong community. That is our national moral purpose. So when I pledge to end child poverty in twenty years, I do so not just as a politician, but as a father.

Can I tell you something? And there are only four other people alive who know this—it's actually a bit odd being Prime Minister. Everyone has views about you, and no hesitation giving them to you. You read things about yourself on a daily basis that are a complete mystery. And you find that a lot of strange new people want to be your friend, and lots of other strange people want to be your enemy.

We're only flesh and blood in the end. Sometimes [we] can't sleep; worry about the job; worry about the kids; worry about growing old; worry about interest rates going up; worry about Newcastle going down.

Then you've got these big worries—when's the health money really going to make a difference? Why are there still people sleeping in doorways? Can't we turn round failing schools more quickly? How many of our pensioners will go cold this winter?

It's a big job. A lonely job. The red boxes really do come at you day and night, papers to read, decisions to make. Sometimes life and death decisions. Often decisions, after all the advice and the consultation, that only the Prime Minister can make.

So it's a pressure. But it's a privilege too. There is no greater privilege than serving your country. And there is no greater purpose than realizing your potential.

I was lucky. A good education, a loving home, a great family, strong beliefs, a great Party in which to give them expression.

Everyone has talent. Everyone has something to offer. And this country needs everyone to make a contribution.

You'll see me on the TV, getting on and off planes, meeting presidents and prime ministers, kings and queens.

It's all part of the job. But the part that matters most to me is getting my sleeves rolled up and pushing through the changes to our country that will give to others by right, what I achieved by good fortune.

Let me read to you the words of someone else who thought ours was a moral purpose, and said this about the people in our Party.

> The men and women who are in it are not working for themselves; they know perfectly well that all they can do is but to create the beginning of a condition of things which will one day bring peace and happiness and freedom and a fuller life for those who are to come after us.

Our very first leader, Keir Hardie.

But hundred years ago, the circumstances of our birth and our political childhood was such we never realized our potential. Born in separation from other progressive forces in British politics, out of the visceral need to represent the interests of an exploited workforce, our base, our appeal, our ideology was too narrow. People were made to feel we wanted to hold them back, limit their aspirations, when in truth the very opposite was our goal.

We were chained by our ideology. We thought we had eternal doctrines, when they are in truth eternal values.

Solidarity, social justice, the belief not that society comes before individual fulfilment but that it is only in a strong society of others that the individual will be fulfilled. That it is these bonds of connection that make us not citizens of one nation but members of one human race.

And wouldn't Keir Hardie have been proud when, under Britain's leadership, this week we cancelled the debt of those African nations deep in poverty so that their people too can realize their potential, have the hopes and dreams for their children we want for ours?

And wouldn't Clem Attlee[10] and Ernie Bevin[11] have applauded when in Kosovo, faced with racial genocide in Europe for the first time since they fought fascism in the Second World War, it was Britain and this government that helped defeat it and set one million people free back to their homeland?

And wouldn't it bring a smile to the faces of all Labour leaders to see how confident our Party is today?

---

[10]Clement Attlee served as Prime Minister of the United Kingdom from 1945–51.
[11]Ernest Bevin was a British unionist and statesman.

Today we stand here, more confident than at any time during our hundred years, more confident because we are winning the battle of ideas; we are putting our values into practice; we are the only political force capable of liberating the potential of our people.

Knowing what we have to do and knowing how to do it.

Arrayed against us: the forces of conservatism, the cynics, the elites, the establishment. Those who will live with decline. Those who yearn for yesteryear. Those who just can't be bothered. Those who prefer to criticize rather than do.

On our side, the forces of modernity and justice. Those who believe in a Britain for all the people. Those who fight social injustice, because they know it harms our nation.

Those who believe in a society of equality, of opportunity and responsibility. Those who have the courage to change. Those who have confidence in the future.

The battleground, the new millennium. Our values are our guide. Our job is to serve. Our workplace, the future.

Let us step up the pace. Be confident. Be radical.

To every nation a purpose.

To every Party a cause.

And now, at last, Party and nation joined in the same cause for the same purpose: To set our people free.

◆

The kaleidoscope has been shaken.*

This speech is regarded as one of the most powerful speeches of Blair's career. The Prime Minister unconventionally used this speech to the Labour Conference on 2 October 2011 to bring home the point that hostility to Osama bin Laden's terrorist network and the Taliban will be uncompromising. Tony Blair as Prime Minister of UK and one of the major allies of the US in its war against terror promised rhetorically in this address to make world a better and safer place.

This is an extraordinary moment for progressive politics.

Our values are the right ones for this age—the power of community, solidarity, the collective ability to further the individual's interests.

People ask me if I think ideology is dead. My answer is: In the sense of rigid forms of economic and social theory, yes.

The twentieth century killed those ideologies and their passing causes little regret. But, in the sense of a governing idea in politics, based on values, no.

The governing idea of modern social democracy is community; founded on the principles of social justice. That people should rise according to merit, not birth, that the test of any decent society is not the contentment of the wealthy and strong, but the commitment to the poor and weak.

But values aren't enough. The mantle of leadership comes at a price—the courage to learn and change, to show how values that stand for all ages, can be applied in a way relevant to each age.

---

*Source: UK Government website

Our politics only succeed when the realism is as clear as the idealism.

This Party's strength today comes from the journey of change and learning we have made. We learnt that however much we strive for peace, we need strong defence capability where a peaceful approach fails. We learnt that equality is about equal worth, not equal outcomes.

Today our idea of society is shaped around mutual responsibility; a deal, an agreement between citizens not a one-way gift, from the well-off to the dependent.

Our economic and social policy today owes as much to the liberal social democratic tradition of Lloyd George, Keynes and Beveridge[1] as to the socialist principles of the 1945 Government.

Just over a decade ago, people asked if Labour could ever win again. Today they ask the same question of the Opposition. Painful though that journey of change has been, it has been worth it, every stage of the way.

On this journey, the values have never changed. The aims haven't. Our aims would be instantly recognizable to every Labour leader from Keir Hardie onwards. But the means do change.

The journey hasn't ended; it never ends. The next stage for New Labour is not backwards; it is renewing ourselves again.

Just after the election, an old colleague of mine said, 'Come on Tony, now we've won again, can't we drop all this New Labour and do what we believe in?'

I said, 'It's worse than you think. I really do believe in it.'

We didn't revolutionize British economic policy—Bank

---

[1] John Maynard Keynes and William Beveridge were noted British economists.

of England independence, tough spending rules—for some managerial reason or as a clever wheeze to steal Tory clothes.

We did it because the victims of economic incompetence—15 per cent interest rates, three million unemployed—are hard-working families.

They are the ones—and even more so, now, with tough times ahead—that the economy should be run for, not speculators or currency dealers or senior executives whose pay packets don't seem to bear any resemblance to the performance of their companies.

Economic competence is the precondition of social justice.

We have legislated for fairness at work, like the minimum wage which people struggled a century for. But we won't give up the essential flexibility of our economy or our commitment to enterprise. Why? Because in a world leaving behind mass production, where technology revolutionizes not just companies but whole industries, almost overnight, enterprise creates the jobs people depend on.

We have boosted pensions, child benefit, family incomes. We will do more. But our number one priority for spending is and will remain education. Why? Because in the new markets countries like Britain can only create wealth by brain power not low wages and sweatshop labour.

We have cut youth unemployment by 75 per cent, by more than any government before us. But we refuse to pay benefit to those who refuse to work. Why? Because the welfare that works is welfare that helps people to help themselves.

The graffiti, the vandalism, the burnt-out cars, the street corner drug dealers, the teenage mugger just graduating from the minor school of crime—we're not old fashioned or right-wing to take action against this social menace.

We're standing up for the people we represent, who play by the rules and have a right to expect others to do the same.

And especially at this time let us say: We celebrate the diversity in our country, get strength from the cultures and races that go to make up Britain today and racist abuse and racist attacks have no place in the Britain we believe in.

All these policies are linked by a common thread of principle.

Now with this second term, our duty is not to sit back and bask in it. It is across the board, in competition policy, enterprise, pensions, criminal justice, the civil service and of course public services, to go still further in the journey of change. All for the same reason—to allow us to deliver social justice in the modern world.

Public services are the power of community in action. They are social justice made real. The child with a good education flourishes. The child given a poor education lives with it for the rest of their life.

How much talent and ability and potential do we waste? How many children never know not just the earning power of a good education but the joy of art and culture and the stretching of imagination and horizons which true education brings? Poor education is a personal tragedy and national scandal.

Yet even now, with all the progress of recent years, a quarter of 11–year–olds fail their basic tests and almost a half of 16-year-olds don't get five decent GCSEs[2].

The NHS meant that for succeeding generations, anxiety was lifted from their shoulders. For millions who get superb

---

[2]The General Certificate of Secondary Education (GCSE) is a qualification taken by 15- and 16-year-olds in the UK, except Scotland.

treatment still, the NHS remains the ultimate symbol of social justice. But for every patient waiting in pain, that can't get treatment for cancer or a heart condition or in desperation ends up paying for their operation, that patient's suffering is the ultimate social injustice.

And the demands on the system are ever greater. Children need to be better and better educated.

People live longer. There is a vast array of new treatment available.

And expectations are higher. This is a consumer age. People don't take what they're given. They demand more.

We're not alone in this. All round the world governments are struggling with the same problems.

So what is the solution? Yes, public services need more money. We are putting in the largest ever increases in NHS, education and transport spending in the next few years and on the police too. We will keep to those spending plans.

And I say in all honesty to the country: If we want that to continue and the choice is between investment and tax cuts, then investment must come first. There is a simple truth we all know.

For decades there has been chronic underinvestment in British public services. Our historic mission is to put that right and the historic shift represented by the election of June 7 was that investment to provide quality public services for all comprehensively defeated short-term tax cuts for the few.

We need better pay and conditions for the staff, better incentives for recruitment and for retention. We're getting them and recruitment is rising.

This year, for the first time in nearly a decade, public sector pay will rise faster than private sector pay.

And we are the only major government in Europe this year to be increasing public spending on health and education as a percentage of our national income.

This Party believes in public services, believes in the ethos of public service and believes in the dedication the vast majority of public servants show and the proof of it is that we're spending more, hiring more and paying more than ever before.

Public servants don't do it for money or glory. They do it because they find fulfilment in a child well-taught or a patient well-cared-for or a community made safer and we salute them for it.

All that is true. But this is also true.

That often they work in systems and structures that are hopelessly old-fashioned or even worse, work against the very goals they aim for. There are schools, with exactly the same social intake—one does well, the other badly. There are hospitals with exactly the same patient mix—one performs well, the other badly.

Without reform, more money and pay won't succeed.

First, we need a national framework of accountability, inspection and minimum standards of delivery. Second, within that framework, we need to free up local leaders to be able to innovate, develop and be creative. Third, there should be far greater flexibility in the terms and conditions of employment of public servants. Fourth, there has to be choice for the user of public services and the ability, where provision of the service fails, to have an alternative provider.

If schools want to develop or specialize in a particular area or hire classroom assistants or computer professionals as well as teachers, let them. If in a Primary Care Trust, doctors can provide minor surgery or physiotherapists see patients otherwise referred to a consultant, let them.

There are too many old demarcations, especially between nurses, doctors and consultants, too little use of the potential of new technology, too much bureaucracy, too many outdated practices, too great an adherence to the way we've always done it rather than the way public servants would like to do it if they got the time to think and the freedom to act.

It's not reform that is the enemy of public services. It's the status quo.

Part of that reform programme is partnership with the private or voluntary sector.

Let's get one thing clear. Nobody is talking about privatizing the NHS or schools.

Nobody believes the private sector is a panacea.

There are great examples of public service and poor examples. There are excellent private sector companies and poor ones. There are areas where the private sector has worked well and areas where, as with parts of the railways, it's been a disaster.

Where the private sector is used, it should not make a profit simply by cutting the wages and conditions of its staff.

But where the private sector can help lever in vital capital investment, where it helps raise standards, where it improves the public service as a public service, then to set up some dogmatic barrier to using it, is to let down the very people who most need our public services to improve.

This programme of reform is huge—in the NHS, education, including student finance; we have to find a better way to combine state funding and student contributions; criminal justice; and transport.

I regard it as being as important for the country as

Clause IV's reform was for the Party, and obviously far more important for the lives of the people we serve.

And it is a vital test for the modern Labour Party.

If people lose faith in public services, be under no illusion as to what will happen.

There is a different approach waiting in the wings. Cut public spending drastically; let those that can afford to buy their own services; and those that can't, will depend on a demoralized, sink public service. That would be a denial of social justice on a massive scale.

It would be contrary to the very basis of community.

So this is a battle of values. Let's have that battle but not amongst ourselves. The real fight is between those who believe in strong public services and those who don't.

That's the fight worth having.

In all of this, at home and abroad, the same beliefs throughout—that we are a community of people, whose self-interest and mutual interest at crucial points merge, and that it is through a sense of justice that community is born and nurtured.

And what does this concept of justice consist of?

Fairness, people all of equal worth, of course. But also reason and tolerance; justice has no favourites, not amongst nations, peoples or faiths.

When we act to bring to account those that committed the atrocity of September 11, we do so not out of bloodlust. We do so because it is just. We do not act against Islam. The true followers of Islam are our brothers and sisters in this struggle.

Bin Laden is no more obedient to the proper teaching of the Koran than those Crusaders of the twelfth century who pillaged and murdered, represented the teaching of the Gospel.

It is time the West confronted its ignorance of Islam. Jews,

Muslims and Christians are all children of Abraham.

This is the moment to bring the faiths closer together in understanding of our common values and heritage, a source of unity and strength.

It is time also for parts of Islam to confront prejudice against America and not only Islam but parts of Western societies too.

America has its faults as a society, as we have ours.

But I think of the Union of America born out of the defeat of slavery. I think of its Constitution, with its inalienable rights granted to every citizen still a model for the world.

I think of a black man, born in poverty, who became Chief of their Armed Forces and is now Secretary of State Colin Powell and I wonder frankly whether such a thing could have happened here.

I think of the Statue of Liberty and how many refugees, migrants and the impoverished passed its light and felt that if not for them, for their children a new world could indeed be theirs.

I think of a country where people who do well, don't have questions asked about their accent, their class, their beginnings but have admiration for what they have done and the success they've achieved.

I think of those New Yorkers I met, still in shock, but resolute; the firefighters and police, mourning their comrades but still head held high.

I think of all this and I reflect: Yes, America has its faults, but it is a free country, a democracy, it is our ally and some of the reaction to September 11 betrays a hatred of America that shames those that feel it.

So I believe this is a fight for freedom. And I want to

make it a fight for justice too.

Justice not only to punish the guilty; but justice to bring those same values of democracy and freedom to people round the world.

And I mean freedom, not only in the narrow sense of personal liberty but in the broader sense of each individual having the economic and social freedom to develop their potential to the full.

That is what community means, founded on the equal worth of all. The starving, the wretched, the dispossessed, the ignorant, those living in want and squalor from the deserts of Northern Africa to the slums of Gaza, to the mountain ranges of Afghanistan—they too are our cause.

This is a moment to seize. The kaleidoscope has been shaken. The pieces are in flux. Soon they will settle again. Before they do, let us reorder this world around us.

Today, humankind has the science and technology to destroy itself or to provide prosperity to all. Yet science can't make that choice for us. Only the moral power of a world acting as a community can.

By the strength of our common endeavour, we achieve more together than we can alone.

For those people who lost their lives on September 11 and those that mourn them, now is the time for the strength to build that community.

Let that be their memorial.

◆

What is perfectly clear is that Saddam is playing the same old games in the same old way.*

This speech was delivered during opening debate on the Iraq crisis in the House of Commons on 18 March 2003.

I beg to move the motion standing on the order paper in my name and those of my right honourable friends.

At the outset I say: It is right that this house debate this issue and pass judgement. That is the democracy, that is our right, but that others struggle for in vain.

And again I say: I do not disrespect the views of those in opposition to mine.

This is a tough choice. But it is also a stark one—to stand British troops down and turn back; or to hold firm to the course we have set.

I believe we must hold firm.

The question most often posed is not why does it matter? But why does it matter so much? Here we are, the government with its most serious test, its majority at risk, the first cabinet resignation over an issue of policy. The main parties divided.

People who agree on everything else, disagree on this and likewise, those who never agree on anything, finding common cause. The country and parliament reflect each other, a debate that, as time has gone on has become less bitter but not less grave.

So, why does it matter so much? Because the outcome of this issue will now determine more than the fate of the Iraqi

---

*Source: UK Government website

regime and more than the future of the Iraqi people, for so long brutalized by Saddam[1]. It will determine the way Britain and the world confront the central security threat of the twenty-first century; the development of the UN; the relationship between Europe and the US; the relations within the EU and the way the US engages with the rest of the world. It will determine the pattern of international politics for the next generation.

But first, Iraq and its WMD[2].

In April 1991, after the Gulf War, Iraq was given fifteen days to provide a full and final declaration of all its WMD.

Saddam had used the weapons against Iran, against his own people, causing thousands of deaths. He had had plans to use them against allied forces. It became clear after the Gulf War that the WMD ambitions of Iraq were far more extensive than hitherto thought. This issue was identified by the UN as one for urgent remedy. Unscom[3], the weapons inspection team, was set up. They were expected to complete their task following the declaration at the end of April 1991.

The declaration when it came was false—a blanket denial of the programme, other than in a very tentative form. So the twelve-year game began.

The inspectors probed. Finally in March 1992, Iraq admitted it had previously undeclared WMD but said it had destroyed them. It gave another full and final declaration. Again the inspectors probed but found little.

In October 1994, Iraq stopped cooperating with Unscom altogether. Military action was threatened. Inspections

---

[1]Saddam Hussein was President of Iraq from 1979–2003.
[2]Weapon (or weapons) of Mass Destruction
[3]United Nations Special Commission

resumed. In March 1995, in an effort to rid Iraq of the inspectors, a further full and final declaration of WMD was made. By July 1995, Iraq was forced to admit that too was false. In August they provided yet another full and final declaration.

Then, a week later, Saddam's son-in-law, Hussein Kamel, defected to Jordan. He disclosed a far more extensive BW—biological weapons—programme and, for the first time, said Iraq had weaponized the programme; something Saddam had always strenuously denied. All this had been happening whilst the inspectors were in Iraq. Kamel also revealed Iraq's crash programme to produce a nuclear weapon in 1990.

Iraq was forced then to release documents which showed just how extensive those programmes were. In November 1995, Jordan intercepted prohibited components for missiles that could be used for WMD.

In June 1996, a further full and final declaration was made. That too turned out to be false. In June 1997, inspectors were barred from specific sites.

In September 1997, another full and final declaration was made. Also false. Meanwhile the inspectors discovered VX nerve agent production equipment, something always denied by the Iraqis.

In October 1997, the US and the UK threatened military action if Iraq refused to comply with the inspectors. But obstruction continued.

Finally, under threat of action, in February 1998, Kofi Annan[4] went to Baghdad and negotiated a memorandum with Saddam to allow inspections to continue. They did. For a few months.

---

[4]Kofi Annan was the UN Secretary General from 1997–2006.

In August, cooperation was suspended.

In December the inspectors left. Their final report is a withering indictment of Saddam's lies, deception and obstruction, with large quantities of WMD remained unaccounted for.

The US and the UK then, in December 1998, undertook Desert Fox, a targeted bombing campaign to degrade as much of the Iraqi WMD facilities as we could.

In 1999, a new inspections team, Unmovic[5], was set up. But Saddam refused to allow them to enter Iraq.

So there they stayed, in limbo, until after resolution 1441 when last November they were allowed to return.

What is the claim of Saddam today? Why exactly the same claim as before: That he has no WMD.

Indeed we are asked to believe that after seven years of obstruction and non-compliance finally resulting in the inspectors leaving in 1998, seven years in which he hid his programme, built it up even whilst inspection teams were in Iraq, that after they left he then voluntarily decided to do what he had consistently refused to do under coercion.

When the inspectors left in 1998, they left unaccounted for 10,000 litres of anthrax; a far-reaching VX nerve agent programme; up to 6,500 chemical munitions; at least 80 tonnes of mustard gas, possibly more than ten times that amount; unquantifiable amounts of sarin, botulinum toxin and a host of other biological poisons; an entire Scud missile programme.

We are now seriously asked to accept that in the last few years, contrary to all history, contrary to all intelligence, he decided unilaterally to destroy the weapons. Such a claim is palpably absurd.

---

[5]United Nations Monitoring, Verification and Inspection Commission

1441 is a very clear resolution. It lays down a final opportunity for Saddam to disarm. It rehearses the fact that he has been, for years, in material breach of seventeen separate UN resolutions. It says that this time compliance must be full, unconditional and immediate. The first step is a full and final declaration of all WMD to be given on 8 December.

I won't to go through all the events since then—the house is familiar with them—but this much is accepted by all members of the UNSC[6]: The 8 December declaration is false. That in itself is a material breach. Iraq has made some concessions to cooperation but no one disputes it is not fully cooperating. Iraq continues to deny it has any WMD, though no serious intelligence service anywhere in the world believes them.

On 7 March, the inspectors published a remarkable document. It is 173 pages long, detailing all the unanswered questions about Iraq's WMD. It lists twenty-nine different areas where they have been unable to obtain information. For example, on VX it says: 'Documentation available to UNMOVIC suggests that Iraq at least had had far reaching plans to weaponize VX...

'mustard constituted an important part (about 70 per cent) of Iraq's CW arsenal...550 mustard filled shells and up to 450 mustard filled aerial bombs unaccounted for...additional uncertainty with respect of 6,526 aerial bombs, corresponding to approximately 1,000 tonnes of agent, predominantly mustard.

'Based on unaccounted for growth media, Iraq's potential production of anthrax could have been in the range of about 15,000 to 25,000 litres... Based on all the available evidence,

---

[6]United Nations Security Council

the strong presumption is that about 10,000 litres of anthrax was not destroyed and may still exist.'

On this basis, had we meant what we said in resolution 1441, the Security Council should have convened and condemned Iraq as in material breach.

What is perfectly clear is that Saddam is playing the same old games in the same old way. Yes there are concessions, but no fundamental change of heart or mind.

But the inspectors indicated there was at least some cooperation; and the world rightly hesitated over war. We therefore approached a second resolution in this way.

We laid down an ultimatum calling upon Saddam to come into line with resolution 1441 or be in material breach. Not an unreasonable proposition, given the history.

But still countries hesitated: How do we know how to judge full cooperation?

We then worked on a further compromise. We consulted the inspectors and drew up five tests based on the document they published on 7 March. Tests like interviews with thirty scientists outside of Iraq; production of the anthrax or documentation showing its destruction.

The inspectors added another test: That Saddam should publicly call on Iraqis to cooperate with them. So we constructed this framework: That Saddam should be given a specified time to fulfil all six tests to show full cooperation; that if he did so the inspectors could then set out a forward work programme and that if he failed to do so, action would follow.

So clear benchmarks; plus a clear ultimatum. I defy anyone to describe that as an unreasonable position.

Last Monday, we were getting somewhere with it. We very nearly had majority agreement and I thank the Chilean

President particularly for the constructive way he approached the issue.

There were debates about the length of the ultimatum. But the basic construct was gathering support.

Then, on Monday night, France said it would veto a second resolution whatever the circumstances. Then France denounced the six tests. Later that day, Iraq rejected them. Still, we continued to negotiate.

Last Friday, France said they could not accept any ultimatum. On Monday, we made final efforts to secure agreement. But they remain utterly opposed to anything which lays down an ultimatum authorizing action in the event of non-compliance by Saddam.

Just consider the position we are asked to adopt. Those on the Security Council opposed to us say they want Saddam to disarm but will not countenance any new resolution that authorizes force in the event of non-compliance.

That is their position. No to any ultimatum; no to any resolution that stipulates that failure to comply will lead to military action.

So we must demand he disarm but relinquish any concept of a threat if he doesn't. From December 1998 to December 2002, no UN inspector was allowed to inspect anything in Iraq. For four years, not a thing.

What changed his mind? The threat of force. From December to January and then from January through to February, concessions were made.

What changed his mind? The threat of force. And what makes him now issue invitations to the inspectors, discover documents he said he never had, produce evidence of weapons supposed to be non-existent, destroy missiles he said he would keep? The imminence of force.

The only persuasive power to which he responds is 2,50,000 allied troops on his doorstep.

And yet when that fact is so obvious that it is staring us in the face, we are told that any resolution that authorizes force will be vetoed. Not just opposed. Vetoed. Blocked.

The way ahead was so clear. It was for the UN to pass a second resolution setting out benchmarks for compliance; with an ultimatum that if they were ignored, action would follow.

The tragedy is that had such a resolution issued, he might just have complied. Because the only route to peace with someone like Saddam Hussein is diplomacy backed by force.

Yet the moment we proposed the benchmarks, canvassed support for an ultimatum, there was an immediate recourse to the language of the veto.

And now the world has to learn the lesson all over again that weakness in the face of a threat from a tyrant, is the surest way not to peace but to war.

Looking back over twelve years, we have been victims of our own desire to placate the implacable, to persuade towards reason the utterly unreasonable, to hope that there was some genuine intent to do good in a regime whose mind is in fact evil. Now the very length of time counts against us. You've waited twelve years. Why not wait a little longer?

And indeed we have.

1441 gave a final opportunity. The first test was the 8th of December. He failed it. But still we waited. Until January 27, the first inspection report that showed the absence of full cooperation. Another breach. And still we waited.

Until February 14 and then February 28 with concessions, according to the old familiar routine, tossed to us to whet our appetite for hope and further waiting. But still no one, not the inspectors nor any member of the Security Council, not any halfway rational observer, believes Saddam is cooperating fully or unconditionally or immediately.

Our fault has not been impatience.

The truth is our patience should have been exhausted weeks and months and years ago. Even now, when if the world united and gave him an ultimatum—comply or face forcible disarmament. He might just do it, the world hesitates and in that hesitation he senses the weakness and therefore continues to defy.

What would any tyrannical regime possessing WMD think viewing the history of the world's diplomatic dance with Saddam? That our capacity to pass firm resolutions is only matched by our feebleness in implementing them.

That is why this indulgence has to stop. Because it is dangerous. It is dangerous if such regimes disbelieve us.

Dangerous if they think they can use our weakness, our hesitation, even the natural urges of our democracy towards peace, against us.

Dangerous because one day they will mistake our innate revulsion against war for permanent incapacity; when in fact, pushed to the limit, we will act. But then when we act, after years of pretence, the action will have to be harder, bigger, more total in its impact. Iraq is not the only regime with WMD. But back away now from this confrontation and future conflicts will be infinitely worse and more devastating.

But, of course, in a sense, any fair observer does not really dispute that Iraq is in breach and that 1441 implies action in such circumstances. The real problem is that, underneath, people dispute that Iraq is a threat; dispute the link between terrorism and WMD; dispute the whole basis of our assertion that the two together constitute a fundamental assault on our way of life.

There are glib and sometimes foolish comparisons with the 1930s. No one here is an appeaser. But the only relevant point of analogy is that with history, we know what happened. We can look back and say: there's the time, that was the moment; for example, when Czechoslovakia was swallowed up by the Nazis, that's when we should have acted.

But it wasn't clear at the time. In fact at the time, many people thought such a fear fanciful. Worse, put forward in bad faith by warmongers. Listen to this editorial from a paper I'm pleased to say with a different position today. But written in late 1938 after Munich when by now, you would have thought the world was tumultuous in its desire to act.

'Be glad in your hearts. Give thanks to your God. People of Britain, your children are safe. Your husbands and your sons will not march to war. Peace is a victory for all mankind. And now let us go back to our own affairs. We have had enough of those menaces, conjured up from the continent to confuse us.'

Naturally, should Hitler appear again in the same form, we would know what to do. But the point is that history doesn't declare the future to us so plainly. Each time is different and the present must be judged without the benefit of hindsight.

So let me explain the nature of this threat as I see it.

The threat today is not that of the 1930s. It's not big powers going to war with each other. The ravages which fundamentalist political ideology inflicted on the twentieth century are memories. The Cold War is over. Europe is at peace, if not always diplomatically.

But the world is ever more interdependent. Stock markets

and economies rise and fall together. Confidence is the key to prosperity; insecurity spreads like contagion. So people crave stability and order.

The threat is chaos. And there are two begetters of chaos—tyrannical regimes with WMD and extreme terrorist groups who profess a perverted and false view of Islam.

Let me tell the House what I know. I know that there are some countries or groups within countries that are proliferating and trading in WMD, especially nuclear weapons technology. I know there are companies, individuals, some former scientists on nuclear weapons programmes, selling their equipment or expertise.

I know there are several countries—mostly dictatorships with highly repressive regimes—desperately trying to acquire chemical weapons, biological weapons or, in particular, nuclear weapons capability. Some of these countries are now a short time away from having a serviceable nuclear weapon. This activity is not diminishing. It is increasing.

We all know that there are terrorist cells now operating in most major countries. Just as in the last two years, around twenty different nations have suffered serious terrorist outrages. Thousands have died in them.

The purpose of terrorism lies not just in the violent act itself. It is in producing terror. It sets out to inflame, to divide, to produce consequences which they then use to justify further terror.

Round the world it now poisons the chances of political progress—in the Middle East; in Kashmir; in Chechnya; in Africa.

The removal of the Taliban in Afghanistan dealt it a blow. But it has not gone away.

And these two threats have different motives and different origins but they share one basic common view—they detest the freedom, democracy and tolerance that are the hallmarks of our way of life.

At the moment, I accept that association between them is loose. But it is hardening.

And the possibility of the two coming together—of terrorist groups in possession of WMD, even of a so-called dirty radiological bomb is now, in my judgement, a real and present danger.

And let us recall: What was shocking about September 11 was not just the slaughter of the innocent, but the knowledge that had the terrorists been able to, there would have been not 3,000 innocent dead, but 30,000 or 300,000 and the more the suffering, the greater the terrorists' rejoicing.

Three kilograms of VX from a rocket launcher would contaminate a quarter of a square kilometre of a city.

Millions of lethal doses are contained in one litre of anthrax. 10,000 litres are unaccounted for. 11 September has changed the psychology of America. It should have changed the psychology of the world. Of course Iraq is not the only part of this threat. But it is the test of whether we treat the threat seriously.

Faced with it, the world should unite. The UN should be the focus, both of diplomacy and of action. That is what 1441 said. That was the deal. And I say to you to break it now, to will the ends but not the means that would do more damage in the long term to the UN than any other course.

To fall back into the lassitude of the last twelve years, to talk, to discuss, to debate but never act; to declare our will but not enforce it; to combine strong language with weak intentions, a worse outcome than never speaking at all.

And then, when the threat returns from Iraq or elsewhere, who will believe us? What price our credibility with the next tyrant? No wonder Japan and South Korea, next to North Korea, have issued such strong statements of support.

I have come to the conclusion after much reluctance that the greater danger to the UN is inaction: That to pass resolution 1441 and then refuse to enforce it would do the most deadly damage to the UN's future strength, confirming it as an instrument of diplomacy but not of action, forcing nations down the very unilateralist path we wish to avoid.

But there will be, in any event, no sound future for the UN, no guarantee against the repetition of these events, unless we recognize the urgent need for a political agenda we can unite upon.

What we have witnessed is indeed the consequence of Europe and the United States dividing from each other. Not all of Europe, Spain, Italy, Holland, Denmark, Portugal have all strongly supported us. And not a majority of Europe if we include, as we should, Europe's new members who will accede next year, all ten of whom have been in our support.

But the paralysis of the UN has been born out of the division there is. And at the heart of it has been the concept of a world in which there are rival poles of power. The US and its allies in one corner. France, Germany, Russia and its allies in the other. I do not believe that all of these nations intend such an outcome. But that is what now faces us.

I believe such a vision to be misguided and profoundly dangerous. I know why it arises. There is resentment of US predominance.

There is fear of US unilateralism. People ask: Do the US

listen to us and our preoccupations? And there is perhaps a lack of full understanding of US preoccupations after 11th September. I know all of this. But the way to deal with it is not rivalry but partnership. Partners are not servants but neither are they rivals. I tell you what Europe should have said last September to the US. With one voice it should have said: We understand your strategic anxiety over terrorism and WMD and we will help you meet it.

We will mean what we say in any UN resolution we pass and will back it with action if Saddam fails to disarm voluntarily, but in return we ask two things of you—that the US should choose the UN path and you should recognize the fundamental overriding importance of restarting the MEPP—Middle East Peace Process—which we will hold you to.

I do not believe there is any other issue with the same power to reunite the world community than progress on the issues of Israel and Palestine. Of course there is cynicism about recent announcements. But the US is now committed, and, I believe genuinely, to the roadmap for peace, designed in consultation with the UN. It will now be presented to the parties as Abu Mazen[7] is confirmed in office, hopefully today.

All of us are now signed up to its vision—a state of Israel, recognized and accepted by all the world, and a viable Palestinian state. And that should be part of a larger global agenda—on poverty and sustainable development; on democracy and human rights; on the good governance of nations.

That is why what happens after any conflict in Iraq is of such critical significance.

---

[7]Mahmoud Abbas, also known as Abu Mazen, briefly served as the Prime Minister of Palestinian Authority in 2003. He is presently the President.

Here again there is a chance to unify around the UN. Let me make it clear.

There should be a new UN resolution following any conflict providing not just for humanitarian help but also for the administration and governance of Iraq. That must now be done under proper UN authorization.

It should protect totally the territorial integrity of Iraq. And let the oil revenues—which people falsely claim we want to seize—be put in a trust fund for the Iraqi people administered through the UN.

And let the future government of Iraq be given the chance to begin the process of uniting the nation's disparate groups, on a democratic basis, respecting human rights, as indeed the fledgling democracy in Northern Iraq—protected from Saddam for twelve years by British and American pilots in the no-fly zone—has done so remarkably.

And the moment that a new government is in place—willing to disarm Iraq of WMD—for which its people have no need or purpose, then let sanctions be lifted in their entirety.

I have never put our justification for action as regime change. We have to act within the terms set out in resolution 1441. That is our legal base.

But it is the reason, I say frankly, why if we do act we should do so with a clear conscience and strong heart.

I accept fully that those opposed to this course of action share my detestation of Saddam. Who could not? Iraq is a wealthy country that in 1978, the year before Saddam seized power, was richer than Portugal or Malaysia.

Today it is impoverished, 60 per cent of its population dependent on food aid. Thousands of children die needlessly every year from lack of food and medicine. Four million people out of a population of just over twenty million are in exile.

The brutality of the repression—the death and torture camps, the barbaric prisons for political opponents, the routine beatings for anyone or their families suspected of disloyalty are well documented. Just last week, someone slandering Saddam was tied to a lamp post in a street in Baghdad, his tongue cut out, mutilated and left to bleed to death, as a warning to others.

I recall a few weeks ago talking to an Iraqi exile and saying to her that I understood how grim it must be under the lash of Saddam. 'But you don't,' she replied. 'You cannot. You do not know what it is like to live in perpetual fear.'

And she is right. We take our freedom for granted. But imagine not to be able to speak or discuss or debate or even question the society you live in. To see friends and family taken away and never daring to complain. To suffer the humility of failing courage in face of pitiless terror. That is how the Iraqi people live. Leave Saddam in place and that is how they will continue to live.

We must face the consequences of the actions we advocate. For me, that means all the dangers of war. But for others, opposed to this course, it means—let us be clear—that the Iraqi people, whose only true hope of liberation lies in the removal of Saddam, for them, the darkness will close back over them again; and he will be free to take his revenge upon those he must know wish him gone.

And if this house now demands that at this moment, faced with this threat from this regime, that British troops are pulled back, that we turn away at the point of reckoning, and that is what it means—what then?

What will Saddam feel? Strengthened beyond measure. What will the other states who tyrannize their people, the terrorists who threaten our existence, what will they take from that? That the will confronting them is decaying and feeble.

Who will celebrate and who will weep?

And if our plea is for America to work with others, to be good as well as powerful allies, will our retreat make them multilateralist? Or will it not rather be the biggest impulse to unilateralism there could ever be. And what of the UN and the future of Iraq and the Middle East peace plan, devoid of our influence, stripped of our insistence?

This House wanted this decision. Well it has it. Those are the choices. And in this dilemma, no choice is perfect, no cause ideal.

But on this decision hangs the fate of many things: Of whether we summon the strength to recognize this global challenge of the twenty-first century and meet it; of the Iraqi people, groaning under years of dictatorship; of our armed forces—brave men and women of whom we can feel proud, whose morale is high and whose purpose is clear; of the institutions and alliances that will shape our world for years to come.

I can think of many things, of whether we summon the strength to recognize the global challenge of the twenty-first century and beat it, of the Iraqi people groaning under years of dictatorship, of our armed forces—brave men and women of whom we can feel proud, whose morale is high and whose purpose is clear—of the institutions and alliances that shape our world for years to come.

To retreat now, I believe, would put at hazard all that we hold dearest, turn the UN back into a talking shop, stifle the first steps of progress in the Middle East; leave the Iraqi people to the mercy of events on which we would have relinquished all power to influence for the better.

Tell our allies that at the very moment of action, at the very moment when they need our determination that Britain faltered. I will not be party to such a course. This is not the time to falter. This is the time for this house, not just this government or indeed this prime minister, but for this house to give a lead, to show that we will stand up for what we know to be right, to show that we will confront the tyrannies and dictatorships and terrorists who put our way of life at risk, to show at the moment of decision that we have the courage to do the right thing.

I beg to move the motion.

◆

They will say the will of the people can't alter. It can. They will say leaving is inevitable. It isn't.[*]

Speech given on 17 October 2017 as former Prime Minister, urging people to rise up against 'Brexit at any cost'.

I want to be explicit. Yes, the British people voted to leave Europe. And I agree the will of the people should prevail. I accept right now there is no widespread appetite to rethink.

But the people voted without knowledge of the true terms of Brexit. As these terms become clear, it is their right to change their mind.

Our mission is to persuade them to do so.

---

*Source: Tony Blair

What was unfortunately only dim in our sight before the referendum is now in plain sight. The road we're going down is not simply Hard Brexit. It is Brexit At Any Cost.

Our challenge is to expose relentlessly what this cost is, to show how the decision was based on imperfect knowledge which will now become informed knowledge, to calculate in 'easy to understand' ways how proceeding will cause real damage to our country; and to build support for finding a way out from the present rush over the cliff's edge.

I don't know if we can succeed. But I do know we will suffer a rancorous verdict from future generations if we do not try.

How hideously, in this debate, is the mantle of patriotism abused. We do not argue for Britain in Europe because we are citizens of nowhere. We argue for it precisely because we are proud citizens of our country—Britain—who believe that in the twenty-first century, we should maintain our partnership with the biggest political union and largest commercial market on our doorstep; not in diminution of our national interest, but in satisfaction of it.

Consider for a moment the surreal situation in which our nation finds itself. I make no personal criticism of the PM or the Government. I know the PM is someone who cares about our country, who is trying to do the right thing as she sees it, and I know how demanding the job of leadership is.

But just consider: Nine months ago both she and the Chancellor, were telling us that leaving would be bad for the country, its economy, its security and its place in the world.

Today it is apparently a 'once in a generation opportunity' for greatness.

Seven months ago, after the referendum result, the Chancellor was telling us that leaving the Single Market would be—and I quote—'catastrophic'.

Now it appears we will leave the Single Market and the Customs Union and he is very optimistic.

Two years ago, the Foreign Secretary was emphatically in favour of the Single Market. Now ditching it is 'brilliant'.

The PM says she wants Britain to be a great open trading nation. Our first step in this endeavour? To leave the largest free trading bloc in the world.

She wants Britain to be a bridge between the EU and the USA. How to begin this worthy undertaking? To get out of Europe thus leaving us with no locus on the terrain where this bridge must be constructed.

We are told that it is high time our capitalism became fairer. And how do we start laying the foundation for such a noble cause? By threatening Europe with a move to a low tax, light regulation economy, the antithesis of that cause.

This jumble of contradictions shows that the PM and the government are not masters of this situation. They're not driving this bus. They're being driven. And as we pass each milestone so the landscape in which we are operating changes not because we have willed the change, but because this is the direction in which the bus is travelling.

We will trigger Article 50 not because we now know our destination, but because the politics of not doing so, would alienate those driving the bus.

The surreal nature of the exercise is enhanced by the curious absence of a big argument as to why this continues to be a good idea.

Many of the main themes of the Brexit campaign barely survived the first weekend after the vote. Remember the £350 million a week extra for the NHS?

Virtually the only practical arguments still advanced—under the general rubric of 'taking back control'—are immigration and the European Court of Justice.

On the ECJ, I would defy anyone to be able to recall any decisions which they might have heard of; as opposed to the decisions of the European Court of Human Rights, a non-EU body.

I can honestly say that during all my time as PM there was no major domestic law that I wanted to pass which Europe told me I couldn't.

It is true ECJ rulings are important on technical issues. Some business likes; some not. But no one would seriously argue that the ECJ alone provides a reason for leaving Europe.

Immigration is the issue. Net immigration into the UK was roughly 3,35,000 in the year to June 2016. But just over half was from outside the EU.

I know, in some parts of the country, there is a real concern about numbers from Europe and the pressures placed on services and wages. However of the EU immigrants, the PM has recently admitted we would want to keep the majority, including those with a confirmed job offer and students.

This leaves around 80,000 who come looking for work without a job. Of these 80,000, a third comes to London, mostly ending up working in the food processing and hospitality sectors.

It is highly unlikely that they're 'taking' the jobs of British-born people in other parts of the country.

The practical impact of Brexit on immigration is on analysis less than 12 per cent of the immigration total. And for many people, the core immigration question—and one which I fully accept is a substantial issue—is immigration from non-European countries, especially when from different cultures in which assimilation and potential security threats can be an issue.

Yet this impacted the Brexit decision.

It was Donald Trump who said without the refugees from Syria, 'you probably wouldn't have a Brexit'.

It is no coincidence that the infamous immigration poster of Leave was a picture of Mr Farage[1] in front of a line of Syrian people.

Thus, we have moved, in few months, from a debate about what sort of Brexit, involving a balanced consideration of all the different possibilities; to the primacy of one consideration—namely controlling immigration—without any real discussion as to why and when Brexit doesn't affect the immigration people most care about.

Now we're told we have to stop debating Brexit and just do it.

Frankly, I would question whether the referendum really provides a mandate for 'Brexit At Any Cost'.

But suppose that it does. The argument is then that the British people have spoken, we must deliver their will and we should just 'get on with it'.

I agree 'getting on with it' is a very powerful sentiment, at present the predominant sentiment.

But were we to be true to the concept of Government through British Parliamentary democracy, rather than Government by one-off plebiscite, we would also feel obliged to point out that it isn't a question of just 'getting on with it'.

This is not a decision that once made is then a mere

---

[1]Nigel Farage is a British politician and Brexit campaigner.

matter of mechanics to implement.

It is a decision which then begets many other decisions. Every part of this negotiation, from money to access to post-Brexit arrangements, is itself an immense decision with consequence.

If we were in a rational world, we would all the time, as we approach those decisions, be asking: Why are we doing this and as we know more of the costs, is the pain worth the gain?

Let us examine the pain.

We will withdraw from the Single Market which is around half of our trade in goods and services. We will also leave the Customs Union, covering trade with countries like Turkey.

Then we need to replace over fifty Preferential Trade Agreements we have via our membership of the EU; for instance with Switzerland. So, EU-related trade is actually two-thirds of the UK total. This impacts everything from airline travel, to financial services to manufacturing industry, sector by sector.

We will pay for previous EU obligations but not benefit from future opportunities, with figures as high as £60 billion as the cost.

We will lose influence in the world's most significant political union; and have to negotiate on our own on issues like the environment where we presently benefit from Europe's collective strength.

There is alarm across sectors as diverse as scientific research and culture as European funding is withdrawn.

And all this then to do an intricate renegotiation of the trading arrangements we have just abandoned. That negotiation is without precedent in complexity. It is even possible that it fails and we end up trading on WTO rules.

This is in itself another minefield: We would need to negotiate the removal not just of tariff barriers, but the prevention of non-tariff barriers which today are often the biggest impediments to trade and pile costs on business.

This could take years.

Our currency is down around 12 per cent against the euro and 20 per cent against the dollar, which is the international financial market's assessment of our future prosperity, i.e. we are going to be poorer.

The price of imported goods in the supermarkets is up and thus the cost of living.

Of course Britain can and would survive out of the EU. This is a great country, with resilient and creative people.

And yes, no one is going to write us off, nor should they. But making the best of a bad job doesn't alter the fact that it isn't smart to put yourself in that position unless you have to.

Most extraordinary of all, the two great achievements of British diplomacy of the last decades in Europe, supported by governments, both Labour and Conservative, namely the Single Market and European Enlargement, are now apparently the two things we most regret and want to rid ourselves of!

The Single Market has been of enormous benefit to the UK bringing billions of pounds of wealth, hundreds of thousands of jobs, and major investment opportunities; our trade with an enlarged European Union has meant for example that trade with Poland has gone from £3 billion in 2004 to £13.5 billion in 2016.

Nations that came out of the Soviet bloc have seen themselves safely within the EU and NATO, so enhancing our own security.

In addition to all this, the possibility of the break-up

of the UK—narrowly avoided by the result of the Scottish referendum—is now back on the table, but this time with a context much more credible for the independence case.

We are already seeing the destabilizing impact of negotiation over border arrangements on the Northern Ireland peace process.

None of this ignores the challenges the country faces which stoked the anger fuelling Brexit: those left behind by globalization; the aftermath of the financial crisis; stagnant incomes for some families; and for sure the pressures posed by big increases in migration which make perfectly reasonable people anxious and feeling unheard in their anxiety.

I always believe that if the centre ground does not deal with the problems, the extremes can exploit them.

But our duty is to give answers, not ride the anger.

Here is the paradox.

As we go through this unique experiment in diplomatic and economic complexity, the entire focus of the government is on one issue—Brexit.

This is a government for Brexit, of Brexit and dominated by Brexit. It is a mono-purpose political entity.

Nothing else truly matters: not the NHS, now in its most severe crisis since its creation; not the real challenge of the modern economy, the new technological revolutions of AI and Big Data; not the upgrade of our education system to prepare people for this new world; not investment in communities left behind by globalization; not the rising burden of serious crime; or bulging prison populations; or social care; not even, irony of ironies, a genuine policy to control immigration.

Governments' priorities are not really defined by white papers or words; but by the intensity of focus.

This government has bandwidth only for one thing—Brexit. It is the waking thought, the daily grind, the meditation before sleep and the stuff of its dreams; or nightmares.

It is obsessed with Brexit because it has to be.

Future historians will be scurrying to investigate the antecedents of these migrants from Europe, for whose restraint we were willing to sacrifice so much.

What will they find—that they were a terrible group of people who threatened the country's stability?

They will find that on the whole they were well-behaved, worked hard, paid their taxes and were a net economic benefit.

So what do we do?

The Leave campaign was a coalition, some against Europe for economic reasons; some for cultural reasons. Some were ideological in their opposition; some had done a cost/benefit analysis and concluded better out than in.

We must expose the agenda of the ideologues, and persuade those interested in the cost–benefit ratio.

For the latter, we must—day in day out—articulate the reality: the pain is large and the gain largely illusory.

But the ideologues are the ones driving this bus.

The economic future which could work outside of Europe is exactly the low tax, light regulation, offshore free market hub, with which Mrs [Theresa] May threatens our European neighbours, but which to the Brexit ideologues is a promise of things to come.

Indeed, this is what many in business say they're being told by Government Ministers, but of course behind the hand, because this is the exact opposite of what the mass of voters are being told when promised a fairer capitalism with a better deal for the workers.

This free market vision would require major restructuring of the British economy and its tax and welfare system.

It will not mean more money for the NHS but less; actually it probably means a wholesale rebalancing of our healthcare towards one based on private as much as public provision.

It will not mean more protection for workers, but less.

And if that were what we wanted to do as a country, we could do it now.

Europe wouldn't stop us.

But as of now the British people would, because they wouldn't vote for it.

So the ideologues know they have to get Brexit first; then tell us this is the only future which works, and by that time they will be right.

In defeating them, we have two major challenges.

There is an effective cartel of media on the right, which built the ramp for pro-Brexit propaganda during the campaign; is now equally savage in its efforts to say it is all going to be 'great' and anyone who says otherwise is a traitor or moaner; and who make it very clear to the PM that she has their adulation for exactly as long as she delivers Brexit.

It hugely skews the broadcast coverage. For example, a week ago there was the annual survey of top business bosses of the leading UK companies. Over half said Brexit was already having an adverse effect on their business. And half did not have confidence in the government negotiating a good deal.

It led the FT[2]. It was barely covered elsewhere. The BBC had it as an item of business news.

Suppose the survey had come to the opposite conclusion.

---

[2]Financial Times

It would have had at least four papers headlining it and would therefore have featured prominently on the broadcasts.

The second challenge is the absence of an Opposition which looks capable on the polls of beating the Government.

The debilitation of the Labour Party is the facilitator of Brexit. I hate to say that, but it is true. What this means is that we have to build a movement which stretches across Party lines; and devise new ways of communication.

There are lots of different groups doing great work, Open Britain naturally being one. These groups must find ways of concerting strategy and tactics effectively.

We should begin to create informal links immediately and then build them into a movement with weight and reach. We need to strengthen the hand of the MPs who are with us and let those against know they have serious opposition to Brexit At Any Cost.

The Institute which I am setting up will play our part. We are creating a policy platform wider than the Europe question. There is an urgent need to reposition the whole debate around globalization and how we make it work for people. In this sense, the Brexit debate is part of something much bigger.

But developing the arguments around Brexit will be an important element of the Institute's work.

We need strong links with the rest of Europe.

If our Government were conducting a negotiation which genuinely sought to advance our country's interests, that negotiation would include the possibility of Britain staying in a reformed Europe.

It is clear the sentiment which led to Brexit is not confined to the UK. There is a widespread yearning for reform across Europe.

Part of our work should be to help build Europe wide alliances to give voice and effect to such an impulse.

So this movement must have many dimensions to it. It requires arguments of detail; and arguments of grandeur.

The case for Europe remains rooted not in understanding the past but the future.

All over the globe, countries are coming together in regional alliances for a very simple reason. As China rises, as India and other large population countries follow and with the USA already so powerful; so to maintain strength and influence, to defend our interests adequately, nations of our size will cooperate based on proximity.

This is true of the nations of Europe. But for Europe there is a more profound reason. The Transatlantic Alliance is needed more than ever; but how much stronger it is with Britain in Europe and Europe an equal partner with America.

Forget the short-term electoral politics there or here. In the long-term, this is essentially an alliance of values—liberty, democracy, the rule of law.

As the world changes and opens up across boundaries of nation and culture, which values will govern the twenty-first century?

Today, for the first time in my adult life, it is not clear that the resolution of this question will be benign.

Britain, because of its history, alliances and character, has a unique role to play in ensuring it is.

How, therefore, can it be wise for us, during this epic period of global evolution, to be focused not on how we build partnerships, but how we dissolve the one to which we are bound by ties of geography, trade, shared values and common interest?

The one incontrovertible characteristic of politics today is its propensity for revolt.

The Brexiteers were the beneficiaries of this wave; now they want to freeze it to a day in June 2016.

They will say the will of the people can't alter. It can.

They will say leaving is inevitable. It isn't.

They will say we don't represent the people. We do, many millions of them and with determination many millions more.

They will claim we're dividing the country by making the case. It is they who divide our country—generation from generation, North from South, Scotland from England, those born here from those who came to our country precisely because of what they thought it stood for and what they admired.

This is not the time for retreat, indifference or despair; but the time to rise up in defence of what we believe—calmly, patiently, winning the argument by the force of argument; but without fear and with the conviction we act in the true interests of Britain.

◆

14

Boris Yeltsin
President of Russia (1991–1999)

We are all guilty.*

Though a Communist Party member for much of his life, Boris Yeltsin eventually came to believe in both democratic and free market reforms, and played an instrumental role in the collapse of the Soviet Union. His tenure was marred by economic hardship, increased corruption and crime, a violent war in the breakaway republic of Chechnya and Russia's diminished influence on world events. This speech was delivered at Czar Nicholas II's funeral on 17 July 1998.

Dear fellow citizens:
It's a historic day for Russia. Eighty years have passed since the slaying of the last Russian emperor and his family. We have long been silent about this monstrous crime. We must

---

*Source: Official website of the Russian President

say the truth: The Yekaterinburg massacre[1] has become one of the most shameful episodes in our history.

By burying the remains of innocent victims, we want to atone for the sins of our ancestors.

Those who committed this crime are as guilty as are those who approved of it for decades. We are all guilty.

It is impossible to lie to ourselves by justifying senseless cruelty on political grounds. The shooting of the Romanov family is a result of an uncompromising split in Russian society into 'us' and 'them'. The results of this split can be seen even now.

The burial of the remains of Yekaterinburg is, first of all, an act of human justice. It's a symbol of unity of the nation, an atonement of common guilt.

We all bear responsibility for the historical memory of the nation. And that's why I could not fail to come here. I must be here as both an individual and the President.

I bow my head before the victims of the merciless slaying.

While building a new Russia, we must rely on its historical experience. Many glorious pages of Russian history were connected with the Romanovs. But with this name is connected one of the most bitter lessons: Any attempts to change life by violence is condemned to failure.

We must end the century, which has been an age of blood and violence in Russia, with repentance and peace, regardless

---

[1]Czar Nicholas II was the last of the Romanov emperors of Russia. During the Russian Revolution, the Czar was forced to abdicate in 1917 and was murdered along with his family by the orders of the revolutionary council. Their bodies were secretly buried in Yekaterinburg. Years later, scientists discovered their remains and identified their bodies through genetic analyses. Thus, on 17 July 2008, eighty years to the day of the massacre, the remains were given a state funeral.

of political views, ethnic or religious belonging.

This is our historic chance. On the eve of the third millennium, we must do it for the sake of our generation and those to come. Let's remember those innocent victims who have fallen to hatred and violence. May they rest in peace.

◆

15

Robin Cook
Foreign Secretary, the United Kingdom
(1997–2001)

**It is for that reason and for that reason alone,
and with a heavy heart,
that I resign from the Government.***

Robin Cook's resignation speech became his swansong. He resigned as the Leader of the House of Commons in protest against Prime Minister Tony Blair's stance against Iraq on 17 March 2003. This speech is widely regarded as one of the best speeches by a statesman, showing resilience, courage and strategy at the same time.

This is the first time for twenty years that I have addressed the House from the Back Benches. I must confess that I had

---

*Source: UK Government website

forgotten how much better the view is from here. None of those twenty years were more enjoyable or more rewarding than the past two, in which I have had the immense privilege of serving this House as Leader of the House, which were made all the more enjoyable, Mr Speaker, by the opportunity of working closely with you.

It was frequently the necessity for me as Leader of the House to talk my way out of accusations that a statement had been preceded by a press interview. On this occasion I can say with complete confidence that no press interview has been given before this statement. I have chosen to address the House first on why I cannot support a war without international agreement or domestic support.

The present Prime Minister is the most successful leader of the Labour Party in my lifetime. I hope that he will continue to be the leader of our Party, and I hope that he will continue to be successful. I have no sympathy with, and I will give no comfort to, those who want to use this crisis to displace him.

I applaud the heroic efforts that the Prime Minister has made in trying to secure a second resolution. I do not think that anybody could have done better than the Foreign Secretary in working to get support for a second resolution within the Security Council. But the very intensity of those attempts underlines how important it was to succeed. Now that those attempts have failed, we cannot pretend that getting a second resolution was of no importance.

France has been at the receiving end of bucketloads of commentary in recent days. It is not France alone that wants more time for inspections. Germany wants more time for inspections, Russia wants more time for inspections; indeed, at no time have we signed up even the minimum necessary to carry a second resolution. We delude ourselves if we think that the degree of international hostility is all the result of President Chirac[1]. The reality is that Britain is being asked to embark on a war without agreement in any of the international bodies of which we are a leading partner—not NATO, not the European Union and, now, not the Security Council.

To end up in such diplomatic weakness is a serious reverse. Only a year ago, we and the United States were part of a coalition against terrorism that was wider and more diverse than I would ever have imagined possible. History will be astonished at the diplomatic miscalculations that led so quickly to the disintegration of that powerful coalition. The US can afford to go it alone, but Britain is not a superpower. Our interests are best protected not by unilateral action but by multilateral agreement and a world order governed by rules. Yet tonight the international partnerships most important to us are weakened: The European Union is divided; the Security Council is in stalemate. Those are heavy casualties of a war in which a shot has yet to be fired.

I have heard some parallels between military action in these circumstances and the military action that we took in Kosovo. There was no doubt about the multilateral support that we had for the action that we took in Kosovo. It was supported by NATO; it was supported by the European Union; it was supported by every single one of the seven neighbours in the region. France and Germany were our active allies. It is precisely because we have none of that support in this case that it was all the more important to get agreement

---

[1]Jacques Chirac served as the President of France from 1995–2007.

in the Security Council as the last hope of demonstrating international agreement.

The legal basis for our action in Kosovo was the need to respond to an urgent and compelling humanitarian crisis. Our difficulty in getting support this time is that neither the international community nor the British public is persuaded that there is an urgent and compelling reason for this military action in Iraq.

The threshold for war should always be high. None of us can predict the death toll of civilians from the forthcoming bombardment of Iraq, but the US warning of a bombing campaign that will 'shock and awe' makes it likely that casualties will be numbered at least in the thousands. I am confident that British servicemen and women will acquit themselves with professionalism and with courage. I hope that they all come back. I hope that Saddam [Hussein], even now, will quit Baghdad and avert war, but it is false to argue that only those who support war support our troops. It is entirely legitimate to support our troops while seeking an alternative to the conflict that will put those troops at risk.

Nor is it fair to accuse those of us who want longer for inspections of not having an alternative strategy. For four years as Foreign Secretary, I was partly responsible for the Western strategy of containment. Over the past decade that strategy destroyed more weapons than in the Gulf War, dismantled Iraq's nuclear weapons programme and halted Saddam's medium- and long-range missiles programmes. Iraq's military strength is now less than half its size than at the time of the last Gulf War.

Ironically, it is only because Iraq's military forces are so weak that we can even contemplate its invasion. Some advocates of conflict claim that Saddam's forces are so weak, so demoralized and so badly equipped that the war will be over in a few days. We cannot base our military strategy on the assumption that Saddam is weak and at the same time justify pre-emptive action on the claim that he is a threat.

Iraq probably has no weapons of mass destruction in the commonly understood sense of the term—namely a credible device capable of being delivered against a strategic city target. It probably still has biological toxins and battlefield chemical munitions, but it has had them since the 1980s when US companies sold Saddam anthrax agents and the then British Government approved chemical and munitions factories. Why is it now so urgent that we should take military action to disarm a military capacity that has been there for twenty years, and which we helped to create? Why is it necessary to resort to war this week, while Saddam's ambition to complete his weapons programme is blocked by the presence of UN inspectors?

Only a couple of weeks ago, Hans Blix[2] told the Security Council that the key remaining disarmament tasks could be completed within months. I have heard it said that Iraq has had not months but twelve years in which to complete disarmament, and that our patience is exhausted. Yet it is more than thirty years since resolution 242 called on Israel to withdraw from the occupied territories. We do not express the same impatience with the persistent refusal of Israel to comply. I welcome the strong personal commitment that the Prime Minister has given to Middle East peace, but Britain's positive

---

[2]Hans Blix was the Executive Chairman of the United Nations Monitoring, Verification and Inspection Commission (Unmovic), which was tasked with searching for WMDs in Iraq.

role in the Middle East does not redress the strong sense of injustice throughout the Muslim world at what it sees as one rule for the allies of the US and another rule for the rest.

Nor is our credibility helped by the appearance that our partners in Washington are less interested in disarmament than they are in regime change in Iraq. That explains why any evidence that inspections may be showing progress is greeted in Washington not with satisfaction but with consternation—it reduces the case for war.

What has come to trouble me most over past weeks is the suspicion that if the hanging chads in Florida had gone the other way and Al Gore[3] had been elected, we would not now be about to commit British troops.

The longer that I have served in this place, the greater the respect I have for the good sense and collective wisdom of the British people. On Iraq, I believe that the prevailing mood of the British people is sound. They do not doubt that Saddam is a brutal dictator, but they are not persuaded that he is a clear and present danger to Britain. They want inspections to be given a chance, and they suspect that they are being pushed too quickly into conflict by a US Administration with an agenda of its own. Above all, they are uneasy at Britain going out on a limb on a military adventure without a broader international coalition and against the hostility of many of our traditional allies.

From the start of the present crisis, I have insisted, as Leader of the House, on the right of this place to vote on whether Britain should go to war. It has been a favourite theme

---

[3]In 2000, George W. Bush narrowly won the presidential election over Vice President Al Gore.

of commentators that this House no longer occupies a central role in British politics. Nothing could better demonstrate that they are wrong than for this House to stop the commitment of troops in a war that has neither international agreement nor domestic support. I intend to join those tomorrow night who will vote against military action now. It is for that reason, and for that reason alone, and with a heavy heart, that I resign from the Government.

◆

16

David Cameron
Prime Minister of the United Kingdom (2010–2016)

A catastrophe for the people of Northern Ireland.*

Statement made on 15 June 2010 to the MPs in the House of Commons on the day the Bloody Sunday report was published.

The Secretary of State for Northern Ireland is publishing the report of the Saville Inquiry—the tribunal set up by the previous government to investigate the tragic events of 30 January 1972, a day more commonly known as Bloody Sunday.

We have acted in good faith by publishing the tribunal's findings as soon as possible after the general election.

Mr Speaker, I am deeply patriotic. I never want to believe anything bad about our country. I never want to call into

---

*Source: UK Government website

question the behaviour of our soldiers and our army, who I believe to be the finest in the world.

And I have seen for myself the very difficult and dangerous circumstances in which we ask our soldiers to serve.

But the conclusions of this report are absolutely clear. There is no doubt, there is nothing equivocal, there are no ambiguities. What happened on Bloody Sunday was both unjustified and unjustifiable. It was wrong.

Lord Saville concludes that the soldiers of the support company who went into the Bogside did so as a result of an order which should not have been given by their commander. He finds that, on balance, the first shot in the vicinity of the march was fired by the British Army. He finds that none of the casualties shot by the soldiers of support company was armed with a firearm.

He finds that there was some firing by Republican paramilitaries but none of this firing provided any justification for the shooting of civilian casualties.

And he finds that, in no case, was any warning given by soldiers before opening fire.

He also finds that the support company reacted by losing their self-control, forgetting or ignoring their instructions and training and with a serious and widespread loss of fire discipline. He finds that despite the contrary evidence given by the soldiers, none of them fired in response to attacks or threatened attacks by nail or petrol bombers.

And he finds that many of the soldiers—and I quote knowingly—put forward false accounts to seek to justify their firing.

Lord Saville says that some of those killed or injured were clearly fleeing or going to the assistance of others who were dying.

The report refers to one person who was shot while crawling away from the soldiers. Another was shot in all probability when he was lying mortally wounded on the ground. The report refers to the father who was hit and injured by army gunfire after going to attend to his son.

For those looking for statements of innocence, Saville says that the immediate responsibility for the deaths and injuries on Bloody Sunday lies with those members of support company whose unjustifiable firing was the cause of those deaths and injuries.

Crucially, that, and I quote, none of the casualties was posing a threat of causing death or serious injury or indeed was doing anything else that could, on any view, justified in shooting.

For those people who are looking for the report to use terms like murder and unlawful killing, I remind the House that these judgements are not matters for a tribunal or politicians to determine.

Mr Speaker, these are shocking conclusions to read and shocking words to have to say. But Mr Speaker, you do not defend the British Army by defending the indefensible. We do not honour all those who have served with such distinction in keeping the peace and upholding the rule of law in Northern Ireland by hiding from the truth.

There is no point in trying to soften or equivocate what is in this report. It is clear from the tribunal's authoritative conclusions that the events of Bloody Sunday were in no way justified.

I know that some people wonder whether, nearly forty years on from an event, [if] a Prime Minister needs to issue an apology. For someone of my generation, Bloody Sunday and the early 1970s are something we feel we have learnt about rather than lived through.

But what happened should never, ever have happened. The families of those who died should not have had to live with the pain and the hurt of that day and with a lifetime of loss.

Some members of our armed forces acted wrongly. The government is ultimately responsible for the conduct of the armed forces and for that, on behalf of the government, indeed, on behalf of our country, I am deeply sorry.

Mr Speaker, just as this report is clear that the actions of that day were unjustifiable, so too is it clear in some of its other findings.

Those looking for premeditation, a plan, those even looking for a conspiracy involving senior politicians or senior members of the armed forces, they will not find it in this report. Indeed, Lord Saville finds no evidence that the events of Bloody Sunday were premeditated, he concludes that the United Kingdom and Northern Ireland governments and the army neither tolerated nor encouraged the use of unjustified lethal force. He makes no suggestion of a government cover up.

Mr Speaker, the report also specifically deals with the actions of key individuals in the army, in politics and beyond, including Major General [Robert] Ford, Brigadier [Pat] MacLellan and Lieutenant Colonel [Derek] Wilford.

In each case, the findings are clear. It does the same for Martin McGuinness. It specifically finds he was present and probably armed with a sub-machine gun but it concludes, and I quote, 'We're sure that he did not engage in any activity that provided any of the soldiers with any justification for opening fire'.

Mr Speaker, while in no way justifying the events of January 30th, 1972, we should acknowledge the background to the events of Bloody Sunday.

Since 1969, the security situation in Northern Ireland had been declining significantly. Three days before Bloody Sunday, two RUC[1] officers, one a Catholic, were shot by the IRA[2] in Londonderry—the first police officers killed in the city during the Troubles.

A third of the City of Derry had become a no-go area for the RUC and the Army. And in the end, 1972 was to prove Northern Ireland's bloodiest year by far, with nearly five hundred people killed.

And let us also remember, Bloody Sunday is not the defining story of the service the British Army gave in Northern Ireland from 1969–2007.

This was known as Operation Banner, the longest continuous operation in British military history, spanning thirty-eight years and in which over 2,50,000 people served.

Our armed forces displayed enormous courage and professionalism in upholding democracy and the rule of law in Northern Ireland. Acting in support of the police, they played a major part in setting the conditions that have made peaceful politics possible. And over 1,000 members—1,000 members—of the security forces lost their lives to that cause.

Without their work, the peace process would not have happened.

Of course, some mistakes were undoubtedly made, but lessons were also learned. And once again, I put on record

---

[1]Royal Ulster Constabulary (RUC) is the state police force in Northern Ireland.
[2]Irish Republican Army

the immense debt of gratitude we all owe to those who served in Northern Ireland.

Mr Speaker, may I also thank the tribunal for its work and all those who displayed great courage in giving evidence.

I would also like to acknowledge the grief of the families of those killed. They have pursued their long campaign over thirty-eight years with great patience. Nothing can bring back those who were killed, but I hope, as one relative has put it, the truth coming out can help set people free.

John Major[3] said he was open to a new inquiry, Tony Blair then set it up. This was accepted by the leader of the Opposition. Of course, none of us anticipated that the Saville Inquiry would take twelve years or cost almost £200 million. Our views on that are well-documented.

It is right to pursue the truth with vigour and thoroughness, but let me reassure the House there will be no more open-ended and costly inquiries into the past.

Today is not about the controversies surrounding the process, it is about the substance, about what this report tells us. Everyone should have the chance to examine its complete findings and that is why it is being published in full. Running to more than 5,000 pages, it is being published in ten volumes.

Naturally, it will take all of us some time to digest the report's full findings and understand its implications. The House will have an opportunity for a full day's debate this autumn, and in the meantime the Secretaries of State in Northern Ireland for Defence will report back to me on all the issues which arise from it.

Mr Speaker, this report and the inquiry itself demonstrate

---

[3]John Major served as the Prime Minister of the United Kingdom from 1990–97.

how a state should hold itself to account and how we should be determined at all times, no matter how difficult, to judge ourselves against the highest standards. Openness and frankness about the past, however painful, they do not make us weaker, they make us stronger.

That is one of the things that differentiates us from the terrorists. We should never forget that over 3,500 people from every community lost their lives in Northern Ireland, the overwhelming majority killed by terrorists.

There were many terrible atrocities. Politically motivated violence was never justified, whichever side it came from. And it can never be justified by those criminal gangs that today want to draw Northern Ireland back to its bitter and bloody past.

No government I lead will ever put those who fight to defend democracy on an equal footing with those who continue to seek to destroy it. But neither will we hide from the truth that confronts us today.

In the words of Lord Saville, what happened on Bloody Sunday strengthened the Provisional IRA, increased hostility towards the Army and exacerbated the violent conflict of the years that followed.

Bloody Sunday was a tragedy for the bereaved and the wounded and a catastrophe for the people of Northern Ireland.

Those are words we cannot and must not ignore. But I hope what this report can also do is mark the moment where we come together in this House and in the communities we represent to acknowledge our shared history, even where it divides us. And come together to close this painful chapter on Northern Ireland's troubled past.

That is not to say we should ever forget or dismiss the past, but we must also move on. Northern Ireland has been transformed over the last twenty years, and all of us in Westminster and Stormont must continue that work of change, coming together with all the people of Northern Ireland to build a stable, peaceful, prosperous and shared future.

And it is with that determination that I commend this statement to the house.

◆

17

Michelle Obama
First Lady of the United States of America
(2009–2017)

...when someone is cruel or acts like a bully, you
don't stoop to their level. No, our motto is,
when they go low, we go high.[*]

This speech was delivered on 25 July 2016 during the Democratic convention.

Thank you all. Thank you so much. You know, it's hard to believe that it has been eight years since I first came to this convention to talk with you about why I thought my husband should be President.

Remember how I told you about his character and convictions, his decency and his grace, the traits that we've

---

*Source: Michelle Obama. Permission to reuse the speech taken from the source.

seen every day that he's served our country in the White House?

I also told you about our daughters, how they are the heart of our hearts, the centre of our world. And during our time in the White House, we've had the joy of watching them grow from bubbly little girls into poised young women, a journey that started soon after we arrived in Washington.

When they set off for their first day at their new school, I will never forget that winter morning as I watched our girls, just 7- and 10-years-old, pile into those black SUVs with all those big men with guns. And I saw their little faces pressed up against the window, and the only thing I could think was, what have we done?

See, because at that moment I realized that our time in the White House would form the foundation for who they would become, and how well we managed this experience could truly make or break them. That is what Barack and I think about every day as we try to guide and protect our girls through the challenges of this unusual life in the spotlight, how we urge them to ignore those who question their father's citizenship or faith.

How we insist that the hateful language they hear from public figures on TV does not represent the true spirit of this country.

How we explain that when someone is cruel or acts like a bully, you don't stoop to their level. No, our motto is, when they go low, we go high.

With every word we utter, with every action we take, we know our kids are watching us. We as parents are their most important role models. And let me tell you, Barack and I take that same approach to our jobs as President and First Lady because we know that our words and actions matter, not just to our girls, but the children across this country, kids who tell us I saw you on TV, I wrote a report on you for school. Kids like the little black boy who looked up at my husband, his eyes wide with hope and he wondered—is my hair like yours?

And make no mistake about it, this November when we go to the polls that is what we're deciding, not Democrat or Republican, not left or right. No, in this election and every election is about who will have the power to shape our children for the next four or eight years of their lives.

And I am here tonight because in this election there is only one person who I trust with that responsibility, only one person who I believe is truly qualified to be President of the United States, and that is our friend Hillary Clinton.

That's right.

See, I trust Hillary to lead this country because I've seen her lifelong devotion to our nation's children, not just her own daughter—who she has raised to perfection—but every child who needs a champion, kids who take the long way to school to avoid the gangs, kids who wonder how they'll ever afford college, kids whose parents don't speak a word of English, but dream of a better life, kids who look to us to determine who and what they can be.

You see, Hillary has spent decades doing the relentless, thankless work to actually make a difference in their lives. Advocating for kids with disabilities as a young lawyer, fighting for children's healthcare as First Lady and for quality childcare in the Senate.

And when she didn't win the nomination eight years ago, she didn't get angry or disillusioned. Hillary did not pack up and go home, because as a true public servant Hillary knows that this is so much bigger than her own desires and disappointments.

So she proudly stepped up to serve our country once again as Secretary of State, travelling the globe to keep our kids safe.

And look, there were plenty of moments when Hillary could have decided that this work was too hard, that the price of public service was too high, that she was tired of being picked apart for how she looks or how she talks or even how she laughs. But here's the thing: What I admire most about Hillary is that she never buckles under pressure. She never takes the easy way out. And Hillary Clinton has never quit on anything in her life.

And when I think about the kind of President that I want for my girls and all our children, that's what I want.

I want someone with the proven strength to persevere, someone who knows this job and takes it seriously, someone who understands that the issues a president faces are not black and white and cannot be boiled down to 140 characters.

Because when you have the nuclear codes at your fingertips and the military in your command, you can't make snap decisions. You can't have a thin skin or a tendency to lash out. You need to be steady and measured and well-informed.

I want a President with a record of public service, someone whose life's work shows our children that we don't chase form and fortune for ourselves, we fight to give everyone a chance to succeed. And we give back even when we're struggling ourselves because we know that there is always someone worse off. And there but for the grace of God, go I.

I want a president who will teach our children that everyone in this country matters, a president who truly believes in the vision that our Founders put forth all those years ago that we are all created equal, each a beloved part of the great American story.

And when crisis hits, we don't turn against each other. No, we listen to each other, we lean on each other, because we are always stronger together. And I am here tonight because I know that that is the kind of President Hillary Clinton will be. And that's why in this election I'm with her.

You see, Hillary understands that the President is about one thing and one thing only—it's about leaving something better for our kids. That's how we've always moved this country forward, by all of us coming together on behalf of our children, folks who volunteer to coach that team, to teach that Sunday school class, because they know it takes a village.

Heroes of every colour and creed who wear the uniform and risk their lives to keep passing down those blessings of liberty, police officers and the protesters in Dallas who all desperately want to keep our children safe. People who lined up in Orlando to donate blood because it could have been their son, their daughter in that club.

Leaders like Tim Kaine who show our kids what decency and devotion look like. Leaders like Hillary Clinton who have the guts and the grace to keep coming back and putting those cracks in that highest and hardest glass ceiling until she finally breaks through, lifting all of us along with her.

That is the story of this country, the story that has brought me to this stage tonight, the story of generations of people who felt the lash of bondage, the shame of servitude, the sting of segregation, but who kept on striving and hoping and doing what needed to be done so that today I wake up every morning in a house that was built by slaves. And I watch my daughters, two beautiful, intelligent, black young women playing with their dogs on the White House lawn.

And because of Hillary Clinton, my daughters and all our sons and daughters now take for granted that a woman can be President of the United States.

So, look, don't let anyone ever tell you that this country isn't great, that somehow we need to make it great again. Because this right now is the greatest country on earth!

And as my daughters prepare to set out into the world, I want a leader who is worthy of that truth, a leader who is worthy of my girls' promise and all our kids' promise, a leader who will be guided every day by the love and hope and impossibly big dreams that we all have for our children.

So in this election, we cannot sit back and hope that everything works out for the best. We cannot afford to be tired or frustrated or cynical. No, hear me. Between now and November, we need to do what we did eight years ago and four years ago.

We need to knock on every door, we need to get out every vote, we need to pour every last ounce of our passion and our strength and our love for this country into electing Hillary Clinton as President of the United States of America!

So let's get to work. Thank you all and God bless.

◆

18

Sheryl Sandberg
Chief Operating Officer, Facebook

We build resilience into ourselves. We build resilience into the people we love. And we build it together, as a community.[*]

This speech was delivered at Virginia Tech Convocation on 12 May 2017.

Hello Hokies![1]

President Sands, esteemed faculty, proud parents, devoted friends, wet siblings…congratulations to all of you. But most

---

[*]Credit: Copyright of the speech is with Sheryl Sandberg. This speech has been reproduced here with permission from Option B.Org.

OptionB.Org is an initiative by Sheryl Sandberg which helps people build resilience and find meaning in the face of adversity.

[1]Hokie was a word made up by a Virginia Tech student for a cheer and has now become a term to describe a student of the university.

importantly, congratulations to the Virginia Tech class of 2017!

I am honoured to be with you and this San Francisco summer day feels just like home, just like it does with anything with 'Tech' in its name.

I'm so delighted to be here with my friend, Regina Dugan. As you just heard, Regina used to run DARPA[2]—for real!—and now she is developing breakthrough technologies at Facebook. In Hokie terms, she's our Bruce Smith. And she is just one of so many alums doing amazing things around the world.

Today, class of 2017, you join them. And I'm thrilled for you. And thrilled for all of the people who are here supporting you—the people who have pushed you, dried your tears and laughed with you from your first day to this day. Let's show them all of our thanks.

Commencement speeches can be pretty one-sided. The speaker—that's me—imparts her hard-earned wisdom...or at least tries to. The graduates—that's you—you sit in the rain today and listen like the thoughtful people you are. Then you hurl your caps in the air, hug your friends, let your parents take lots pictures of you—post them on Instagram, just one idea—and head off into your amazing lives...maybe swinging by Sharkey's for one last plate of wings before you go.

Today's going to be a little bit different because I'm not going to talk about something I know and you don't. I want to talk about something the Virginia Tech community knows all too well.

Today, I want to talk about resilience.

This university is known for so many things. Your kindness

---

[2]Defense Advanced Research Project Agency (DARPA) is a US Department of Defense agency that facilitates research in technology for national security.

and decency. Your academic excellence. Your deeply felt school spirit. I've spent a lot of time at colleges—yes for work, but also because I might want to relive my 20s just a little.

Few people talk about their school the way Hokies talk about Virginia Tech. There is so much pride and unity here. Such a deep sense of identity, and I am going to prove it by asking you one simple question: What's a Hokie? [I am!]

That's it! What you might not realize is that that Hokie spirit has made all of you more resilient. I've spent the last two years studying resilience because something happened in my life that demanded more of it than I ever would have thought possible.

Two years and eleven days ago, I lost my husband, Dave, suddenly and unexpectedly. Sometimes I still have a hard time saying the words because I can't quite believe it actually happened. I woke up on what I thought would be a totally normal day. And my world just changed forever.

I know, important day—it's raining, and I'm up here talking about death. But I promise you there's a reason—and even one that's not even sad.

Because what I've learned since losing Dave has fundamentally changed how I view this world and how I live in it. And I want to share it with you on this day because I think it's going to help you lead happier, healthier and more joyful lives. And you deserve all of that.

Each of you walked a very unique path to reach this day. Some of you faced real trauma. All of you faced challenges, disappointment, heartache, loss, illness—all of these are so personal when they strike, but they are also so universal.

And then there are the shared losses. The Virginia Tech community knows this. You've stopped for a quiet moment by the thirty-two Hokie stones on the Drillfield, as I did with President Sands just this morning. You've joined your friends for the 'Run in Remembrance'. You know that life can turn in an instant. And you know what it means to come together, to pull together, to grieve together, but, ultimately, to overcome together.

After Dave died, I did something I've done at other hard times in my life: I hit the books. With my friend Adam Grant, a psychologist who studies how we find meaning in our lives, I dove into the research on resilience and recovery.

The most important thing I learned is that we are not born with a certain amount of resilience. It is a muscle, and that means we can build it.

We build resilience into ourselves. We build resilience into the people we love. And we build it together, as a community. That's called 'collective resilience'. It's an incredibly powerful force—and it's one that our country and our world need a lot more of right about now. It is in our relationships with each other that we find our will to live, our capacity to love and our ability to bring change into this world.

Class of 2017, you are particularly suited to the task of building collective resilience because you are graduating from Virginia Tech. Communities like this don't just happen. They are formed and strengthened by people coming together in very specific ways. You've been part of that here, whether you knew it or not. As you go off and become leaders—and yes, you will lead, you are destined to lead—you can make the communities you join, and the communities you form, stronger.

Here's where you start.

You can build collective resilience through shared experiences. You've had lots of those: jumping to 'Enter

Sandman'—I saw that this morning, it's incredible; enduring the walk across the Drillfield in the winter—kind of like Jon Snow at the Wall; finding new loves and then new, new loves; being there for each other through triumph and through disappointment. Every class, every meal, every all-nighter has added another strand to a vast web that connects you to each other and to Hokies everywhere.

These ties do more than connect—they support. Nearly thirty years ago, a very talented young man made it from a very underprivileged background all the way to college, but then he didn't finish. And when he dropped out, he said, 'If only I had my posse with me, I would have graduated.' That insight led an amazing woman named Deborah Bial to create The Posse Foundation, which recruits high-potential students in teams of ten to go from the same city to the same college. Posse kids have a 90 per cent graduation rate from some of the best schools in the country.

We all need our posses, especially when life puts the obstacles in our path. Out there in the world, when you leave Virginia Tech, you're going to have to build your own posse, and sometimes that's going to mean asking for help.

This was never easy for me. Before Dave died, I tried to bother people as little as possible—and yes, 'bothering people' is what I thought it was. But then my life changed and I needed my friends and family and colleagues more than I ever could have thought I would. My mom, who along with my dad is here with me today just like yours are here with you, stayed with me for the very first month, literally holding me as I cried myself to sleep. I had never felt weaker. But I learned that it takes strength to rely on others. There are times to lean in and there are times to lean on.

Building a posse also means acknowledging our friends' challenges. Before I lost Dave, if a friend was going through something hard, I would usually say I am sorry—once. And then I wouldn't bring it up again because I didn't want to remind them of their pain. Losing my husband taught me how absurd that was—you can't remind me I lost Dave. But like I had done with others, when people failed to mention it, it felt like there was a big, old elephant following me around everywhere I went.

It's not only death that ushers in the elephant. You want to completely silence a room? Say you have cancer, that your father went to jail, that you just lost your job. We retreat into silence just when we need each other the most. Now, not everyone is going to want to talk about everything all the time. But saying to a friend, 'I know you are suffering and I am here with you', can kick a very ugly elephant out of any room.

If you are in someone's posse, don't just offer to help in a generic way. Before I lost Dave, when a friend was in need, I would say, 'Is there anything I can do?' And I meant it kindly. The problem is, that question kind of shifts the burden to the person in need. And when people asked me, I didn't know how to answer the question. 'Can you make Father's Day go away?' Here's a different approach. When my friend Dan Levy's son was sick in the hospital, a friend texted him and said, 'What do you not want on a burger?' Another friend texted from the lobby and said, 'I'm in the lobby of the hospital for a hug for the next hour whether you come down or not.'

You don't have to do something huge. You don't have to wait for someone to tell you exactly what they need. And you do not have to be someone's best friend from the first grade to show up. If you are there for your friends, and let them be there for you—if you laugh together until your sides ache, if you hold each other as you cry, and maybe even bring them a burger with the wrong toppings before they ask—that won't just make you more resilient, it will help you lead a deeper and more meaningful life.

We also build collective resilience through shared narratives. That might sound light—how important can a story be? But stories are vital. They're how we explain our past and they are how we set expectations for our future. And they help us build the common understanding that creates a community in the first place.

Every time your friends tell their favourite tales, like, I don't know, when Tech beat UVA in double overtime, you strengthen your bonds to each other.

Shared narratives are critical for fighting injustice and creating social change. A few years ago, we started LeanIn. org to help work towards gender equality. Helping women and men form Lean In Circles—small groups that support each other's ambitions. There are now more than 33,000 Circles in 150 countries. But it wasn't until I lost Dave that I understood why Circles are thriving—it's because they build collective resilience.

Not long ago, I was in Beijing and I had a chance to meet with women from Lean In Circles across China. Like in a lot of places, it's not always easy to be a woman in China. If you're unmarried past age 27, you're called 'sheng nu'—a leftover woman. And I thought the word 'widow' was bad! The stigma that comes from being a leftover woman can be intense. One woman—a 36-year-old economics professor—was rejected by fifteen men because—wait for it—she was too educated! After that, her father forbade her younger sister from going to graduate school.

But more than 80,000 women have come together in Lean In Circles to create a new narrative. One Circle created a play, *The Leftover Monologues*, which celebrates being 'leftover' and tackles the topics too often unspoken, like sexual harassment, date rape and homophobia. The world told them what their stories should be, and they said, actually, we're writing a different story for ourselves. We are not leftover. We are strong and we will write our own story together.

Building collective resilience also means trying to understand how the world looks to those who have experienced it differently, because they are a different race, come from a different country, have an economic background unlike yours. We each have our own story but we can write new ones together; and that means seeing the values in each other's points of view and looking for common ground.

Anyone here a little bit anxious about your future? Not sure where the future is taking you? Sometimes me too. And you know what helps you combat that fear? A very big idea captured in a very tiny word: Hope.

There are many kinds of hope. There's the hope that she wouldn't swipe left. Sorry. There's the hope that as you sit here your stuff will magically pack itself. Sorry. There's the hope that it would stop raining. Double sorry. But my favourite kind of hope is called grounded hope—the understanding that if you take action you can make things better.

We normally think of hope as something that's held in individual people. But hope, like resilience, is something we grow and nurture together. Just two days ago, I visited Mother Emanuel church in Charleston. We all know about the shooting that took place there just two years ago, claiming the lives of a pastor and eight worshippers. What happened afterwards was extraordinary. Instead of being consumed by hatred, the community came together to stand against racism and violence. As a local pastor, Jermaine Watkins, beautifully put it: 'To hatred, we say no way, not today. To division, we say no way, not today. And to loss of hope, we say no way, not today.'

That was the theme of maybe the most touching Facebook post I've ever read—and let's face it, I've read a lot of Facebook posts. This one was written by Antoine Leiris, a journalist in Paris whose wife Hélène was killed in the 2015 Paris attacks. Two days later—two days—he wrote an open letter to his wife's killers: 'On Friday night, you stole the life of an exceptional being, the love of my life, the mother of my son. But you will not have my hate. My 17-month-old son will play as we do every day, and all his life this little boy will defy you by being happy and free. Because you will not have his hate either.'

Strength like that makes all of us who see it stronger. Hope like that makes all of us more hopeful. That's how collective resilience works. We lift each other up. This might seem very intuitive to you Hokies because these qualities of collective resilience—shared experiences, shared narratives and shared hope—shine forth from every corner of this university. You are a testament to courage, faith and love. And that's been true, not just for these past ten years, but for over a century before then. This university means a lot to you, graduates, but it also means a lot to America and to the world. So many of us look to you as an example of how to stay strong and brave and true.

This is your legacy, Class of 2017. You will carry it with you—that capacity for finding strength in yourselves and building strength in the people around you.

Virginia Tech has given you a purpose, reflected in your motto, 'That I May Serve'. An important way you can serve and lead is by helping build resilience in the world. We have a responsibility to help families and communities become more resilient, because none of us get through anything alone. We get through it together.

As you leave this beautiful campus and set out into the world, build resilience in yourselves. When tragedy or disappointment strikes, know that deep inside you, you have the ability to get through anything. I promise you do. As the saying goes, we are more vulnerable than we ever thought, but we are stronger than we ever imagined.

Build resilient organizations. Speak up when you see injustice. Lend your time and your passion to the causes that matter. My favourite poster at Facebook reads, 'Nothing at Facebook is someone else's problem'. When you see something that's broken and there is a lot that is broken out there, go fix it. Your motto demands that you do.

Build resilient communities. Virginia Tech founded the Global Forum on Resilience four years ago, and it's doing outstanding work in this field. Be there for your friends and family. And I mean in person, not just in a message with a heart emoji—even though those are pretty great too. Be there for your neighbours; it's a divided time in our country, and we need you to help us heal. Lift each other up and celebrate each and every moment of joy. Because one of the most important ways you can build resilience is by cultivating gratitude.

Two years ago, if someone had told me that I would lose the love of my life and become more grateful, I would have never have believed them. But that's what happened. Because today I am more grateful now than I ever was before—for my family and especially my children. For my friends. For my work. For life itself.

A few months ago, my cousin, Laura, turned 50. Graduates, you may not appreciate that turning 50 happens soon and feels old, but your parents do. I called her that morning and I said, 'Happy Birthday, Laura. But I am also calling to say in case you woke up this morning with that "Oh my God, I'm 50" thing. Don't do that. This is the year Dave doesn't turn 50.' Either we get older, or we don't. No more jokes about growing old. Every year, every moment—even in the pouring rain—is an absolute gift.

You don't have to wait for special occasions, like graduation, to feel and show your gratitude to your family, your friends, your professors, your baristas—everyone. Counting your blessings increases them. People who take the time to focus on the things they are grateful for are happier and healthier.

My New Year's resolution last year was to write down three moments of joy before I went to bed each night. This very simple thing has changed my life. Because I realize I used to go to bed every night thinking about what I did wrong and what I was going to do wrong the next day. Now I go to sleep thinking of what went right. And when those moments of joy happen throughout the day, I notice them more because I know they'll make the notebook. Try it. Start tonight, on this day full of happy memories—but maybe before you hit Big Al's.

Graduates, on the path before you, you will have good days and you will have hard days. Go through all of them together. Seek shared experiences with all kinds of people. Write shared narratives that create the world you want to live in. Build shared hope in the communities you join and the communities you form. And above all, find gratitude for the gift of life itself and the opportunities it provides for meaning, for joy and for love.

Tonight, when I write down my three moments of joy, I will write about this. About the hope and the amazing resilience of this community. And maybe you'll write that I finally stopped talking.

You have the whole world in front of you. I cannot wait to see what you do with it.

Congratulations and go Hokies!

♦

19

John McCain
United States Senator

Let's leave the history of who shot first to the historians.[*]

This speech was delivered by Senator John McCain after his recuperation from brain cancer. On 25 July 2017, the 80-year-old Arizona Republican took the floor with a scar above his left brow and some bruising underneath his eye. As McCain entered the Senate to vote, senators on both sides of the aisle rose in a standing ovation.

Mr President:

I've stood in this place many times and addressed as president many presiding officers. I have been so addressed when I have sat in that chair, as close as I will ever be to a presidency.

---

*Source: US Federal Government

It is an honorific we're almost indifferent to, isn't it. In truth, presiding over the Senate can be a nuisance, a bit of a ceremonial bore, and it is usually relegated to the more junior members of the majority.

But as I stand here today—looking a little worse for wear I'm sure—I have a refreshed appreciation for the protocols and customs of this body, and for the other ninety-nine privileged souls who have been elected to this Senate.

I have been a member of the United States Senate for thirty years. I had another long, if not as long, career before I arrived here, another profession that was profoundly rewarding, and in which I had experiences and friendships that I revere. But make no mistake, my service here is the most important job I have had in my life. And I am so grateful to the people of Arizona for the privilege—for the honour—of serving here and the opportunities it gives me to play a small role in the history of the country I love.

I've known and admired men and women in the Senate who played much more than a small role in our history, true statesmen, giants of American politics. They came from both parties, and from various backgrounds. Their ambitions were frequently in conflict. They held different views on the issues of the day. And they often had very serious disagreements about how best to serve the national interest.

But they knew that however sharp and heartfelt their disputes, however keen their ambitions, they had an obligation to work collaboratively to ensure the Senate discharged its constitutional responsibilities effectively. Our responsibilities are important, vitally important, to the continued success of our Republic. And our arcane rules and customs are deliberately intended to require broad cooperation to function well at all.

The most revered members of this institution accepted the necessity of compromise in order to make incremental progress on solving America's problems and to defend her from her adversaries.

That principled mindset, and the service of our predecessors who possessed it, come to mind when I hear the Senate referred to as the world's greatest deliberative body. I'm not sure we can claim that distinction with a straight face today.

I'm sure it wasn't always deserved in previous eras either. But I'm sure there have been times when it was, and I was privileged to witness some of those occasions.

Our deliberations today, not just our debates, but the exercise of all our responsibilities—authorizing government policies, appropriating the funds to implement them, exercising our advice and consent role—are often lively and interesting. They can be sincere and principled. But they are more partisan, more tribal, more of the time than any other time I remember. Our deliberations can still be important and useful, but I think we'd all agree they haven't been overburdened by greatness lately. And right now they aren't producing much for the American people.

Both sides have let this happen. Let's leave the history of who shot first to the historians. I suspect they'll find we all conspired in our decline—either by deliberate actions or neglect. We've all played some role in it. Certainly I have. Sometimes, I've let my passion rule my reason. Sometimes, I made it harder to find common ground because of something harsh I said to a colleague. Sometimes, I wanted to win more for the sake of winning than to achieve a contested policy.

Incremental progress, compromises that each side criticize but also accept, just plain muddling through to chip away at problems and keep our enemies from doing their worst isn't glamorous or exciting. It doesn't feel like a political triumph. But it's usually the most we can expect from our system of government, operating in a country as diverse and quarrelsome and free as ours.

Considering the injustice and cruelties inflicted by autocratic governments, and how corruptible human nature can be, the problem-solving our system does make possible, the fitful progress it produces and the liberty and justice it preserves, is a magnificent achievement.

Our system doesn't depend on our nobility. It accounts for our imperfections and gives an order to our individual strivings that have helped make ours the most powerful and prosperous society on earth. It is our responsibility to preserve that, even when it requires us to do something less satisfying than 'winning'. Even when we must give a little to get a little. Even when our efforts manage just three yards and a cloud of dust, while critics on both sides denounce us for timidity, for our failure to 'triumph'.

I hope we can again rely on humility, on our need to cooperate, on our dependence on each other to learn how to trust each other again, and by so doing better serve the people who elected us. Stop listening to the bombastic loudmouths on the radio and television and the Internet. To hell with them. They don't want anything done for the public good. Our incapacity is their livelihood.

Let's trust each other. Let's return to regular order. We've been spinning our wheels on too many important issues because we keep trying to find a way to win without help from across the aisle. That's an approach that's been employed by both sides, mandating legislation from the top down, without any support from the other side, with all the parliamentary manoeuvres that requires.

We're getting nothing done. All we've really done this year is confirm Neil Gorsuch to the Supreme Court. Our healthcare insurance system is a mess. We all know it, those who support Obamacare and those who oppose it. Something has to be done. We Republicans have looked for a way to end it and replace it with something else without paying a terrible political price. We haven't found it yet, and I'm not sure we will. All we've managed to do is make more popular a policy that wasn't very popular when we started trying to get rid of it.

I voted for the motion to proceed to allow debate to continue and amendments to be offered. I will not vote for the bill as it is today. It's a shell of a bill right now. We all know that. I have changes urged by my state's governor that will have to be included to earn my support for final passage of any bill. I know many of you will have to see the bill changed substantially for you to support it.

We've tried to do this by coming up with a proposal behind closed doors in consultation with the administration, then springing it on sceptical members, trying to convince them it's better than nothing, asking us to swallow our doubts and force it past a unified opposition. I don't think that is going to work in the end. And it probably shouldn't.

The Obama administration and congressional Democrats shouldn't have forced through Congress without any opposition support a social and economic change as massive as Obamacare. And we shouldn't do the same with ours.

Why don't we try the old way of legislating in the Senate, the way our rules and customs encourage us to act. If this process ends in failure, which seem likely, then let's return to regular order.

Let the Health, Education, Labor, and Pensions Committee under Chairman [Lamar] Alexander and Ranking Member [Patty] Murray hold hearings, try to report a bill out of committee with contributions from both sides. Then bring it to the floor for amendment and debate, and see if we can pass something that will be imperfect, full of compromises and not very pleasing to implacable partisans on either side, but that might provide workable solutions to problems [that] Americans are struggling with today.

What have we to lose by trying to work together to find those solutions? We're not getting much done apart. I don't think any of us feels very proud of our incapacity. Merely preventing your political opponents from doing what they want isn't the most inspiring work. There's greater satisfaction in respecting our differences, but not letting them prevent agreements that don't require abandonment of core principles, agreements made in good faith that help improve lives and protect the American people.

The Senate is capable of that. We know that. We've seen it before. I've seen it happen many times. And the times when I was involved even in a modest way with working out a bipartisan response to a national problem or threat are the proudest moments of my career, and by far the most satisfying.

This place is important. The work we do is important. Our strange rules and seemingly eccentric practices that slow our proceedings and insist on our cooperation are important. Our founders envisioned the Senate as the more deliberative, careful body that operates at a greater distance than the other body from the public passions of the hour.

We are an important check on the powers of the Executive. Our consent is necessary for the President to appoint jurists and powerful government officials and in many respects to conduct foreign policy. Whether or not we are of the same party, we are not the President's subordinates. We are his equal!

As his responsibilities are onerous, many and powerful, so are ours. And we play a vital role in shaping and directing the judiciary, the military and the cabinet, in planning and supporting foreign and domestic policies. Our success in meeting all these awesome constitutional obligations depends on cooperation among ourselves.

The success of the Senate is important to the continued success of America. This country—this big, boisterous, brawling, intemperate, restless, striving, daring, beautiful, bountiful, brave, good and magnificent country—needs us to help it thrive. That responsibility is more important than any of our personal interests or political affiliations.

We are the servants of a great nation, 'a nation conceived in liberty and dedicated to the proposition that all men are created equal'. More people have lived free and prosperous lives here than in any other nation. We have acquired unprecedented wealth and power because of our governing principles, and because our government defended those principles.

America has made a greater contribution than any other nation to an international order that has liberated more people from tyranny and poverty than ever before in history. We have been the greatest example, the greatest supporter and the greatest defender of that order. We aren't afraid. We don't covet other people's land and wealth. We don't hide behind walls. We breach them. We are a blessing to humanity.

What greater cause could we hope to serve than helping

keep America the strong, aspiring, inspirational beacon of liberty and defender of the dignity of all human beings and their right to freedom and equal justice? That is the cause that binds us and is so much more powerful and worthy than the small differences that divide us.

What a great honour and extraordinary opportunity it is to serve in this body.

It's a privilege to serve with all of you. I mean it. Many of you have reached out in the last few days with your concern and your prayers, and it means a lot to me. It really does. I've had so many people say such nice things about me recently that I think some of you must have me confused with someone else. I appreciate it though, every word, even if much of it isn't deserved.

I'll be here for a few days, I hope managing the floor debate on the defense authorization bill, which, I'm proud to say is again a product of bipartisan cooperation and trust among the members of the Senate Armed Services Committee.

After that, I'm going home for a while to treat my illness. I have every intention of returning here and giving many of you cause to regret all the nice things you said about me. And, I hope, to impress on you again that it is an honour to serve the American people in your company.

Thank you, fellow senators.

Mr President, I yield the floor.

◆

20

Joe Biden
Vice President of the United States of America
(2009–2017)

Globalization has cost some of them their livelihood. As your President can tell you.[*]

This speech was delivered at Cornell University Convocation on 27 May 2017.

Thank you. Thank you. Thank you. Thank you very much. Thank you. Thank you.

Madam president, standing here in this field my first words that come to mind are: 'Put me in coach I'm ready to play.' What a great, great, great, great university. And congratulations madam president on your impending inauguration. And I hope they've warned you about selfies.

---

[*]Permission for the transcript taken from The Ithaca Voice.

And I want to say to my mom who's looking down and to the moms here, I did offer Lauren [Lang][1] my coat. She's got goosebumps but she wouldn't take my coat. But I did offer. My mother would kill me had I not. Y'all think I'm kidding. I'm not kidding.

And I want to, I want to thank the senior class and the convocation committee for inviting me to speak here today. I am truly, and I mean this sincerely, I'm honoured, I'm honoured to be asked.

I have loved Cornell. Cornell is one of the great, great universities in the world. And I want you to know that there are three great ones—they're all land grant schools—MIT, Cornell and Delaware. And we're all land grant schools.

I almost came here for law school, but I couldn't get enough financial aid and so I—y'all think I'm kidding. I'm not, but I—part of that was I barely got in. So I ended up going to Syracuse University. Everybody thinks I went because they gave me a full scholarship, which they did. That's not the reason. I went to Syracuse because they get more snow than you get here off the lake.

And I married a Skaneateles girl. I think this is, when the sun is shining, the most beautiful part of the world. She lived on Skaneateles Lake, and I, I really do.

And I got a chance to talk to some of the Cornell grads, soon to be grads, beforehand.

I, madam president and I...I tell you what, this child [Lang] is going to end up, I told her when she's President of the United States and I bring my great grandchildren by and they say that Joe Biden is in the waiting room, I don't want her to

---

[1]Students Lauren Lang and Matthew Baumel were part of the ceremony.

say, 'Joe who?' That's the only promise I ask for her.

And Chuy [Matthew Baumel], I can tell you something man, you're never getting rid of that nickname. You can go to Wall Street, you can go to Japan, you can go to China [...] you're going to be Chuy and people are going to be proud to know you. They're going to be proud to know you.

I also got a chance to meet Rebecca Schwartz, your valedictorian of your comms department who was in the line, and I'm sure there's a lot of other people, if I get [a] chance I'd like to meet as well, who are graduating.

You guys are a truly impressive group. Ladies and gentlemen, but I gotta admit to you the real reason I came today: I love ice cream.

I'm the only Irishman you guys know who's never had a drink and loves ice cream. And your dean of the school of agriculture told me that this is the best ice cream because y'all have the smartest cows up here. So good to see you Big Red. It's good to be here.

To all the family members and loved ones in the audience, particularly the moms and dads, congratulations you all get a pay raise today. No more undergraduate tuition. Look at it that way man. Look at it that way.

And I'm going to tell you something you think is corny, but I mean it. All you graduates, stand up and give your parents a round of applause and thank them. Thank them for what they've done for you.

But I don't know man, do you guys know what your kids have been doing up here? You know what the most popular course on this campus is? Wines. Wines. Pass, fail. Wines.

I don't know about that man, I...I hope some of you forgive me. I was, a couple days ago, I was speaking at another one of your Ivy League rivals earlier this week. I hope you don't hold it against me. And I hope you sure and hell don't throw any fish at me.

I know you know the school. It's that safety school. At least that's what my son at Yale and my son and daughter at Penn called it.

I...I tell you what, how many opposing goalies have the Lynah[2] faithful tormented over all the years here. I mean you guys are tough, man. I married a Philadelphia girl. They are the meanest, smartest, lousiest fans in the world.

But throwing fish at them, that's, I tell you, you all are good, man. You all are good. I tell you the Philadelphia Flyers would love you. They'd love you.

It's amazing what all of you all that snow has done to your temperament. As I said, I understand snow. I understand it's the first time you've had what, three, four snow days in fifteen years or so or a long time. I just want you all to know, they didn't do that for you. They did that for your professors.

Look, it's, it's time to celebrate. No more prelims. You're about to graduate.

And God knows I know you'll miss Olin Library. I know you'll miss it badly but except maybe for the two guys I saw as I flew over Lake Cayuga as I landed here, trying to pass their swimming test.

I hope to hell you fish them out, you know, this is...Cornell is a great place. It's one of the most beautiful campuses, I think, in the entire country and I've been on hundreds literally over the last forty years and I hope it's been full of great memories for you.

---

[2]Lynah Rink is the ice hockey arena at Cornell University.

I hope this last week you've spent some time reliving some of the great memories you've had [in] the last four years. Your last trip to the CTB. Your last scoop at the Dairy Bar. Maybe a tray ride down the Libe slope. I hope to hell you didn't try it this year in the spring, but some of you probably did.

The friends you've made here are likely to be with you for the rest of your life. They're people you're going to be able to look to, so hold on tight to the memories you have here. This has been a wonderful trip for the vast majority of you.

No graduating class gets to choose the world into which they graduate. Tomorrow, when you walk across the stage to receive your diploma, you're going to enter a world where there are a lot of Americans uncertain and anxious about their futures.

Globalization has cost some of them their livelihood. As your President can tell you. Digitalization, Moore's law, artificial intelligence, with overwhelming significant promise, are also generating great anxiety among the great working middle-class of this country.

Some communities are struggling to get by and they're worried that they won't be able to keep up. And we saw how playing to their fears rather than their hopes, rather than their better angels, can still be a powerful political tool.

As I said several times this commencement season, this past election cycle churned up some of the ugliest realities that still remain in this country. Civilized discourse and real debate gave way to some of the coarsest rhetoric, stroking our darkest emotions.

I thought we had passed the days when it was acceptable for political leaders at local and national levels to bestow legitimacy to hate speak and fringe ideologies. But the world is changing so rapidly. There are a lot of folks out there who are both afraid and susceptible to this kind of negative appeal.

We saw the forces of populism, not only here but around the word, call to close our nation's gates against the challenges of a rapidly changing world. The immigrant, the minority, the transgender—anyone not like me became a scapegoat.

'Just build a wall. Keep Muslims from coming into the United States. They're the reason I can't compete. That's why I don't have a job. That's why I worry about my safety.'

And imagine, I imagine, like me, many of you seeing this unfold was incredibly disorienting and disheartening. Your reaction, you graduates in particular, is understandable.

But I assure you that this is a temporary state of affairs. The American people will not sustain this attitude for long. I promise you.

And the moment like this, it's more important than ever that we get back to basics. That we hold fast to what has always made America great and unique.

To me, at its basic, it's down to a simple idea: That every single person is entitled to be treated with dignity and respect. It's in our DNA. It's in the fabric of our Declaration and our Constitution. It sounds corny but we do hold these truths, self-evident that all men and women are created equal. It's the uniting feature of what makes us who we are.

You cannot define an American based on ethnicity, religion, race. America is an idea. That's the uniqueness of who we are and it's embodied in what we say we believe.

Even when we haven't live[d] up to our ideals, dignity has been part of our national ethic because we know that if people are treated with respect, if we equip them with care—the capability to care for their families—to maintain their dignity, it's harder for the politics of fear to find a home.

For when a person is stripped of their dignity, they lose hope.

My dad, who moved from Scranton because the job he had in the mid-50s wasn't enough to take care of the family...set up in Delaware and was able to take care of us again. Every time he'd hear someone [had] lost their job, my dad would look at me and say, 'Joey—and I mean this sincerely, my word as a Biden—Joey, a job is about a lot more than a paycheck. It's about your dignity. It's about respect. It's about your place in the community. It's about being able to look your child in the eye and say, "Honey it's going to be okay."' It's that basic.

Your parents can tell you. The single most helpless thing a parent can face is looking in the eyes of their child with an enormous opportunity or a significant problem and know there's nothing they can do to help.

Look folks, the American people aren't looking for a hand out. They're not looking for government to solve their problems. But at a minimum they expect their government to understand their problems. Just understand their problems.

And it helps when this generation that's emerging reaches out because all this is personal and tries to understand, understand the people you're dealing with, understand their problems.

It's an awful lot harder to dislike someone when you know their dad is dying of prostate cancer or they have a brother with a drug problem. Or they just lost their mom. You may fundamentally disagree with them, but it's hard to dislike them. It's hard to question motive. And that's all we do today—is question motive. And when you do that you can never get to a resolution.

If I say your motive is that you are in the pocket of this or you are unethical about that, it's awful hard to reach a consensus, and you can't govern this country without consensus.

It's the way we talk to one another, the way we act towards one another that really matters. You don't need years of experience or even an Ivy League degree to put this into practice.

It's pretty basic stuff.

Everything, from your marriage, to your job, to your neighbourhood, to your country, works better when we actually take time to look out for the other guy. Just treat them with a little bit of dignity and decency in our neighbourhoods, as well as our national institutions.

Everything works better when we honour that uniquely American, uniquely egalitarian ideal: Access to opportunity and recognize that everyone [is] entitled to be treated with dignity. It's not that complicated.

I believe from that uniquely American perspective sprung this outstanding university: 'I would found an institution where any person, any person could find instruction in any study.'

Cornell wasn't just talking about white men. He wasn't just talking about those born in the United States, not just the wealthy. He was talking about any person with the desire, the drive and the capacity to excel. And Ezra Cornell meant what he said.

His response to a letter he received asking if a young black man could enrol was unequivocal: 'Send him. Send him. Send him.'

And look what's been sent.

Who knows? They may be the next Ruth Bader Ginsburg

or the next Janet Reno or the next Edmund Muskie or Gabby Giffords, who I'll see in two days. The next Toni Morrison, Kurt Vonnegut. The next Mae Jemison or even, or even, Bill Nye the Science Guy.

But really and truly think about it. And by the way so can you can be. So can you, the graduating class be. I hope you know that in no uncertain terms.

I know you expect graduation speakers to tell you what you're capable of and give you advice. I don't have a lot of advice, but I tell you what, I know one thing: the people I know who are successful and happy are the people who treat others with the same dignity that they demand for themselves.

To do that...to do that, you're going to have to fight the urge to build a self-referential, self-reinforcing and self-righteous echo chamber of yourself online. No, I mean this, I mean this sincerely. Living in your screens encourages shallow and antiseptic relationships that make it too easy to reduce the other...to reduce the other...to stereotypes.

They're not flattened versions of humanity. They're not flattened versions...faster... They're a whole person, flawed, struggling to make the world better just like you. To make it in the world just like you. And you have to ascribe to those with whom you disagree the same emotional complexity you know yourself and that you possess.

At the end of the day, for a person to be afforded dignity, there must be an absolute intolerance of the abuse of power. My father had another expression...he really did. He said, 'Joey, the greatest sin you can commit is the abuse of power, whether it's economic manipulation, social manipulation or physical intimidation.'

Everybody always asks why did I write the Violence

Against Women Act. Was my mother abused, was my…no. My father, my father was a gentle man but he said the cardinal sin of all sins was to raise your hand to a child or to a woman. That's what ignited my political passion throughout my life.

When I was a high school kid and a college kid in Delaware, I got involved with the civil right[s] movement because my state was still struggling. That's why I joined the environmental movement as I ran to push back companies polluting the Delaware River and our bay, and I ran for United States Senate.

That's why I got criticized, but I make no apologies for looking at the president of a country named Slobodan Milošević and he asked what do you think of me and I said, 'I think you're a damn war criminal, and I will spend the rest of my life seeing you tried as one.'

That's why I wrote and worked to pass the Violence Against Women Act. Because look, if you can't be free from physical abuse, the ability to reach the capacity that you have is diminished in a significant way.

Today, today we're on a verge—in my view—of being able to fundamentally change the culture in this country—to fundamentally change the culture.

The press always asks me, 'When will you know you've succeeded?'

I've succeed[ed] when not one single woman who is abused ever ask themselves: 'What did I do?' Not one single woman ever ask[s]: 'What did I do?'

And so folks…folks, you know as you go into the world you're going to have an enormous amount of pressure, temptations along the way to rationalize and to make choices that other people want you to make.

And as you move through life, you may notice yourself

slipping into a bubble that prioritizes social trappings of success rather than doing what you know is right, what you feel in your heart is what you should do.

Take this job, live in this place, hang out with people just like me, take no real risk and have no real impact. Living a life of dignity is going to require more than just watching out for your success. It's going to require...you can't erect a bubble around you and your family.

This degree won't protect you from the pressures of a changing world. And don't fool yourself into thinking that disengaging from the system that you believe is broken is going to hold you harmless from its failures. What happens in your country, your community, your neighbourhood affects you.

If the nation is permanently riddled with as much income inequity today as it is and unable to create good middle-class paying jobs in an age of artificial intelligence and automation, you're not going to thrive economically either.

If you sister is the victim of domestic violence, you are violated. If your brother can't marry the man he loves, you are lessened. If your best friend...if your best friend has to worry about being profiled racially, you live in a circumstance unworthy of us. If the global rules that undermine our security for the last seventy years break down, we'll all be less free. We'll all be less safe. If the air we breathe is not clean, the water we drink is not pure, there's no way for you to hide. There's no way to hide.

You are the most engaged, tolerant, talented and technologically advanced generation in the history of the United States of America. But none of that will matter very much if you don't engage in public affairs. I'm not saying you all have to go out and run for office.

A recent study done by Harvard Kennedy School of the millennial generation shows it's the most engaged, tolerant, et cetera. But it also shows something else.

Fifty eight per cent say [that they] know what happens in public affairs can fundamentally affect their lives but only 7 per cent of the women, only 9 per cent of the whole population thinks they are going to get engaged at all. You have a responsibility to engage and incredible opportunity, as well, when you do.

It's only in moments of great change and upheaval, moments like this, you have a chance to actually bend history just a little bit to the way you want the nation to be. I know that sounds like a tall order. But sometimes perspective can be helpful.

I remember sitting not far from here, where you are today, on Syracuse University's campus on their football field in June of 1968. I was graduating from law school. As we began our semester, we were certain that the war in Vietnam was about to end and we wouldn't all have to go. But then the Viet Cong launched the Tet Offensive[3] in an effort to end the war in one seismic, two-day assault.

Two days into the offensive, a bullet fired in streets of Saigon by a Vietnam police officer went into [the] skull of a handcuffed Vietnam soldier and a photographer captured that mayhem. That one bullet not only pierced that soldier's skull, it pierced America's consciousness. Even those of you graduating today probably have seen that iconic photo all these years later.

---

[3]Vietnam War (1954–75): A conflict that pitted the communist government of North Vietnam and its allies in South Vietnam (Viet Cong) against the government in South and its main ally, the US that was concerned over the possible spread of communism in Southeast Asia.

Viet Cong or Vietnamese Communists was the guerrilla force in the South; Tet Offensive were attacks staged on 31 January 1968 against cities in South Vietnam.

It brought home to everybody in my generation that there was no light at the end of the tunnel. That the comedian Lenny Bruce was right when he would say, 'It's a freight train.'

Peaceful anti-war demonstrations turned violent all across America and the violence in Vietnam exploded. That year alone…17,000 of my generation died that year alone in Vietnam.

Shortly after that, Lyndon Baines Johnson, who coveted the presidency, announced he would not seek re-election.

In April, Dr King[4] was assassinated—a major political icon, a moral compass for the country—gunned down on a balcony in Memphis.

Cities, including my home town of Wilmington, went up in flames. My city was the only city since Reconstruction [that was] occupied by National Guard with drawn bayonets on every corner for nine months.

And in June when I walked across that stage, my only political hero of my life, Robert Kennedy, was gunned down in a hotel in California after winning the primary and becoming the de facto nominee for president. I can remember my colleagues and I looking at each other as we graduated thinking, 'How could this be happening?'

But in spite of it all, I never doubted for one instant that we could rewrite the outcome we were careening towards. We got involved. We turned our anger and disappointment into resolve, and I would argue, into positive change.

Four years later, after I walked off that stage, I was being sworn in as a United States Senator determined to end the war in Vietnam. Not long after that, I sat across from President

---

[4]Dr Martin Luther King Jr., who led the civil rights movement in the US, was assassinated on 4 April 1968.

Ford[5] as a Freshman senator—the youngest person in the room—as they explained finally with Secretary Schlesinger and Kissinger[6] the plan to end the war in Vietnam.

Five weeks later the rooftop at the embassy at Saigon was evacuating people and the war was over.

So ladies and gentleman, graduating seniors, never doubt your capacity to make a difference. There's no reason why you and your generation and the class of '17 can't have a similar and more profound impact on this country than my generation did. And I mean it.

As I said, you're the most tolerant, talented, engaged generation in American history. You have better tools to tackle the challenges that lie ahead than my generation did.

There's more power in that cell phone you have in your pocket or purse than the computer that put the man on the moon; 3-D printers are restoring tissue after traumatic injury; scientists are racing to figure out how to print human organs for transplant; technology—technology is there to fight climate change. Cornell scientists are figuring to suppress the growth of brain cancer by inhibiting the ability to recruit other cells into a deadly malignancy.

So make no mistake about it, we're going to be able to end the scourge of cancer and do so much more. There's so many opportunities. I'm so optimistic about your generation and I'm optimistic about this country. The United States has ever been better positioned to lead the world than we are at this moment.

We have the most productive workers in the world, three

---

[5]Gerald Ford served as the 38th President of the United States of America from 1974–77.
[6]James Schlesinger and Henry Kissinger served as Secretary of Defence and Secretary of State, respectively, under President Ford's administration.

times [more] productive than in Asia. The most agile venture capitalist system in the world; the greatest research universities in the world—thanks to Dwight Eisenhower. We have more great research universities in America than the rest of the world combined, and that's not hyperbole. And we're at the epicentre of energy in this new century.

And like I said folks, I've met every major world leader. I know every one of them leading their country now in a major country. I've spent more time with President Xi [Biden may have been talking about Chinese President Xi Jinping], for example, than any world leader. I've had twenty-five hours of private dinners with him. I've not met a single leader who wouldn't change places with the President of the United States in a heartbeat, in a heartbeat.

We have problems, but my God.

And I'm so tired of both political parties. I'm so tired of the incrementalism. I'm so tired of thinking small. When has America ever thought small? We never have. It's time for America to get up. It's time to regain our sense of unity and purpose and remember who we are.

With all the brainpower and energy I see in front of me, I know that nothing and no one in this world can beat us. And we want these other nations to do well, but God, the idea that we are somehow behind the eight ball...it's time for the country to wake up.

And ladies and gentlemen, the graduating class of '17, go out and wake us up.

God bless us all. May God protect our troops and give my regard to Davy.

◆

Donald Trump

President of the United States of America

A new national pride is sweeping across our nation.*

Joint Address to the Congress on 28 February 2017.

Thank you very much. Mr Speaker, Mr Vice President, members of Congress, the First Lady of the United States and citizens of America:

Tonight, as we mark the conclusion of our celebration of Black History Month, we are reminded of our nation's path towards civil rights and the work that still remains to be done. Recent threats targeting Jewish community centres and vandalism of Jewish cemeteries, as well as last week's shooting in Kansas City, remind us that while we may be a nation

---

*Source: White House website

divided on policies, we are a country that stands united in condemning hate and evil in all of its very ugly forms.

Each American generation passes the torch of truth, liberty and justice in an unbroken chain all the way down to the present. That torch is now in our hands. And we will use it to light up the world. I am here tonight to deliver a message of unity and strength, and it is a message deeply delivered from my heart. A new chapter of American Greatness is now beginning. A new national pride is sweeping across our nation. And a new surge of optimism is placing impossible dreams firmly within our grasp.

What we are witnessing today is the renewal of the American spirit. Our allies will find that America is once again ready to lead. All the nations of the world—friend or foe—will find that America is strong, America is proud and America is free.

In nine years, the United States will celebrate the 250th anniversary of our founding—250 years since the day we declared our independence. It will be one of the great milestones in the history of the world. But what will America look like as we reach our 250th year? What kind of country will we leave for our children?

I will not allow the mistakes of recent decades past to define the course of our future. For too long, we've watched our middle-class shrink as we've exported our jobs and wealth to foreign countries. We've financed and built one global project after another, but ignored the fates of our children in the inner cities of Chicago, Baltimore, Detroit and so many other places throughout our land.

We've defended the borders of other nations while leaving our own borders wide open for anyone to cross and for drugs to pour in at a now unprecedented rate. And we've spent trillions and trillions of dollars overseas, while our infrastructure at home has so badly crumbled.

Then, in 2016, the earth shifted beneath our feet. The rebellion started as a quiet protest, spoken by families of all colours and creeds—families who just wanted a fair shot for their children and a fair hearing for their concerns.

But then the quiet voices became a loud chorus as thousands of citizens now spoke out together, from cities small and large, all across our country. Finally, the chorus became an earthquake, and the people turned out by the tens of millions, and they were all united by one very simple, but crucial demand: That America must put its own citizens first. Because only then can we truly make America great again.

Dying industries will come roaring back to life. Heroic veterans will get the care they so desperately need. Our military will be given the resources its brave warriors so richly deserve. Crumbling infrastructure will be replaced with new roads, bridges, tunnels, airports and railways gleaming across our very, very beautiful land. Our terrible drug epidemic will slow down and, ultimately, stop. And our neglected inner cities will see a rebirth of hope, safety and opportunity. Above all else, we will keep our promises to the American people.

It's been a little over a month since my inauguration, and I want to take this moment to update the nation on the progress I've made in keeping those promises.

Since my election, Ford, Fiat Chrysler, General Motors, Sprint, SoftBank, Lockheed, Intel, Walmart and many others have announced that they will invest billions and billions of dollars in the United States, and will create tens of thousands of new American jobs.

The stock market has gained almost $3 trillion in value since the election on November 8th—a record. We've saved taxpayers hundreds of millions of dollars by bringing down the price of a fantastic—and it is fantastic—new F-35 jet fighter, and we'll be saving billions more on contracts all across our government. We have placed a hiring freeze on non-military and non-essential federal workers.

We have begun to drain the swamp of government corruption by imposing a five-year ban on lobbying by executive branch officials and a lifetime ban [...] and a lifetime ban on becoming lobbyists for a foreign government.

We have undertaken a historic effort to massively reduce job-crushing regulations, creating a deregulation task force inside of every government agency. And we're imposing a new rule which mandates that for every one new regulation, two old regulations must be eliminated. We're going to stop the regulations that threaten the future and livelihood of our great coal miners.

We have cleared the way for the construction of the Keystone and Dakota access pipelines, thereby creating tens of thousands of jobs. And I've issued a new directive that new American pipelines be made with American steel.

We have withdrawn the United States from the job-killing Trans-Pacific Partnership[1]. And with the help of Prime Minister Justin Trudeau[2], we have formed a council with our neighbours in Canada to help ensure that women entrepreneurs have access to the networks, markets and capital

---

[1]Trans-Pacific partnership was the trade accord signed by twelve countries that border the Pacific Ocean in 2016. The pact would have represented nearly 40 per cent of the world's economic output.
[2]Justin Trudeau is the Prime Minister of Canada since 2015.

they need to start a business and live out their financial dreams.

To protect our citizens, I have directed the Department of Justice to form a Task Force on Reducing Violent Crime. I have further ordered the departments of Homeland Security and Justice, along with the Department of State and the Director of National Intelligence, to coordinate an aggressive strategy to dismantle the criminal cartels that have spread all across our nation. We will stop the drugs from pouring into our country and poisoning our youth, and we will expand treatment for those who have become so badly addicted.

At the same time, my administration has answered the pleas of the American people for immigration enforcement and border security. By finally enforcing our immigration laws, we will raise wages, help the unemployed, save billions and billions of dollars, and make our communities safer for everyone. We want all Americans to succeed, but that can't happen in an environment of lawless chaos. We must restore integrity and the rule of law at our borders.

For that reason, we will soon begin the construction of a great, great wall along our southern border. As we speak tonight, we are removing gang members, drug dealers and criminals that threaten our communities and prey on our very innocent citizens. Bad ones are going out as I speak, and as I promised throughout the campaign.

To any in Congress who do not believe we should enforce our laws, I would ask you this one question: What would you say to the American family that loses their jobs, their income or their loved one because America refused to uphold its laws and defend its borders?

Our obligation is to serve, protect and defend the citizens of the United States. We are also taking strong measures to protect our nation from radical Islamic terrorism. According to data provided by the Department of Justice, the vast majority of individuals convicted of terrorism and terrorism-related offenses since 9/11 came here from outside of our country. We have seen the attacks at home—from Boston to San Bernardino to the Pentagon, and, yes, even the World Trade Center.

We have seen the attacks in France, in Belgium, in Germany and all over the world. It is not compassionate, but reckless to allow uncontrolled entry from places where proper vetting cannot occur. Those given the high honour of admission to the United States should support this country and love its people and its values. We cannot allow a beachhead of terrorism to form inside America. We cannot allow our nation to become a sanctuary for extremists.

That is why my administration has been working on improved vetting procedures, and we will shortly take new steps to keep our nation safe and to keep out those out who will do us harm.

As promised, I directed the Department of Defense to develop a plan to demolish and destroy ISIS—a network of lawless savages that have slaughtered Muslims and Christians, and men, and women and children of all faiths and all beliefs. We will work with our allies, including our friends and allies in the Muslim world, to extinguish this vile enemy from our planet.

I have also imposed new sanctions on entities and individuals who support Iran's ballistic missile programme, and reaffirmed our unbreakable alliance with the State of Israel.

Finally, I have kept my promise to appoint a Justice to the United States Supreme Court, from my list of twenty judges, who will defend our Constitution.

I am greatly honoured to have Maureen Scalia with us in the gallery tonight. Thank you, Maureen. Her late, great husband, Antonin Scalia, will forever be a symbol of American justice. To fill his seat, we have chosen Judge Neil Gorsuch, a man of incredible skill and deep devotion to the law. He was confirmed unanimously by the Court of Appeals, and I am asking the Senate to swiftly approve his nomination.

Tonight, as I outline the next steps we must take as a country, we must honestly acknowledge the circumstances we inherited. Ninety-four million Americans are out of the labour force. Over forty-three million people are now living in poverty, and over forty-three million Americans are on food stamps. More than one in five people in their prime working years are not working. We have the worst financial recovery in sixty-five years. In the last eight years, the past administration has put on more new debt than nearly all of the other Presidents combined.

We've lost more than one-fourth of our manufacturing jobs since NAFTA[3] was approved, and we've lost 60,000 factories since China joined the World Trade Organization in 2001. Our trade deficit in goods with the world last year was nearly $800 billion dollars. And overseas we have inherited a series of tragic foreign policy disasters.

Solving these and so many other pressing problems will require us to work past the differences of party. It will require us to tap into the American spirit that has overcome every challenge throughout our long and storied history. But to accomplish our goals at home and abroad, we must restart the engine of the American economy—making it easier for

---

[3]North American Free Trade Agreement

companies to do business in the United States, and much, much harder for companies to leave our country.

Right now, American companies are taxed at one of the highest rates anywhere in the world. My economic team is developing historic tax reform that will reduce the tax rate on our companies so they can compete and thrive anywhere and with anyone. It will be a big, big cut.

At the same time, we will provide massive tax relief for the middle-class. We must create a level playing field for American companies and our workers. We have to do it. Currently, when we ship products out of America, many other countries make us pay very high tariffs and taxes. But when foreign companies ship their products into America, we charge them nothing, or almost nothing.

I just met with officials and workers from a great American company, Harley-Davidson. In fact, they proudly displayed five of their magnificent motorcycles, made in the USA, on the front lawn of the White House. And they wanted me to ride one and I said, 'No, thank you.'

At our meeting, I asked them, 'How are you doing, how is business?' They said that it's good. I asked them further, 'How are you doing with other countries, mainly international sales?' They told me—without even complaining, because they have been so mistreated for so long that they've become used to it—that it's very hard to do business with other countries because they tax our goods at such a high rate. They said that in the case of another country, they taxed their motorcycles at 100 per cent. They weren't even asking for a change. But I am.

I believe strongly in free trade but it also has to be fair trade. It's been a long time since we had fair trade. The first Republican President, Abraham Lincoln, warned that the 'abandonment of the protective policy by the American government...will produce want and ruin among our people.' Lincoln was right—and it's time we heeded his advice and his words. I am not going to let America and its great companies and workers be taken advantage of us any longer. They have taken advantage of our country. No longer.

I am going to bring back millions of jobs. Protecting our workers also means reforming our system of legal immigration. The current, outdated system depresses wages for our poorest workers, and puts great pressure on taxpayers. Nations around the world, like Canada, Australia and many others, have a merit-based immigration system. It's a basic principle that those seeking to enter a country ought to be able to support themselves financially. Yet, in America, we do not enforce this rule, straining the very public resources that our poorest citizens rely upon. According to the National Academy of Sciences, our current immigration system costs American taxpayers many billions of dollars a year.

Switching away from this current system of lower-skilled immigration, and instead adopting a merit-based system, we will have so many more benefits. It will save countless dollars, raise workers' wages, and help struggling families—including immigrant families—enter the middle-class. And they will do it quickly, and they will be very, very happy, indeed.

I believe that real and positive immigration reform is possible, as long as we focus on the following goals: To improve jobs and wages for Americans; to strengthen our nation's security; and to restore respect for our laws. If we are guided by the well-being of American citizens, then I believe Republicans and Democrats can work together to achieve an outcome that has eluded our country for decades.

DONALD TRUMP ◆ 295

Another Republican President, Dwight D. Eisenhower, initiated the last truly great national infrastructure programme—the building of the Interstate Highway System. The time has come for a new programme of national rebuilding. America has spent approximately $6 trillion in the Middle East—all the while our infrastructure at home is crumbling. With this $6 trillion, we could have rebuilt our country twice, and maybe even three times if we had people who had the ability to negotiate.

To launch our national rebuilding, I will be asking Congress to approve legislation that produces a $1 trillion investment in infrastructure of the United States—financed through both public and private capital—creating millions of new jobs. This effort will be guided by two core principles: Buy American and hire American.

Tonight, I am also calling on this Congress to repeal and replace Obamacare with reforms that expand choice, increase access, lower costs, and, at the same time, provide better healthcare.

Mandating every American to buy government-approved health insurance was never the right solution for our country. The way to make health insurance available to everyone is to lower the cost of health insurance, and that is what we are going do.

Obamacare premiums nationwide have increased by double and triple digits. As an example, Arizona went up 116 per cent last year alone. Governor Matt Bevin of Kentucky just said Obamacare is failing in his state—the state of Kentucky—and it's unsustainable and collapsing.

One-third of counties have only one insurer, and they are losing them fast. They are losing them so fast. They are leaving, and many Americans have no choice at all. There's no choice left. Remember when you were told that you could keep your doctor and keep your plan? We now know that all of those promises have been totally broken. Obamacare is collapsing, and we must act decisively to protect all Americans.

Action is not a choice, it is a necessity. So I am calling on all Democrats and Republicans in Congress to work with us to save Americans from this imploding Obamacare disaster.

Here are the principles that should guide the Congress as we move to create a better healthcare system for all Americans: First, we should ensure that Americans with preexisting conditions have access to coverage, and that we have a stable transition for Americans currently enrolled in the healthcare exchanges.

Secondly, we should help Americans purchase their own coverage through the use of tax credits and expanded Health Savings Accounts—but it must be the plan they want, not the plan forced on them by our government.

Thirdly, we should give our great state governors the resources and flexibility they need with Medicaid to make sure no one is left out.

Fourth, we should implement legal reforms that protect patients and doctors from unnecessary costs that drive up the price of insurance, and work to bring down the artificially high price of drugs, and bring them down immediately.

And finally, the time has come to give Americans the freedom to purchase health insurance across state lines, which will create a truly competitive national marketplace that will bring costs way down and provide far better care. So important.

Everything that is broken in our country can be fixed.

Every problem can be solved. And every hurting family can find healing and hope.

Our citizens deserve this, and so much more. So why not join forces and finally get the job done, and get it done right? On this and so many other things, Democrats and Republicans should get together and unite for the good of our country and for the good of the American people.

My administration wants to work with members of both parties to make childcare accessible and affordable, to help ensure new parents that they have paid family leave, to invest in women's health, and to promote clean air and clean water and to rebuild our military and our infrastructure.

True love for our people requires us to find common ground, to advance the common good and to cooperate on behalf of every American child who deserves a much brighter future.

An incredible young woman is with us this evening, who should serve as an inspiration to us all. Today is Rare Disease Day, and joining us in the gallery is a rare disease survivor, Megan Crowley.

Megan was diagnosed with Pompe disease, a rare and serious illness, when she was 15 months old. She was not expected to live past 5. On receiving this news, Megan's dad, John, fought with everything he had to save the life of his precious child. He founded a company to look for a cure, and helped develop the drug that saved Megan's life. Today she is 20 years old and a sophomore at Notre Dame.

Megan's story is about the unbounded power of a father's love for a daughter. But our slow and burdensome approval process at the Food and Drug Administration keeps too many advances, like the one that saved Megan's life, from reaching those in need. If we slash the restraints, not just at the FDA but across our government, then we will be blessed with far more miracles just like Megan. In fact, our children will grow up in a nation of miracles.

But to achieve this future, we must enrich the mind and the souls of every American child. Education is the civil rights issue of our time. I am calling upon members of both parties to pass an education bill that funds school choice for disadvantaged youth, including millions of African American and Latino children. These families should be free to choose the public, private, charter, magnet, religious or home school that is right for them.

Joining us tonight in the gallery is a remarkable woman, Denisha Merriweather. As a young girl, Denisha struggled in school and failed third grade twice. But then she was able to enrol in a private centre for learning—a great learning centre— with the help of a tax credit and a scholarship programme.

Today, she is the first in her family to graduate, not just from high school, but from college. Later this year she will get her master's degree in social work. We want all children to be able to break the cycle of poverty just like Denisha.

But to break the cycle of poverty, we must also break the cycle of violence. The murder rate in 2015 experienced its largest single-year increase in nearly half a century. In Chicago, more than 4,000 people were shot last year alone, and the murder rate so far this year has been even higher. This is not acceptable in our society.

Every American child should be able to grow up in a safe community, to attend a great school and to have access to a high-paying job. But to create this future, we must work with, not against...not against...the men and women of law enforcement. We must build bridges of cooperation and trust—not drive the wedge of disunity and, really, it's what it is, division. It's pure, unadulterated division. We have to unify.

Police and sheriffs are members of our community. They're friends and neighbours, they're mothers and fathers, sons and daughters—and they leave behind loved ones every day who worry about whether or not they'll come home safe and sound. We must support the incredible men and women of law enforcement.

And we must support the victims of crime. I have ordered the Department of Homeland Security to create an office to serve American victims. The office is called VOICE—Victims of Immigration Crime Engagement. We are providing a voice to those who have been ignored by our media and silenced by special interests. Joining us in the audience tonight are four very brave Americans whose government failed them. Their names are Jamiel Shaw, Susan Oliver, Jenna Oliver and Jessica Davis.

Jamiel's 17-year-old son was viciously murdered by an illegal immigrant gang member who had just been released from prison. Jamiel Shaw, Jr., was an incredible young man, with unlimited potential who was getting ready to go to college where he would have excelled as a great college quarterback. But he never got the chance. His father, who is in the audience tonight, has become a very good friend of mine. Jamiel, thank you. Thank you.

Also with us are Susan Oliver and Jessica Davis. Their husbands, Deputy Sheriff Danny Oliver and Detective Michael Davis, were slain in the line of duty in California. They were pillars of their community. These brave men were viciously gunned down by an illegal immigrant with a criminal record and two prior deportations. Should have never been in our country.

Sitting with Susan is her daughter, Jenna. Jenna, I want you to know that your father was a hero, and that tonight you have the love of an entire country supporting you and praying for you.

To Jamiel, Jenna, Susan and Jessica, I want you to know that we will never stop fighting for justice. Your loved ones will never, ever be forgotten. We will always honour their memory.

Finally, to keep America safe, we must provide the men and women of the United States military with the tools they need to prevent war—if they must—they have to fight and they only have to win.

I am sending Congress a budget that rebuilds the military, eliminates the defence sequester and calls for one of the largest increases in national defence spending in American history. My budget will also increase funding for our veterans. Our veterans have delivered for this nation, and now we must deliver for them.

The challenges we face as a nation are great, but our people are even greater. And none are greater or braver than those who fight for America in uniform.

We are blessed to be joined tonight by Carryn Owens, the widow of a US Navy Special Operator, Senior Chief William 'Ryan' Owens. Ryan died as he lived—a warrior and a hero, battling against terrorism and securing our nation. I just spoke to our great General [Jim] Mattis, just now, who reconfirmed that—and I quote—'Ryan was a part of a highly successful raid that generated large amounts of vital intelligence that will lead to many more victories in the future against our enemies.' Ryan's legacy is etched into eternity. Thank you. And Ryan is looking down right now—you know that—and he is very happy because I think he just broke a record.

For as the Bible teaches us, 'There is no greater act of love than to lay down one's life for one's friends.' Ryan laid down his life for his friends, for his country and for our freedom. And we will never forget Ryan.

To those allies who wonder what kind of a friend America will be, look no further than the heroes who wear our uniform. Our foreign policy calls for a direct, robust and meaningful engagement with the world. It is American leadership based on vital security interests that we share with our allies all across the globe.

We strongly support NATO, an alliance forged through the bonds of two world wars that dethroned fascism, and a Cold War and defeated communism.

But our partners must meet their financial obligations. And now, based on our very strong and frank discussions, they are beginning to do just that. In fact, I can tell you, the money is pouring in. Very nice. We expect our partners—whether in NATO, the Middle East or in the Pacific—to take a direct and meaningful role in both strategic and military operations, and pay their fair share of the cost. Have to do that.

We will respect historic institutions, but we will respect the foreign rights of all nations, and they have to respect our rights as a nation also. Free nations are the best vehicle for expressing the will of the people, and America respects the right of all nations to chart their own path. My job is not to represent the world. My job is to represent the United States of America.

But we know that America is better off when there is less conflict, not more. We must learn from the mistakes of the past.

We have seen the war and the destruction that have ravaged and raged throughout the world—all across the world. The only long-term solution for these humanitarian disasters, in many cases, is to create the conditions where displaced persons can safely return home and begin the long, long process of rebuilding.

America is willing to find new friends and to forge new partnerships, where shared interests align. We want harmony and stability, not war and conflict. We want peace, wherever peace can be found.

America is friends today with former enemies. Some of our closest allies, decades ago, fought on the opposite side of these terrible, terrible wars. This history should give us all faith in the possibilities for a better world. Hopefully, the 250th year for America will see a world that is more peaceful, more just and more free.

On our hundredth anniversary, in 1876, citizens from across our nation came to Philadelphia to celebrate America's centennial. At that celebration, the country's builders and artists and inventors showed off their wonderful creations: Alexander Graham Bell displayed his telephone for the first time; Remington unveiled the first typewriter; an early attempt was made at electric light; Thomas Edison showed an automatic telegraph and an electric pen. Imagine the wonders our country could know in America's 250th year.

Think of the marvels we can achieve if we simply set free the dreams of our people. Cures to the illnesses that have always plagued us are not too much to hope. American footprints on distant worlds are not too big a dream. Millions lifted from welfare to work is not too much to expect. And streets where mothers are safe from fear, schools where children learn in peace and jobs where Americans prosper and grow are not too much to ask.

When we have all of this, we will have made America greater than ever before—for all Americans. This is our vision. This is our mission. But we can only get there together. We are one people, with one destiny. We all bleed the same blood. We all salute the same great American flag. And we all are made by the same God.

When we fulfil this vision, when we celebrate our 250 years of glorious freedom, we will look back on tonight as when this new chapter of American Greatness began. The time for small thinking is over. The time for trivial fights is behind us. We just need the courage to share the dreams that fill our hearts, the bravery to express the hopes that stir our souls and the confidence to turn those hopes and those dreams into action.

From now on, America will be empowered by our aspirations, not burdened by our fears; inspired by the future, not bound by the failures of the past; and guided by our vision, not blinded by our doubts.

I am asking all citizens to embrace this renewal of the American spirit. I am asking all members of Congress to join me in dreaming big, and bold, and daring things for our country. I am asking everyone watching tonight to seize this moment. Believe in yourselves, believe in your future, and believe, once more, in America.

Thank you, God bless you, and God bless the United States.

◆

www.ingramcontent.com/pod-product-compliance
Lightning Source LLC
Chambersburg PA
CBHW051045060526
44539CB00047B/1522